NEGATIVE TILT

NEGATIVE TILT

ADVANCED PRAISE
NEGATIVE TILT
BY BOBBY MATHEWS

"Bobby Mathews is a hell of a Southern storyteller conjuring stories with brutal honesty and truth. He writes about a world of jilted lovers, down on their luck journalists, and desperate men seeking revenge. A wild and haunting ride from start to finish."

> —**Ace Atkins**, New York Times bestselling author of ***Don't Let the Devil Ride***

"***Negative Tilt*** unveils Bobby Mathews as a modern, powerful, and versatile voice of modern noir, with a collection that will weave readers through a tangled cast of characters that reflect the lonesome, hard-fought, and relatable that populate Mathews's tales of struggle and revenge. ***Negative Tilt***'s stark, chiseled prose shoots through you from the first story. Next thing you know, you've burned through the entire book. Don't miss this collection."

> —**Alex Segura**, award-winning and bestselling author of ***Secret Identity*** and ***Alter Ego***

"Mixing gimlet-eyed intensity, a poet's gift for the perfect phrase, and a breathtaking depth of humanity, Bobby Mathews offers one stunner after another in ***Negative Tilt***, illuminating the lives of characters haunted by what they've done, what's been done to them, and the fierce weight of what they might do next."

> —**Art Taylor**, Edgar Award-winning author of ***The Adventure of the Castle Thief and Other Expeditions and Indiscretions***

"This gripping, wide-ranging collection encompasses backwoods vengeance, Parisian tricksters, a mirror that reflects the crimes of the past, and so much more. Bobby Mathews' versatility is matched only by the humanity he invests in even his most broken, desperate characters."

> —**Scott Von Doviak**, Edgar Award-nominated author of ***Lowdown Road*** and ***Charlesgate Confidential***

"Most crime writers come on hard, like they want to show the world how tough they are. Bobby Mathews is a different kind of cat: in *Negative Tilt*, he wants to show you how even the worst of us have a vulnerable heart. This insightfulness and empathy make him one of the best writers working today."

—**Nick Kolakowski**, author of *Payback Is Forever* and *Love & Bullets*

"*Negative Tilt* is more than a collection, it's a body, sprawled out on the table, open and sensitive and bleeding yet furiously, gloriously, alive. With a reporter's eye for detail, a barbarian's taste for chaos, a poet's sense of soul, and a conman's mastery for turns of phrase, Bobby Mathews announces himself as a vital voice, not just to crime fiction, but also as an heir to Portis, Woodrell, and Hiaasen."

—**Paul J. Garth**, author of *The Low White Plain*

BOBBY MATHEWS

NEGA TIVE TILT

NEGATIVE TILT

STORIES

SHOTGUN HONEY

2024

Some of the stories in this collection have appeared elsewhere:
"Negative Tilt," *Rock & A Hard Place,* Issue 7; "The Swahili Word For Hope," *The Dillydoun Review,* Issue 4; "My Father's Guns," *Reckon Review*; "The Ghost of Buxahatchee Creek," *Reckon Review*; "Love Seat," T*he Dillydoun Review,* Issue 2; "Visitation at Nine," *The Dillydoun Review,* Issue 3; "Room for an Hour," *The Sandy River Review*; "A Little Push," *All Due Respect 2020*; "The Big Gamble," *Bristol Noir*; "All Debts Paid," *The Dark City Crime & Mystery Magazine*, Vol. 5, Issue 2; "Dance the Night Away," *Reckon Review*; "Trap House," *Under the Thumb: Stories of Police Corruption*; "Whipping Post," *Trouble No More*; "The Handyman." *Yellow Mama*; "Every Night I Tell Him," *Yellow Mama*; "Never See the Stars," *Flash Fiction Magazine*; "Quitman County Ambush." *Bristol Noir*; "Two in the Street," *Shotgun Honey*, "One in the Chamber," *Shotgun Honey*; "A Good Night's Sleep," *Crimeucopia: We're All Animals Under the Skin*.

Published by **Shotgun Honey Books**

215 Loma Road
Charleston, WV 25314
www.ShotgunHoney.com

Cover by Bad Fido.

First Printing 2024.

ISBN-10: 1-956957-65-0
ISBN-13: 978-1-956957-65-5

9 8 7 6 5 4 3 2 1   24 23 22 21 20 19

For Darlene Mock and Samm Hamilton.

We know heartbreak.

STORIES

MORE STORIES

NEGATIVE TILT: STORIES

NEGATIVE-TILT STORIES

FOREWORD

I'm a lucky guy.

As I write those words, I'm sitting in my parents' house listening to my Dad cough in the living room. It's a crisp December day, maybe forty degrees. The house is thick with cigarette smoke, and I hate the way it clings to everything—especially me. Dad has been diagnosed with stage 4 lung cancer, and the treatment—chemo, radiation, and now immunotherapy—is very nearly as bad as the disease. Over the past two years, I've lost my mom, lost my brother, and I'm now playing Sancho Panza to a tough-as-nails Vietnam veteran's Don Quixote. Bring on those windmills, because I know he'll fight until there's no fight left. There's been drama all through my personal life, and yet the words haven't stopped flowing. I've always been able to get lost in the page.

Over the course of the past three-and-a-half years, I've had thirty stories published, and about two-thirds of those have found their way into this collection. There are also eight stories finding their first daylight within these pages, and I hope you enjoy reading them as much as I enjoyed writing them.

But why do I say that I'm lucky?

It's pretty easy to explain, I think. I have friends in this insane publishing world, and they make all of the difference. There are people who haven't let me quit, who have encouraged me and stuck with me, who have cared and loved me and given me the space to be the messy, complicated human that I am.

With your indulgence, dear reader, let me thank Jessy Minney — for never letting me quit, even when I so desperately wanted to — and Paul J. Garth, Chad Williamson and his alter ego, James D.F. Hannah for their wise counsel, crucial edits, and putting up with random dirty jokes when I call. Mark Westmoreland is the little brother I never wanted, and Rob D. Smith is a great bunkie and writing talent in his own right. Morgan Hayworth and Holly West are aces, and I love them both fiercely. Neither of them takes any shit from me. Beau Johnson is a wonderful human being whose only flaw appears to be putting ice in his beer; and Nikki Dolson, who is the absolute queen of the modern noir short story and a fabulous friend as well. Of course, Libby Cudmore is a joy who eggs me on at every opportunity. I'd be completely remiss if I didn't single out S.A. Cosby for his repeated kindness and friendship. He knows, better than most, what the struggle is like. The fact that he continues to lift others up is a testament to his character and love of writing and writers.

I was also going to mention Hector Acosta, but I don't want to.

All right. Let's talk about the stories in this collection. There are award-winners and award nominees in here. I've been very lucky that way, and the collection kicks off with its namesake, "Negative Tilt," which won the Derringer for best long story published in 2022 from the Short Mystery Fiction Society. I've broken them down into more literary stories—the first nine or so—and then the hard-and-fast crime and mystery stories. From there, there are four flash stories—think of them as a palate cleanser—and then we end with the final four, which are all tales of suspense, and I'd argue that the last two are probably straight-up horror. Consider them a little poisoned bon-bon, a bitter mint with that telltale scent of almonds on your pillow when you turn back the covers at night.

I feel so fortunate to still be here. To still be writing and publishing at a (hopefully) high level. Despite all of the hardship and all of the pain, good things still happen. You're holding the proof in your hands.

Thank you for reading, for supporting small presses like Shotgun Honey and small press authors like me. Now, what the heck are you waiting for? Dive right in.

Bobby Mathews
Dec. 19, 2023

Editor's note: On January 9, 2024, Bobby's father lost his battle with lung cancer.

NEGATIVE TILT

COREY LIKED THE WORK, talking people into giving up their friends and family members, finding out where they'd moved. He'd prop one steel-toed Wellington on the bumper of his tow truck, come on with that good-old-boy attitude that it was so hard to say no to, and stay one step ahead of the skip tracers in the corporate office. Those conversations were the best part of his day, a bittersweet reminder of his old life, a life cut off with no apparent way back.

Corey spent less time in the truck than the other drivers. The big tow truck—a Dodge 4500 with a boom folded atop its fore-shortened rear end like Jesus carrying a hydraulic steel cross—put people on guard. Being outside the cab made him seem harmless, like someone who could be shined on. It would only be later, after the unit had been scooped up sometime in the middle of the night, that some of them might realize the unassuming, bespecta-cled driver had put one over on them.

If the conversations were the best part, the constant driving was the worst. He dreaded the long stretches of highway, driving for hours at a time, like a hungry shark churning the water in search of the next meal. That was when his calves swelled painfully in his boots, constricting the blood flow until his feet began to tingle. Diabetes ran in his family, but he'd always tested negative. Now, as the years and the pounds piled up, he worried about his blood sugar as if it were an ancestral curse.

He treated this new career—he'd been doing it for more than a year now, so that counted as a new career as far as he was concerned—like his first newspaper job, working swing-shift hours so that he could talk to debtors during the day and sweep the city at night. He used the conversations like interviews, jotting down notes as soon as he got back into his own vehicle to keep his memory fresh.

That led him to his second-favorite part of the job: slipping through the deserted streets after midnight, using his GPS locator to compare addresses and locate the missing units. Professionally, they never called their prey "cars." In the repo industry, agents always referred to cars or trucks as units—as in, *find the wanted unit*—in everything from official reports to casual telephone conversations. Sometime around 2 a.m. was the magic time of night for Corey, listening to podcasts and letting his mind wander. The company had six trucks working the greater Birmingham area, from Trussville down to Calera, all the way up to Cullman and Jasper.

Mostly, Corey worked southwestern Birmingham, despoiled and rotting neighborhoods like Ensley, Brighton, Midfield, Fairfield, Bessemer, and Roosevelt.

The other agents based out of his office—Corey couldn't quite think of them as co-workers, because they never saw each other—thought he ran the most dangerous territory. But Corey didn't care. He hadn't cared about much at all since the old life had up and left him.

Buyouts, they called them. A month's severance pay for every year a journalist had worked for the paper. For Corey, who had been there twenty-four years, it was a sizable chunk of change. He didn't leap at the money, not at first. He thought about it for a couple of weeks, would have talked it over with Jeanne if she and the kids hadn't already left.

Twenty-four years was a long time in any business. He was only forty-seven, in the news business for nearly half his life. If he wasn't a journalist, what the hell was he?

Upper management increased the pressure. They wanted to hire younger people, get some of the heavier paychecks off the books for whatever merger they could finagle next. The advertising manager was the first one to go. The circulation manager got the ax when he wouldn't take the buyout. A twenty-two-year-old kid took his place.

As the longest-tenured member of the newsroom, Corey carried a heftier salary than most. If he took the buyout, he could take a year off, work on the novel he kept telling himself he should write. He did the math, and then sent an email to the publisher.

"I can't believe it," Nancy Boyette told him while he boxed up the few personal items on his desk. Nancy, his direct supervisor, with her glossy black hair and piercing blue eyes and bottle of Crown Royal in the bottom left-hand drawer of her big cherry desk. She'd been with the paper for eighteen months and always looked a little lost. "I thought you were a lifer."

But that was the problem. Newspaper work was a life sentence. It got in your blood, chasing the story down and wrestling it into print. As the deputy managing editor, he was the one who worked late and put the paper to bed. His phone was the first to ring in the morning if the shit hit the fan. The years made his skin sallow, and his hair had all but disappeared. There were lines on his face and ulcers in his stomach from the long nights and the short deadlines.

"It's time to get out," he told her, patting the check folded carefully in his breast pocket. "I was treading in deep water for a long time, and they finally threw me a lifeline."

"Probably the most money anyone's ever made from this

paper," she said. Her voice sounded wistful. "You want to go out back for one last smoke?"

"Sure," Corey said. He left the half-filled cardboard box in his desk chair. There wasn't much left there, anyway. Once he'd decided to take the buyout, he'd started sifting his personal stuff out of the building a little at a time, so as not to cause alarm to the reporters who worked under him.

Corey and Nancy strode back to the loading dock together. This had been an end-of-day ritual for her, and a beginning of shift ritual for him. Each day they'd meet and discuss the budget items for the evening, sketching out the front page, talking through major and minor points like which stories still needed art, or what stories might break overnight and necessitate a flash page on the paper's website.

But that wasn't his problem anymore.

"We're going to miss you around here," Nancy said. She drew hard on her cigarette, which drew the tiny vertical lines along her lips into sharp relief. The first two fingers of her right hand, the ones that held the cigarette, were slightly yellowed, stained with nicotine. When she'd come to work at the paper, her nails had been perfectly lacquered. Now, most of the time the polish was chipped and peeling, and she picked at her fingers absently while the newsroom died its slow silent death around her.

"I've been missing it for a while now already," Corey said. His voice echoed around the open loading dock. When he first started, the dock was where the printers had taken the papers off of the press in freshly wrapped bundles that were warm to the touch. When Corey first started up in the newsroom on the main floor of the building, he could always tell when the press started running because the floor would vibrate softly, bringing even more life into the building. But in some buyout or other down the line, the old web press had been broken down and sold for parts. Now all that was left was the hollowed-out, oil-stained cavern where it had once been. All that is left of the dinosaurs are the bones, petrified relics of a bygone era.

• • •

The car was pointed nose-out down a steep driveway, a nearly new Honda Accord, hadn't been off the lot for six months before the debtor fell behind on payments. He hopped out, checked the Vehicle Identification Number—a little metal plate visible on the driver's side of the dash—to make sure he had the right vehicle. Back in the truck, the rumble of the engine under his ass, lower the boom. He had the newest truck in the fleet, with a hydraulic system that would drop the boom down past zero degrees—they called it negative tilt—so that it could recover units parked down steep driveways like this. Corey used the hydraulic controls to slide the boom under the Honda and lock onto the front wheels.

Corey engaged the boom and lifted the Honda so that only its rear wheels were touching the ground. He shifted the truck into drive and pulled out. No lights in the house behind him came on. No dogs barked. He'd gotten away with it again.

By the time the third day of unemployment rolled around, Corey knew he wasn't going to be able to write anything. It was the noise, or the lack of it. In the newsroom, with a deadline beating down on him and the hum of other journalists doing their own work, he could pound out a thousand words in an hour. No typos. No rewrites. The first draft of history, even if that history was just a recap of a county commission meeting that ended late.

In his sunny little home office, where he'd never done much more than write out checks for the monthly bills, writing anything as vast as a novel seemed impossible. He put the TV on in the living room, just for some noise, but found it impossible to concentrate. He found himself wandering into the living room, plopping down on the couch to check out the second half of The

View and staying put for the judges, Judy and Mathis. By the time Ellen DeGeneres's show ended each afternoon, he'd be disgusted with himself for another wasted day.

He got a police scanner and placed it on his desk, hoping its familiar noise would help him find that Zen-like place in his mind where the world went away and the words came. It helped for a couple of days, and then it was just background noise. He started lurking on social media, checking out the paper's website. He wanted to be reassured that his work there had meant something, that all of the hours he'd sacrificed, the marriage and family he'd thrown over the side, was worth it; that he was—unlike everyone else who had left—irreplaceable. To his dismay, the paper continued to publish without him.

Nancy would occasionally text, gossiping about who else had gotten the ax. She was safe, of course. She hadn't been with the paper long enough to command a decent salary, and she was young enough that the long hours and the low pay must have seemed sort of romantic to her. But Corey could tell some cracks were appearing at the edges.

"No bonuses this quarter," she messaged one night, out of the blue. "We're still in austerity, whatever that means. FFS, I was counting on that money."

As for Corey, he blew through the buyout money. It wasn't real to him. He applied to other newspapers, but the only one that wanted to hire him was out in the Big Horn mountains of Wyoming. What the hell did he know about Wyoming? He flew out for the interview anyway—on their dime, not his—and found the little shop charming and quaint. The town, about five thousand people total, was mostly one- or two-story buildings, and the mountains surrounding the place painted a blue haze on the horizon. The high plains were scoured by constant wind, and in places bare rock was left scraped raw. The deep folds and creases in the earth looked like something Georgia O'Keefe might have imagined in her earlier and unfinished work.

The first thing he did with the publisher was to settle down on the man's back deck with three months' worth of newspapers and a supply of red Sharpie pens. Corey scanned the papers. He caught typos in headlines and cutlines. He questioned why certain stories got play, and why others didn't. Instead of being embarrassed, the publisher looked eager.

"This is just what we need here," the publisher said. "You understand local. You understand what I want."

He brought out a bottle of Maker's Mark and they toasted one another. Several times after that, they found reasons to lift a glass until the bottle was empty and they were not. The publisher put him on a plane back to Alabama the next day, with a promise that he'd make an offer soon. But when the offer came, Corey's heart fell. They wanted him to work for half of what he'd been making in Birmingham.

"I can't do it," he finally told the publisher. His voice was calm, but tears flowed freely down his face. "I can't figure out how to make the money work."

Money. That's what it all came down to. Eleven months after he took the buyout, Corey was out of money, so stone-broke that his debit and credit cards were declined at the convenience store where he stopped to buy a soft drink.

He began perusing job websites harder, expanding his search parameters until he found something that caught his eye. DRIVER WANTED IMMEDIATELY, it said and listed a phone number. That was all. He called the number, and a woman's voice answered.

"I'm calling about the job you listed," he said, and then she cut him off.

"Can you pass a drug test?"

Corey grinned at the phone. He'd never done any kind of illegal drug—not ever—the only one of his friends from high school and college who could say that. He'd often wondered at the lure of a forbidden high. But it had simply never appealed to him, so he never did it. Peer pressure, it seemed, wasn't so inevitable after all.

"Yes," Corey said, and he could feel cool relief flush down his neck. "I can pass it."

"Good," the woman said. "The last three guys who wanted this job couldn't." She gave him an address in Pinson, a small town northeast of Birmingham. He read it back to her.

"All right, so you're not illiterate," she said. "Come in and fill out the application."

"Wait. How much does it pay?"

There was a pause on the woman's end.

"Hundred-and-twenty-five a car." The line went dead. She'd hung up, or gotten cut off. Corey still didn't understand what kind of work it was, but the promise of *hundred-and-twenty-five a car* rang in his ears.

That was the interview. He passed the drug screen and the background check. The woman who'd spoken to him on the phone—Bailey—ran the office for American Repossessors United. She pushed Corey's application through, sent him for a week of training at the company headquarters just outside Memphis, Tennessee, and within two weeks he was behind the wheel of an $80,000 tow truck. He was, in fact, paid $125 for every vehicle— every *unit*—he repossessed, and nothing at all if he didn't find anything. Feast or famine from the get-go.

He seemed to have a natural aptitude for it. Within the first three months on the job, he became the top agent in the Birmingham office, pulling in twenty to thirty units in a week. He ran the new accounts on his list every night, inputting updates on the laptop computer anchored to the dash of the truck while his right foot pressed the gas pedal. He used social media platforms to stalk and find debtors, and he cross-referenced license plate numbers that repeatedly showed up at addresses he was monitoring. He found that he was using the relentless approach he'd taken with journalism, spending hours upon hours behind the wheel. He was in the Dodge or in the Toyota for sometimes twenty hours a day.

Nancy kept in touch. As the paper's ownership kept chopping

staff like loggers felling logs in a dwindling forest, she talked less about what was going on in the newsroom, and more about herself.

"I don't know how much more of this I can take," she texted him one night. It was just after 11 p.m., and he assumed she'd just put the paper to bed. "It's like a ghost town around here. Do you want to meet for a drink?"

Corey had a Tesla on the boom and an angry debtor to sooth when he got her message. He left her on read until the next morning.

"I was already in bed," he told her. "Sorry I missed you. Maybe next time."

The obscene part was that repo work paid better than newspaper work ever had or ever would. The most he'd ever made as a journalist was forty thousand dollars in a year. In six months as a repo agent, he'd passed that benchmark. But as much as he liked the money and genuinely enjoyed the investigative aspect of the job, he still hated parts of the work. He was an anomaly in this new world, college educated and soft, a man with no feel for the lockout kit, a hard plastic wedge used to pry open a unit's window and a long metal rod with a half-hook at the end that the other agents wielded with the deft diplomacy of long use. When they saw one another, which was infrequently, the other agents teased him about his education and his political views.

"Stop being a damned liberal," Nick would say, and laugh. Nick who was not yet thirty and sported a sleeve of tattoos from his left wrist to his shoulder, who chain-smoked Marlboros and listened to artists Corey had never heard of, who would take a shit on a debtor's lawn if he couldn't find the wanted unit at their address.

"Hell, he can't help it," Stevie might chime in, pronouncing can't as *cain't*. Stevie who wore basketball shorts and muscle shirts year-round, no matter how cold it got, who had lost the hearing in his left ear when he was nine when his brother struck him upside the head with a hard pine two-by-four, who would laugh and point at the thick rope of scar tissue that wrapped from behind the ear all the way up to the top of his closely-shorn head. "They done educated him up at that college, and then the newspaper ruined him. He'll be aight if we can keep him in a truck for the next five years. He'll get it outta his system."

Javier, who was also teased by the other agents, rarely said anything either way. He just looked on in silence, sometimes laughing, sometimes watching with dark and brooding eyes that never let on what he was thinking. Javier had come to Alabama as a small child and still spoke with the melodic lilt of his native Dominican Republic, even though he'd never been out of the United States. He learned the music of his country's language at home with his mother and three sisters, and it was his dream to visit Paris one day.

"You should go," Corey told him one day. "There's nothing like it anywhere."

Corey had taken his ex-wife to Paris on their honeymoon, a fact that impressed the other agents with its extravagance and romance even if the marriage itself hadn't lasted. But Javier only shook his head sadly.

"I think I'll stay here," he said, casting a sidelong glance at Nick. "I think if I go overseas, they maybe don't let me come back."

Nick laughed.

"I knew you was illegal," he said, his voice full of mirth. "Hey, Stevie—"

"I'm not," Javier said, and the way he said it made the laughter in Nick's words die. Nobody said anything for a minute, so Javier said, "I got a green card and then I got a citizenship test and then I got a Social Security card. I'm as American as you are."

Nick, who was embarrassed that Javier hadn't let his joke go, shook his head and said "Bullshit" in a low voice.

"Hey, fuck you," Javier said. "I earned it. All you had to do was be born here."

Nick threw down a half-smoked cigarette and stepped over to Javier. It might have gotten serious, but Corey and Stevie stepped between them, hustling them out of each other's face and away toward their respective trucks.

Once Nancy called to pick his brain on where to go with a story a young reporter was pursuing. He was good enough to consult for free, but not good enough to pay for his years of experience. Corey was ninety-nine percent sure the consulting call hadn't been her idea. He knew she was getting squeezed, too.

"What are you doing these days?" She asked him when they were done talking about the story.

"Oh, this and that," he said. He didn't know why he didn't talk to her about the new job, the new career. Was he ashamed of it? No. Well, okay, maybe a little. But he also liked it, the silent shark thrashing through the dark waters of the Birmingham night, feasting or starving, depending on how the night went, but always swimming forward.

"I bet you're still living high off the buyout," she said. The jealousy in her voice was thick with pain, like a lonely child. "Jesus, it must have been like hitting the lottery."

If it had, the lottery he'd won had been poisonous, killing off his career, his previous life, as surely as a cyanide capsule would kill the captured spy in a war movie. They hung up, and Corey felt his chest loosen like a clenched fist finally opening.

"We never got that drink," Nancy said. It felt like an invitation.

"You buying?" He asked, hoping that she heard the smile on his face.

She snorted, a wised-up cynical veteran newspaper sound.

"We're in austerity right now," she said, "whatever that means. I gotta take a furlough, a whole week off without pay."

"Well," Corey said. "Maybe I'll run into you soon."

None of the Birmingham agents had ever been shot—not yet—but they'd all had close calls. Stevie had showed up one morning with two neat bullet holes drilled through the glass in the rear windshield of his truck and a pair of slugs buried in the dashboard.

"Probably did it himself," Javier said, checking Stevie's truck. "You know that cracker ain't right in the head."

Corey and Nick watched from a distance. He didn't want to get close to the spent rounds. Just looking at the bullet holes made him feel a little weak below his belt line. Javier reached into his back pocket and brought out a heavy folding knife, which he flicked open with one hand. Peering at the dash, he worked the sharp blade carefully around in first one hole and then another until he plucked out two deformed lead mushrooms. He walked over to them and held the shrapnel in his palm for the others to see.

"Twenty-twos," Nick said. "Well, that's not so bad."

"Maybe twenny-fives," Javier said. "Probably just sting a little, you know, from a distance."

They were straight-faced, not looking at Corey. He couldn't tell if they were kidding or not. Probably a little of both. The job required a lot of balls, to go onto someone else's property in the middle of the night, skulk out and pop a VIN on the dashboard with a flashlight, maybe hook up the loud and heavy hydraulic lift, and then scoot away like a thief in the night. They each walked a line somewhere between confident and cocky, but the bullet holes were a reminder of how things could go wrong, and how close Stevie had come to a bad end somewhere in Outer Bumfuck. Corey could picture it in his head, Stevie, half his head blown away, gut sagging in his sleeveless muscle shirt, basketball shorts filling with shit and piss after his bowels let go, sitting in the leather seat behind the steering wheel as the truck leaned cantilevered in a ditch somewhere.

He shook his head to clear the image and walked away. He couldn't think about things like that and continue to do the job.

When her name came up on his hot list, Corey wasn't too surprised. The GPS took him to a large apartment complex off of Highway 150 in Hoover, the largest suburb of Birmingham. The suburbs meant less security than in the city proper, and this particular complex had no gate, no guard. Easy pickings, unless she'd moved and the skip tracers were a step behind.

But he found her building, and then he found her unit, a two-year-old Mazda 3, a sporty hatchback that looked small enough to fit in his palm. But no, better to use the truck. He took the Mazda from behind, raising it up and pulling it deftly from its parking space before leaving it in the middle of the parking lot. He released the hooks and slid away from the unit, circling back around until he could lock onto it from the front, so that he wouldn't have to throw straps over the rear wheels. He drove away with her car trailing behind him like a remora suctioned tight to the back of an apex predator.

His phone was in his lap, his text messages open to Nancy's last missive, the one where she talked about the budget cuts that had come down the pike. The new owners were slashing news-room salaries by fifteen percent. She was hanging in there, but just barely. In the meantime, she was looking for a new position, she said, but so far there was no good news on the horizon. Corey thought about texting her. He could tell her everything.

He could tell her about the new job, about the top-of-the-line truck with the negative tilt and the hydraulic winch. He could tell her about the money, explain the absurdity of what he did now and how the newspaper business had unexpectedly prepared him for this new life. But it was almost four in the morning, and she would know soon enough that there was no good news anywhere, not anymore.

THE SWAHILI WORD FOR HOPE

FOGERTY WAS LATE, but that was to be expected. The old man kept only a passing acquaintance with time, and he could have gotten lost in a dozen different ways on the walk to his office, from a turn of phrase in Ozymandias to the meaning of a soliloquy by Captain America. For all Bertrand knew, the geezer was sitting out on one of the benches on the quad, playing his damned silver harmonica and watching the clouds move across the sky.

But the third floor of Ellison Hall wasn't a bad way to spend half an hour; the hall itself wasn't much, just cinderblock walls painted oyster white and warrens of tiny offices for professors. But the coeds were wearing Uggs and yoga pants against the chill, and Bertrand paid careful, if covert, attention. He caught a couple of them staring at him as well, and was pleased. He had scrupulously cultivated his look — the two-day growth of mustache and beard, the tattered jeans and Vans, the fisherman's sweater and scally cap — in order to catch the interest of a young English major. It hadn't worked yet, but it was only the end of the first semester.

They all knew about him, of course. If the story in The Times hadn't caught their attention, then the Pushcart Prize nomination and the Lannan Award almost certainly had. Bertrand saw himself as a rising star. He had to be, considering who his mother was.

Katarine Fournier was a woman who, like Athena, might have sprung directly from the forehead of Zeus himself. Fiercely independent and the wielder of an otherworldly talent, she'd won the National Book Award at the unbelievable age of twenty-three years old, and since then she'd been a finalist for the Pulitzer twice and the Nobel once. If there was such a thing as literary royalty, she was it.

Bertrand knew that his mother considered him the crown prince of the literary fiction world, even if his own publication list was limited to small journals that no one but other academics read. He wanted to please his mother, who had raised him — by her choice — alone. She had dreamed her dreams for him, had pushed him toward the pursuit of whatever talent he possessed, and he mustn't fail her now. Not when the curtain was just now rising on the stage of his own literary career.

This was to be his third conversation with Fogerty. The other TAs all called him Foggy, but Bertrand had never gotten the courage to call him anything but Professor Fogerty. The man wasn't just some has-been word jockey eking out a comfortable retirement in academe. He'd won a Man Booker, a Pushcart, and he'd been a finalist for the National Book Award three times. If Katarine Fournier was literary royalty, Foggy was at least a minor duke in the small, insular kingdom of working writers. Fogerty was the real goods; he was why Katarine made Bertrand apply to this MFA program, where she had once taught. She knew Foggy, Katarine told Bertraind, and knew that the old lion would love his work.

So Bertraind expected the prof to be blown away by his writing, that they would become more than student and teacher. Perhaps they'd sit in Foggy's office and sip single-malt scotch as the afternoon wound down outside and discuss the Johns — Updike, Cheever, and Irving — or Raymond Carver and Eudora Welty.

It hadn't happened that way.

Instead of a kindly old professor — maybe not Dumbledore, but certainly in that same zip code — Bertrand had found his own personal Snape. Their first short story assignment — there were two due during the semester — had come back with so much green ink spilled across it ("Foggy" didn't believe in red pens) that the prof might have slain the Jolly Green Giant. DERIVATIVE was scribbled at the bottom of the last page, along with a note that Bertrand needed to read further in order to develop whatever small seedling of talent he might have.

Bertrand's face still burned in shame at that first assignment. He'd poured his heart out into thirty-six pages of double-spaced narrative about a young boy orphaned on an Oklahoma farm, too young — too small — to properly bury his parents, and each night the wolves and coyotes and other dust-bowl creatures would come to feast on the bodies while the orphaned child could do nothing to stop them. Bertrand thought the symbolism was clear.

"I wanted to talk to you about my story," Bertrand told Fogerty at that first meeting, once they'd closed the door to the old man's spare little office. All three walls were lined with bookshelves from floor to ceiling, and the desk was piled high with advance copies of books due to be published within the next year, from publishers seeking reviews or writers seeking blurbs. Fogerty got himself seated behind his department-issued blond wood desk without toppling any of the precariously stacked volumes and plucked a meerschaum pipe from its stand.

"I'm sure you do," Fogerty said, and stuck the stem of the cold pipe between his teeth. He didn't smoke anymore, but he puffed dreams of tobacco past as he listened.

"I think you were a little too, you know, hard on me," Bertrand said. "I mean, how can you say that what I wrote was derivative? I don't even know what you mean. Do you mean I copied it from somewhere? Because I didn't."

When Fogerty smiled, he looked like a forgetful Santa Claus.

His beard was white and trimmed neatly, a counterpoint to the hazy cloud of thinning hair atop his head. The professor leaned back in his chair and removed the pipe from between his lips, holding it absently in one hand.

Then he shook his head.

"No," he said. "I mean that you know too much of the wrong things and not enough of the right ones."

Bertrand didn't know what to say to that, so he didn't say anything for a moment. He was unsurprised to find that his rage at the professor's comments had cooled into an icy diamond of resolve. His temper was a gift directly from his mother, and he must hold onto it, cram everything he felt down into his gut and let it turn cold. He would show this old man, show him where he could push that Pushcart, by God.

"I still don't know what that means."

"I know your mother," Fogerty said. "Did you know that?"

"My mom knows a lot of people. We are talking about my story."

"Actually, we're talking about your failure," Fogerty said, his voice gentle. "Where did you grow up?"

"I—why?"

"Just answer the question," Fogerty said, not unkindly.

"Saddle River, New Jersey. If you know my mother, you should know that."

"And you completed your undergrad at Rutgers, I believe?"

"Yes."

"Good university," Fogerty said, and Bertrand brightened a little. For a moment, he thought his background, the summa cum laude, Phi Beta Kappa, all of it, was working in his favor. But then Fogerty asked, "Have you ever been to Oklahoma?"

Bertrand was quiet. He looked down at the artfully torn knees of his blue jeans and didn't meet the prof's eyes.

"No," he mumbled.

The chair creaked again as Fogerty leaned forward and placed his elbows on the desk.

"So why write about a farm-boy in the Dust Bowl?"

Bertrand didn't know what to say. The idea had simply come to him, as ideas always had, and he had written it on his Royal manual typewriter—why would a real writer ever want to use anything else?—and agonized over the setting and word choice. He had sweated over the dialogue and description, trying to find a perfect balance. When it was done, when it was absolutely perfect—or so he thought—he'd turned it in. And gotten slapped in the face.

"You've clearly read Steinbeck," Fogerty said. "Certainly *The Grapes of Wrath* and *Of Mice and Men*, probably *The Pearl*, too. Am I right?"

"Yes," Bertrand said, looking at the vinyl floor tile between his shoes. He could see where the professor was going.

"Your piece doesn't bring anything new to that conversation. Sure there's some lovely writing in it, but anybody can string together a few pretty words. Fitzgerald did it pickled off his ass every day of his life. But the only Oklahoma you know is the fictional one someone else has described to you. The story has no heart. And anyone worth a good goddamn can tell."

Bertrand's mouth gaped. He'd never had anyone say something like that about his writing. His writing had heart, damn it. It did. He had published sixteen stories over the course of his undergraduate career, and while not one of them had achieved even a percentage of his mother's acclaim, every piece published was another brick in the foundation of the tower that he would build to reach the constellation of his mother's fame. He knew that it would happen; Katarine expected it. And what Katarine Fournier expected, she got.

But Fogerty didn't know that.

"I don't understand," Bertraind said finally.

"I don't expect you to," Fogerty said. "Not yet, at any rate. If you want to be a writer, it's your job to find understanding. Find empathy. No matter who you're writing about. Find something real—Hemingway called it 'one true sentence' and hang your story on it like a hat on a nail. If the one true thing holds, then everything you build around it will hold."

Bertrand had nodded like he'd known what the professor meant, all the while the word DERIVATIVE blinked on and off in neon green cursive in the front of his mind. He couldn't stop thinking about it, couldn't stop thinking about what his mother would say if she could have heard that conversation. When he left the office, he'd gone back to his spartan apartment near campus and drunk all the beer in the fridge. He missed class the next day — it was a lot of beer — but by the morning after that, he felt good enough to TA for the English 101 class. All freshmen were required to turn in a personal essay, and the TAs got to grade them (because the professors sure as hell weren't going to do that).

He was still thinking over his talk with Foggy while he was grading, and Bertrand's own pen (his RED pen, dammit) was bleeding all over the essays, making the pages a crime scene. There was one, though, that looked pretty good.

In it, the author described his family's emigration from Entebbe, in Uganda, across the treacherous waters of Lake Victoria, how the momentum of the waves carried them past Kisumu, where they were supposed to land, all the way down to the port at Musoma, in Tanzania. It detailed how the student's family had finally moved up the coast, sneaking into Kenya — first to Kisumu, then Nairobi — scrimping and scraping to save enough money to eventually flee to the United States, where the student — Nbushe Okeke was his name — was born. It was a fascinating bit of personal history, written in an open and completely guileless manner. Before Bertrand allowed himself to think about what he was doing, he went to the photocopier hidden in the TA's anteroom and ran off a copy of the essay.

Over the next two weeks, Bertrand ignored his typewriter. Instead, he bent over his laptop, eyes straining against the harsh glow of the screen. His fingers flew across the keys as he stripped the essay down, switching from first person to third, adding some dialogue, making the arduous trek across Lake Victoria seem even more dangerous than the student described it. For the final draft, he hunched over his typewriter, the posture of a thief, and made the last smooth motions to transfer Nbushe Okeke's story to himself. At the top of page one, he titled the piece simply "Tumaini," the Swahili word for hope.

The next meeting in Foggy's office was much more pleasant.

"You did the research," the professor said. He wasn't effusive, and Bertrand got the feeling that the old man would never warm up to him, that he was judging Bertrand's talent against Katarine's, and his work would never measure up. "This story is much stronger than your first attempt. The details feel real in a way that your Dust Bowl story didn't. I must say that I didn't expect this from you, Mr. Fournier."

"Thank you, sir."

"Of course, there are still places where you can improve. The dialogue, for instance."

Bertrand stiffened. That was one of the few things he had actually written himself. And it needed improvement?

"It sounds too American," Foggy said. "The ease of idiom, the phrasing. Think of how you can punch that dialogue up a little bit, how you can reveal character with it. This is a kid who grew up speaking Swahili at home but English at school, right?"

Bertrand nodded. Foggy leaned back in his chair and put a foot up on the corner of his desk.

"If I were writing it, I would probably make him sound much more formal when he speaks in English. His native language is probably what he thinks in, but English is the language of his classmates, his professors, right?"

"I guess," Bertrand said.

Foggy dropped his foot to the floor and leaned forward. His usually mild blue eyes were crackling with intensity.

"Don't guess," he said. "Know."

But Bertrand did know. Nbushe Okeke's spoken English was

always formal, nearly archaic. He began to think about how the student acted, the way he gathered the thoughts in his mind before speaking. It was like watching a thundercloud build above Okeke's browline.

By the end of that meeting, Foggy had encouraged Bertrand to submit 'Tumaini' for publication in a small but well-regarded literary journal. Pending dialogue changes, of course.

Then the damned story was published. It won a Lannan Award and the prize money that came with it. The money — quite a lot of it — was nice, but the real victory came when Katarine called to congratulate him.

"I knew you had it in you," she said. "I have a friend at The Times who's going to call you to do an interview."

"What? Mother, no. That's not necessary."

"Of course it is. You'll have to get used to doing these kinds of interviews, you know. The press is going to expect a lot from you, but you can use that to your advantage. And I don't have to tell you that ink sells books. You know that already."

His mouth was dry, his stomach hollow. But at last he agreed to the interview with a feeling of impending doom hanging over his head.

It had gone surprisingly well. The questions were easy, most of them the sort of growing-up-with-a-famous-mother softball questions that he'd answered before. The only thing that shook him was when the reporter asked where he'd gotten the idea for the story.

"Ideas come from everywhere," Bertrand said. "Sometimes you just let your imagination fly."

And sometimes when that doesn't work, you steal with both hands, he thought but did not say.

Bertrand hadn't met with Fogarty since the day the professor encouraged him to submit 'Tumaini' for publication. Then, this morning the professor had emailed and asked to meet with him this afternoon. The Pushcart announcements were nearing, and

Bertrand wondered if the story could have won. No, that was too much to hope for, too much to fear.

Near the end of the semester, with the hallways mostly empty, and here came Foggy, walking along like a man twenty years his junior. He was accompanied by a young Black professor, Harriet Unjohn, who taught a different track in the MFA program. Bertrand had never met her, but he'd heard good things, and she had some really strong MFA candidates under her watchful eye.

Foggy nodded to Bertrand and introduced Professor Unjohn. The woman nodded curtly, her lips in a hard line like a tightrope stretched between buildings. Foggy unlocked the office door, and ushered them in. Harriet took the seat across from Foggy's desk, angling it slightly so that she could look at Bertrand, who was looking around for somewhere to sit.

"Don't worry about it," Foggy said, dropping heavily into his own chair. He looked tired. "You won't be staying long."

Bertrand cocked his head. He felt his heart sink, and he understood at once that Foggy had found out about the stolen piece. He didn't know how, but that didn't matter. The old professor was staring him down, practically mad-dogging him, like a physical challenge. Professor Unjohn was sitting quietly, one side of her mouth now quirked upward. Not quite a smile, but some small satisfactory amusement.

It was she who spoke next.

"I'm going to say a name," she said. "When I do, you are going to leave this office. You will withdraw from this program."

Bertrand tried not to let anything show, but he could feel the heat rising in his face. He didn't say anything, imagining himself a prisoner, offered a blindfold and final cigarette before the firing squad did its mortal duty.

"Nbushe Okeke."

Bertrand pushed down the urge to say "bless you." He was in enough trouble as it was. So he didn't say anything. Instead, he stood there, a dead man waiting to fall.

"Do you have anything to say for yourself?"

Bertrand shook his head.

"Withdraw from the program," Professor Unjohn said. "If you try to return for Spring semester, I'll make sure you are formally dismissed, that your name is publicly dragged through every bit of goddamned mud I can find. Every Google search for your name will detail how you stole that young man's essay, and how you were thrown out of this university."

Tears formed at the corners of Bertrand's eyes and tracked slowly down his cheeks. He didn't mean to cry. He didn't *want* to cry. But the tears came anyway. When Fogerty and Unjohn didn't say anything else, Bertrand opened his mouth to defend himself, but all that came out was a harsh, guttural sob.

"What about me?" Bertrand asked when he could find his voice. His gaze bounced back and forth between the professors. There was no sympathy anywhere. "What will happen to me?"

Fogerty stared at him a long time, those flinty blue eyes holding no warmth, no mercy, not an ounce of compassion.

"I'm sure we don't care," he said. "I have already called your mother, so don't think that whining to her will do you any good. You are done here. And if I have any favors left, you are done forever."

Fogerty dismissed Bertrand with a wave of his fingers and turned away to talk with Professor Unjohn about the department's literary magazine.

Bertrand left the door open behind him and fled into the hall, down the stairs to the first floor, and out into the dying afternoon light. His phone buzzed in his pocket. When he freed it and hit the unlock button, he looked at the screen and saw it was his mother calling.

MY FATHER'S GUNS

MY FATHER BEGAN PREPARING for his funeral while he was still in his sixties, back when his shock of salt-and-pepper hair was still trending mostly toward pepper. He drove to other family members' funerals both far and wide: Uncle Silam down in Texas, Aunt Katherine in Louisville, cousin Sherman in Orlando. It didn't matter how far or how distantly related, Dad always showed up at the funeral in his black three-piece suit flecked with cigarette ashes, his hair freshly shaved in the flat-top he'd maintained since his earliest days in the Army, his unruly handlebar mustache trimmed down to something presentable instead of a bristle-brush that could have placed third in a Sam Elliot look-alike contest.

The joke, of course, was that he outlived nearly all of his contemporaries. At eighty-seven, he'd finally cashed in his chips and moved on to whatever happens next. Natural causes, the coroner said. The old man had finally worn down until there wasn't enough left to continue.

It was a shock, of course. Maybe it shouldn't have been, but Dad always seemed like a force of nature. Even when he was feeling unwell, the flip sides of his personality—his humor and his temper—always made him seem somewhat larger than life. He'd survived being shot in Vietnam, survived falling from a forty-foot scaffold with nothing more than a broken arm. Even though I knew that his time would eventually come, that was just academic. In reality, I was sure that my father would live forever.

I guess there was a good turnout at the funeral. You'd have to ask my sister to be sure. I was too busy staring at the casket and wondering what the hell I was going to do now. Mom had passed two years before. Now it was Dad's turn. Forty-nine years old seems awful old to find yourself an orphan in the world, but there I was. The funeral director was quiet and unobtrusive, bland and non-confrontational in his platitudes, just like the sanctuary where we held the service. At the gravesite, a bugler blew Taps and a detail of pink-cheeked soldier boys served as pallbearers and honor guard, solemnly firing their 21-blank salute harmlessly toward the clear October sky above us.

I don't know when the soldier handed me the flag, but I remember what the cloth felt like that day, soft and smooth, folded tightly into a triangle from which it would never be unfolded. The soldier—a lieutenant, maybe?—stepped back and snapped a salute. I still don't know if he was saluting me or the flag. I guess it doesn't really matter a whole hell of a lot, does it? After they lowered Dad's casket into the freshly dug grave, I still had to stand around and wait while the few well-wishers and mourners who made the trek from the funeral home came by to express their condolences. I stared down at the graves. My father and mother, side-by-side for eternity.

They'd never really liked one another that much while they'd been alive. Now they could bicker for eternity.

My sister, Charlene, and my brother, Jay, stood with me. We didn't say a whole lot until after the service, when everyone else was gone and we were alone.

"I wish the boys could have made it," Charlene said, meaning of course my boys, who were still in elementary school. I'd married late, had children even later, and now almost everything I did here in middle age was contingent upon them. While my friends had children going off to college—and some of them even had grand-children by now—my boys were concentrating on Pokémon and Power Rangers, and occasionally showing the slightest interest in baseball and soccer. I had carefully chosen not to have them with me for the trip down from Birmingham. They loved their grand-father so much, and I didn't want their last memory of him to be the body in the box that we'd all witnessed at the funeral home.

It may have looked like my father, but it wasn't him. Whatever spark that had been inside of him was gone now, and we all knew it.

"You'll be going back now?" Jay asked, and I nodded in a non-committal way. There were things I needed to do back at the house, some things Mom and Dad had both asked me to take care of once they were gone. I'd see those things through, and then I'd go home to my boys.

My parents' house is a brick bungalow on the wrong side of the tracks in a small Southern town where that kind of thing still mat-ters. I'd grown up in that little house set alongside a dirt road. That house had always been the true North in the compass of my life. I could always find my way back to it. Even in the bad years, the ones that had taken me to Manhattan and Wyoming and Atlanta, I could feel that small house tugging at my heart and telling me to come back home.

Someone said you can't go back home, and I guess they're right. It's even truer when your parents are dead.

I used Dad's key to unlock the door from the carport into the house and was immediately assaulted with the thick and clogging scent of cigarette smoke. I'd grown up in it, of course, and in the seventies and eighties it seemed like everyone smoked, so my par-ents' house was no better or worse than anyone else's. But now that I had my own home—my own life to go back to—the smoke here was like an invisible attacker determined to choke me down and smother me into oblivion. The first thing I did was open every window in the place and let the fall breeze waft its way through.

I stood in the dark kitchen and listened. No sound. Nothing. Not my father's hacking cough from too many cigarettes, not the subtle shift as he sought a more comfortable place on the couch for one of his frequent afternoon naps. The TV didn't boom with the sound of a late-season baseball game, the volume turned up as Dad's hearing worsened.

If there are ghosts in this world—and I believe there are—they were quiet and welcoming in my parents' house.

The last room facing east had been my bedroom. Since Mom died it had become the gun room. I don't remember when my father began collecting firearms, but I'm pretty sure it started in earnest when Obama won re-election. That's when I remember seeing the first NRA magazines showing up in his mailbox, and when he told me more than once that the blacks and the queers and the Jews were "coming to take our guns."

The firearms started showing up, almost of their own volition. A Sig-Sauer .9-millimeter semiautomatic, a chrome-plated .38 revolver with walnut grips, an AR-15. Instead of the hunting guns I remembered from my childhood, my father was building an arsenal in the little house that had been my home growing up. At more than eighty years old, my father had become a gun nut.

I learned to shoot early, maybe six years old, standing in a deep gully beside the dirt road where we lived. That first gun was a .410 shotgun, a single-shot off-brand weapon that would have exploded if you tried to shoot a load of buckshot. My father broke the weapon open at the breech to show me that the gun was unloaded. He was a soldier, and he'd been badly wounded in Vietnam, so he taught me first how to treat a firearm with respect. Dad drew a couple of fat, stubby shells from one of the bulging pockets of his hunting vest and taught me how to load the gun. Then he snapped it closed.

He held the weapon in a position I would come to know as

port arms, the long gun held diagonally across his body, the barrel end pointing up and safely away from us.

"See that pine cone?" He asked. "The one hanging from the tree?"

I didn't; even then, my eyes were weak. But it didn't matter. Dad wasn't really asking. Even though I was only six, I already knew that my dad sometimes talked only for his own ears, illustrating what he was doing not to me but to himself. So even if I didn't see the pine cone, it was still important that I listen to what he was saying. He raised the shotgun level with his shoulders, socking the butt of the long gun deep into the natural hollow caused by the movement. He looked perfectly comfortable, as if he could stand that way all day. Then he sighted down the barrel.

The long gun boomed, the shot ringing and redoubling against the deep and crumbling red clay walls of the gully, and fifty yards away a pine cone that had been hanging from a bare limb, minding its own business, exploded. Dad broke open the shotgun and ejected the spent shell casing.

Then he handed the gun to me.

See one, do one. That was Dad's motto. I don't know if it was something he picked up during his twenty years in the Army, or if had been with him longer than that. I held the gun carefully, and with some distaste, as if my father had just handed me a live possum or a dead snake. I took one of the fat red shells from him and loaded the gun, just as I had seen him do it. I tried to snap the gun closed with the same authoritative movement that he had used, but couldn't manage it. The weapon did close, but not with that same snicking sound of finality. I held the gun across my body, pointed at nothing, just as I had seen him do it, and waited for him to pick out the target.

"Look to your right," he said. "There's a beer bottle on the ground. Try for that."

And there it was, about ten yards away, half buried in the soft red clay. The thin, late-autumn sun glinted off the dark brown bottle. I raised the gun, bringing it up and up and up, settling it into the pocket, that little hollow between my chest and shoulder, and looked down the sights. It was easy. Line up the front sight on your target. Make sure the rear sight—that little notch—is lined up, too. Breathe out. Hold steady. Aim. Take up the slack on the trigger. Then squeeze off the shot.

"Don't pull the trigger," Dad had told me while we were walking down to the makeshift firing range. "If you pull the trigger, you'll miss. Just squeeze it gently and let the weapon do the rest." I nodded, as if I had some idea of what he was talking about. But when the shotgun fired and became a living thing in my hands, roaring and bucking like a wild thing, I nearly dropped it. Thirty feet away, the beer bottle disintegrated into a shower of glass, and Dad whooped in delight.

I was shaking when I handed the shotgun back to him. If Dad noticed, he didn't say anything.

By that winter, I had my own gun, something a lot bigger than that little .410: a 12-gauge bolt-action that kicked and bellowed like a sinner trying to escape the grip of a hardshell Baptist preacher's sermon. Dad and I would take off for the woods every weekend in deer season, meeting up with our cousins, Henry and Mayorn, and a Yankee transplant they all liked regardless of where he was from. We used Mayorn's dogs to hunt, loosing them on one side of the woods and letting them catch the deer scent and take up the chase while we waited and watched. The dogs would drive the deer toward us and could take our time shooting down the panicked bucks—or does, if they were in season.

I hated it, of course. The cold was miserable, and the wet, and every time I'd line up for a shot at a deer, it seemed like one of the adults had already put it down. I didn't mind the tramping about in the woods, but all in all, I would have preferred to be sprawled in the warmth of our living room on a Saturday morning, watching the Super Friends battle the Legion of Doom on our little color TV set.

Sometimes Jay would join us if he hadn't stayed out drinking all the night before. If he had, if the drink was still sloshing around in him, numbing his brain and his reflexes, he'd stay in bed when Dad tried to get him up, the smell of Jim Beam wafting from his bedroom. I had no such shield, of course, so I'd get up and wriggle into the long johns and muck boots, throw on a T-shirt and a long-sleeved flannel over it. Before we'd leave the house, I'd slip into an insulated jacket and an orange hunter's vest. Dad would have a thermos of coffee and something for me to eat on the drive. We'd put our weapons carefully into the gun rack in the back of his truck and pile ourselves onto the long bench seat.

In those days, it seemed like we never had money. The truck was old, with three gears on the steering column -- the legendary three on the tree -- and cracks all along the dashboard. The heater worked, at least sometimes, and we'd ride out to meet the rest of the hunters at the spot they'd designated the week before.

Eventually my Dad tired of the cold and the wet and the hiking. He'd marched mile upon mile upon mile in the Army, and I doubt the woods held much allure for him anymore after the tours of duty in-country, as the veterans I knew called it. But Dad was always safe and sure with his guns. He locked them away in the tall cedar gun cabinet he'd made himself, a beautiful thing with fitted strips of cedar pegged together and sealed with clear-coat to let the wood shine even in the dimmest of lights. He kept both of our shotguns locked in there, and a fiberglass recurve bow, and the barrel of his own father's .22 rifle.

In the unlocked bottom portion of the cabinet, he kept a nine-shot .22-caliber revolver. I could have taken it out and played with it anytime I wanted. But even though I was fascinated with the cowboys and gunfighters of the Old West, I never played with my father's guns. He had instilled in me a deep respect for weapons, and I understood—even as a small child—that these weren't toys. They were tools.

"Nothing more and nothing less," Dad told me over and over

again. "Like an ax, or a hoe or wrench. The only difference is that a gun is a tool made to kill. Treat it careful."

At some point during the 1980s, the guns began to disappear. I really didn't notice much at first. But when my 12-gauge went missing, I asked about it. The big green recurve bow was gone, too, and so was Dad's pump-action shotgun.

"Sold 'em," he said. He seemed serene about it.

"But why?"

We were still poor, that was why. Of course. The only Christmas presents we had that year came because Dad sold his guns, or at least most of them. The only things left in that cedar gun cabinet were the revolver in the unlocked bottom compartment and the barrel of his own father's rifle. He couldn't bear to part with either of them.

For a long time then, my father owned no other weapons. But old age and the fear and uncertainty that comes with it had driven him back to the weapons. He got a concealed carry permit, and whenever he would go out, he wore the Sig on his hip, the little clamshell holster secured to his belt and a nylon safety strap snapped tight over the butt.

The year he turned 80, I drove down from Birmingham to take him to lunch at Ito's, his favorite Chinese restaurant. Over egg rolls and Mongolian beef, he told me that he'd begun carrying a five-shot .32 revolver on his ankle in addition to the semi-automatic on his hip.

"What do you need with all of those guns?" I asked. A mistake, of course. He made a face at me, a look that said that even at nearly fifty years old, I didn't understand the dog-eat-dog nature of the world. But I couldn't let it go.

"Pretty soon you'll be carrying a derringer up your sleeve," I said.

Dad looked down at his lunch, moving the food around with his fork like a toddler trying to hide how little he was eating. It made me take a longer look at my father. He was thinner than I'd remembered. His gray mustache was streaked with yellow nicotine, and his gray eyes were hazier than I ever could recall them being. His hands, always brown and freckled from long hours exposed to the sun, were thinner, too. They were no longer the thick, rough hands of a framing carpenter. They belonged to an old man.

But his hands didn't shake. Give the tough old bastard that much.

We went to the range afterward. It was a long, low cinderblocks building with a red neon sign in one window that blinked OPEN in constant, nearly soothing monotony. A sign on the door stated that every customer had to enter with their weapons unloaded. Dad and I stood in the cold November air and unloaded every gun, clearing the breeches and passing the weapons back and forth to check one another's work.

If the unloading had been awkward, the shooting wasn't. We put a few hundred rounds through white targets with a vaguely man-shaped silhouette printed on it, cycling through each weapon a couple of times each. The old man my father had become disappeared while we shot. His aim was sure, even when we broke out my .270 bolt-action rifle that had a kick like a pissed-off mule. When we were done, we made sure the guns were clear, and went back home to clean them.

It wasn't the last good time we had, but it's probably the clearest one in my memory. Soon the cancer that we hadn't known about was eating him alive, metastasizing from his lungs and into his spinal cord and brain. The last thing he told me was that I was to have his guns.

"I don't want Jay to get them," he said. "You know why."

Oh, hell. I had kind of hoped the old man had forgotten, but of course he hadn't.

After Mom passed, Dad and Charlene went to the funeral home to make the arrangements. I was out of the country at the time and fighting like hell with Delta to change my flight and get back home as quickly as possible.

With no one at home, Jay snuck in the house and stole every one of Mom's prescription medications. While he was in there, he found her little cache of cash, too, and that disappeared. We all knew he did it, even though we had no proof. Jay was an addict, and had been one for most of his adult life. It had cost him jobs and cars and houses, and once we discovered what he'd done, it had cost him his relationship with the rest of the family, too.

The funeral was hard, but what came after was harder. By this time we'd learned our lesson, and the house was locked up tighter than Queen Victoria's corset. Only Charlene and I had a key. As I stood in the living room with the ghosts of my parents so near, I saw my sister pull up in her late-model Altima. When she got out, her face was streaked with tears. I met her at the carport door. There was history there, and I felt the weight of it as I hugged her tightly.

"It's just us now," she said, her voice muffled as she buried her face in my chest.

"I know," said. "It's going to be okay."

It wasn't, and we both knew it. But what else can you do except go on? We went into the house. Charlene turned on the lights; she wasn't as comfortable with the ghosts as me. Even though we were physically similar--both short with blonde hair and blue eyes, and the kind of Northern European complexion that reddens easily and burns even more so--we were incredibly different. She was always the practical one, with plans and contingencies for everything. I was the dreamer, the one most comfortable living in a world of possibility. I'm sure that explains why it was so hard for me to settle down for so many years.

For a long time, I had been the baby of the family. Now I was a middle-aged (very nearly old) man myself, a fact that startled me every time I thought about it.

Charlene put on coffee, and we got to work.

My father never owned a gun safe. By the time he became an old gun nut, it was just him and Mom in the house together.

Whenever my wife and I visited with the boys, he locked their bedroom so that my sons couldn't get near the loaded firearms. Charlene and I unloaded the weapons one at a time, again passing them back and forth to one another to make sure neither of us had missed anything important like a round in the chamber; then we gathered the guns into a black plastic garbage bag and put them behind the washer and dryer that sat in a small alcove off the dining room.

By the time Jay got there, we were sitting at the round blond kitchen table my parents had kept all of my life. We heard him pull up in the decrepit Dodge pickup truck he drove everywhere. When I was ten or twelve, one of the legs on the stout wooden pedestal had broken, and I remember being excited that we were going to get some new furniture in the place.

But Dad was a carpenter. And even more than that, he had grown up in a time where people made do, where they fixed things that could be fixed, and didn't throw things away simply because they were broken.

He had me help him turn the table over so that its surface was flat on the floor. I watched him use a ratchet wrench to remove the remaining piece of the broken pedestal, and then we took the separate pieces out to his woodshop behind the house. He placed the broken piece against the pedestal and said, "Hold this here."

I did, and Dad used a heavy electric drill to bore a hole through the thickest part of the broken piece and into the larger trunk. He coated the broken sides with Gorilla Glue and used heavy metal clamps to hold the pieces together. Two days later, he ran a steel bolt into the hole he had bored. Then we took the pedestal back into the house, ratcheted the separate sections of the table together, flipped it over, and the table was as good as new.

"Do you think we're doing the right thing?" Charlene asked.

"I don't know," I said, "but it's what Dad wanted."

Jay's heavy stride clomped up the wooden ramp to the carport entrance. He tried the door, but I had locked it. The knob rattled, and for a moment there was silence. Charlene and I looked at one another as his footsteps retreated.

A few seconds later, there was a long blast from the truck's horn, and then another. I went to the door, unlocked it, and stuck my head out. Jay saw me, stopped beeping the damned horn, and came back to the house. I had half a mind to lock the door again.

"Hey, brother," he smiled.

"Normal people knock," I said.

"Normal people don't lock their family out," he countered.

He shoved past me and went straight to Dad's bedroom. Charlene shot me a look, one that said *don't start anything*. It was a look I was used to. Once upon a time, *starting something* was one of my strongest traits, but that was back before I had children of my own. Before I had a family.

We followed Jay back to my father's bedroom, pausing in the doorway to watch as he scanned the bookshelves and yanked open the night table's drawers. His knees popped as he got down on all fours to look under the bed. When he stood up, his face was red, and he was sweating.

"Where's Daddy's guns?" He wasn't quite yelling at us, but he wasn't quiet, either.

"He didn't want you to have them," Charlene said.

"What?" *Now* he was yelling. "Are you two trying to cut me out? I'm supposed to get something. He's my Daddy, too. After everything I did--"

That's when I couldn't stay silent any more.

"Yes," I said. "After everything you did. You called him every week, asking for money. Money for gas, money for food--you think you deserve something? You nickel-and-dimed him into the goddamn grave."

We would have come to blows then except for Charlene. She was two years older than Jay, and a full twelve years older than me, but she put her body between the two of us so that neither one of us could take a swing at the other without hitting her. Jay and I stared at one another over her head. His eyes were murderous, and I realized that mine probably were, too.

That's something they don't tell you about grief. Anger runs along with it, a poisonous, fast-rushing stream underneath the placid, nearly calm reality of the pain. Rage bubbles up like an eddy, swirling dangerously and ready to grab the nearest swimmer and take them down, down, down and never let them go.

"Let's go sit at the table," Charlene said. "Jay, have some coffee with us."

Jay and I kept staring at one another for a long moment when things could have gone either way. Then I turned on my heel and went back to the kitchen table. My own coffee had cooled to the point of being lukewarm, but I sat down anyway. My brother and sister followed, Jay taking a space at the table directly opposite me. Charlene poured him a cup of coffee and brought it to the table.

He spooned heaps of sugar from the bowl on the table, stirring them into the black coffee hard enough to slop the liquid onto the table.

"I'll get it," Charlene said, and went away to fetch a roll of paper towels. When the mess was cleaned up, she came back and sat with us. If the cold coffee in her cup bothered her at all, Charlene didn't let it show.

I started to say something, but my sister shot me a look, and I shut up. If she wanted to be the one to wade into the hornet's nest, so be it.

"Daddy didn't want you to have his guns," Charlene said. "He told Bradley and me both, several times. He was very clear on it."

"Goddamn," Jay said. His fingers had turned white where he gripped the coffee cup. "What am I supposed to do, sit back while the two of you split it all? How's that fair?"

Of course my father hadn't left a will. To put something on paper would have been unlike him. He didn't write. He spoke, and he expected you to pay attention when he did. He had told Charlene and me what he wanted, at length.

"He wanted you to have the Hyundai," she said.

"Why in the world?"

Because you can't pay your bills. Because you've had three or four cars repossessed. Because if you'll take care of it, it'll get you where you need to go. Because, goddamn it, he wanted you to have something of his, and you ought to be fucking grateful that he left you anything at all, you fucking leech.

Those words were nearly out of my mouth before I caught them, but I was able to round them out and stuff them back down my throat. The only thing that escaped was a soft grunt of effort as I willed my mouth to stay shut.

"He wanted you to have his boat, too."

Jay looked at her.

"I don't get it."

Charlene drew in a deep breath, then let it out slowly. Her eyes were swollen from the effort of not crying at the funeral and from the difficulty of being the older sibling, the one who had to explain to Jay that he wasn't getting what he wanted. I felt ashamed. My sister was exhibiting more of the iron control with which she lived her life, having carved out a place for herself and her own family from the chaos of the world around her, but here I was, ready to make the situation worse, just to have the satisfaction of seeing Jay crumble beneath the venom of my words.

I kept silent. Damn it.

"He wanted you to have *something*," Charlene said. "He left the guns to Bradley, and he left the house to Bradley and me, to keep or sell, whichever we decide."

Jay shoved back from the table, standing up to his full height.

"The hell he did."

I don't remember standing up, but there I was on my feet, too. I wasn't going to let Jay pitch a fit or act a fool. We had put my father--our father--in the ground less than an hour ago, and the memory of it was heavy upon me. My face was wet with tears, and I saw that Jay was crying, too. Charlene was the only one of us who managed to maintain control.

Jay came around the table, trying to put his hands on me. There was a time when I would have been afraid of that, but he was an old man now, his hands weak and his rough skin baggy at the jawline and belly. He grabbed at me, desperate, and I shoved him away. He hit the kitchen table--the one our father had so meticulously repaired when I was a child--and fell against it with all of his weight. A tremendous crack sounded as the pedestal gave way and the tabletop split. The whole thing crashed to the floor.

Charlene leapt back out of the way, swiping at her coffee cup, hoping to save it. But the white china mug hit the floor and shattered, spilling what was left of her coffee in a wide brown stain.

Jay shoved away from the table, his knees popping with the effort. He looked at the kitchen, at the mess we had made, at the broken table lying in two parts on the floor, and for a moment he was frozen and I could see the guilt and shame in his face. Then he walked out the door without saying anything.

We let him go. Beside me, Charlene looked at the damaged, broken thing that had once been the place where our whole family had gathered. It was the place where anyone had been welcome, where we had shared a thousand meals, where Thanksgiving and Christmas dinners had been served, where endless conversations had taken place, where pinochle and hearts and spades had ruled the evenings before the Internet. Her shoulders hitched once, and then she lowered her head and began to cry.

I went off to find a broom and dustpan, ignoring my own tears. Some things are easier to fix than others.

THE GHOST OF BUXAHATCHEE CREEK

CALEB WHITE HAS BEEN DRAGGING around behind me ever since I chained his body to an anvil and dropped the whole mess into the deep water near the base of the railroad trestle that spans Buxahatchee Creek.

Ain't no telling where the little bastard will show up. Last week, he was behind me in line at the Pic-N-Go while I paid for gas. His flickering ghost appears in the grimy plate glass of empty stores as I walk around downtown. He lay next to me in bed in the dark every night for three months, the cords in his rotting neck rasping against the rusty logging chain I looped around it before I sent him down into the black, cold water.

I tell myself that it's all in my head. But if that's true, why were the sheets damp on the other side of the bed?

I felt the cold and clammy touch of wet chain links on the back of my neck on the night Taylor Davis finally let me get her into bed. As my lips skated down the slender line of her thigh, her back arched with readiness and need. Then there was the shiver of wet steel at the small of my back and the smell of slowly decaying water in my nostrils. I rolled away from Taylor, gasping, every

43

last bit of lust and excitement leaving my body like geese headed south for the winter. It took a couple of seconds for Taylor to catch up, but the moment was over.

"I don't know what's wrong with you," Taylor said after she rolled off of the bed and started to dress. Nothing sexy now, just a striptease in reverse. Taylor stared me down while she put on her bra and shirt, her mouth a thin line of frustration and disappointment.

"People get over things, Mike. They let things go, they move on. I'm talking about people here. Normal people."

"Yeah," I said. I couldn't look at her. "Other people."

When Taylor walked out, Caleb crouched in a cobwebbed corner and grinned his lipless yellow smile at me, a glistening length of chain clotted with rust dangling from a finger.

He never says anything. He doesn't have to.

I guess I'd known Caleb most of his life. His family moved down here from somewhere outside Cullman, real white trash. They lived in a single-wide trailer, and you could never tell how many of the Whites there were, maybe ten of them with about seventeen teeth between the whole bunch and Caleb hogging four or five teeth all to himself.

No surprise that Caleb dropped out of high school. I guess a lot of us do. There ain't a whole lot to do in Chilton County but grow peaches and cook methamphetamine. We used to go fish the Buxahatchee, but the water's brown and ugly and dead thanks to the chemical companies treating it like their own personal shitter.

Caleb cooked meth at a canted-over trailer and chased girls at the Skate Shack, only place that's left around here to go since the movie house closed. We all hung out there, country boys playing pool and eyeing the girls eyeing us, everyone alert to the possibility that someone might be looking right at them. The music was loud and the multicolored lights strobed relentlessly, giving the place and everyone in it a faintly madhouse look.

My brother Victor was two years younger than me, and

everybody made a fuss over him. He had long, dark brown hair that fell in natural waves over the back of his collar, and he had these green eyes that always looked faintly amused. His teeth weren't perfect, but that just made him look human instead of like a Greek god.

Was Caleb jealous of him? I guess so, because Victor was handsome and Caleb was not, but all I remember is how they circled around each other like a pair of big cats, wary and ready to fight over the slightest perceived insult. It all came to a head that night at the Skate Shack when Caleb tried to drag Cady Alberson out to the parking lot with him.

Cady wasn't much to look at herself, but to a lot of the boys in the trailer parks around town, she was ol' Miss Reliable. But that night when Caleb wanted to take her out to the parking lot, she didn't want to go. She didn't want to go just as bad as he wanted her to come, and they ended up in a shouting match near the entrance. Victor was shooting pool and I was shooting the shit, but I knew my brother was going to step in. Maybe I knew it before he did. Victor may have been the younger brother, but he was the leader. I walked where he walked and watched everything he did.

I pushed myself away from the wall of the building where I was talking to Taylor, but Victor straightened up from the table where he'd been lining up the three-ball for the side pocket.

He tossed me the cue and told me to take care of it for him.

I wanted to tell him that he didn't have to get involved. But Victor knew that already, just like he knew that the tension between himself and Caleb White had been building and building, and that at some point the genie would come out of the bottle and the fight would be on. By the time Victor got to them, Caleb gripped Cady's arm so tight that his knuckles were white.

Victor didn't wait around. He didn't say a word to Caleb, didn't tell him to let the girl go. My brother was always a straight-ahead kind of guy. He hit Caleb in the mouth with his right fist, and one of that boy's few candy-corn colored teeth went flying. Caleb went down and bounced right back up like a rubber ball. He charged at Victor with his head down, and Victor put a knee right into the middle of Caleb's face. It pulverized his nose, and he stood up with both hands plastered to his ruined face.

Victor hit him again, and this time Caleb went backwards and stumbled against the Skate Shack door. One more shot with the side of his fist against Caleb's temple, and the boy went through the door and fell to the weedy and cracked concrete parking lot.

You could have knocked Cady Alberson over with a feather. Her eyes were full of tears, shining in that ugly yellow fluorescent light. She might as well have been carrying a sign with MY HERO in bold letters and surrounded by hearts and stars.

"You good?" Victor asked her. She didn't say anything, just clasped her arms around his waist and squeezed the hell out of him. He gave her a small pat on the back and then gently disengaged himself.

"He shouldn't have done that," Taylor said as she watched Victor come back and take the cue from me. He dropped the three in the side pocket but whiffed on the seven in the corner. His hands, the knuckles skinned from Caleb's bony face, trembled. I put my hand on his shoulder when he came by, and it was like touching a marble statue.

Afterward, Taylor and I sat outside in the quiet, humid night and slapped idly at mosquitoes. Her shoulder was brushing mine. We weren't quite holding hands, but weren't quite *not* holding hands, either. We seemed to be drifting closer, like planets whose gravitational pull had aligned.

"Your brother should have minded his own business," she said, and that knocked me out of orbit and back to reality. I leaned away from her. I had been in love with Taylor since the second grade, and usually the only thing we fought over was college football. But Victor was off-limits.

She felt the connection between us break, a nearly tangible snap. I still didn't say anything.

"I'm just saying. Bad things happen to people who mess with the Whites. They don't forget and they don't forgive. You remember Alex Sadler."

I did. Alex was a little older than us, and he had burned up when he missed a curve along Dug Holler Road and crashed into a tree. By the time the cops and the firefighters had arrived on the scene, there wasn't nothing left of him to save.

"That was an accident," I said.

"You're so innocent sometimes," Taylor said. "It's sweet."

She tried to move closer to me, but the moment was gone.

The word around town was that Caleb White or one of his family had done something, but no one knew exactly what. He'd bled the brakes on Alex's car. He'd cut the fuel line to make the car burn hotter and faster. Caleb never said anything about it, just kind of smirked around whenever anyone talked about Alex, like he knew the punchline to a joke that no one else had figured out yet. Victor and I always thought Caleb was just trying to act inscrutable to make himself look tougher and meaner.

But the word got around. You didn't mess with the Whites unless you wanted war. And now Victor had started one. For the right reasons, maybe, but there was no way Caleb White would look at it that way. Victor had embarrassed him and left him laying bloody and beaten.

When I drove us home that night, Victor kept looking in the passenger mirror. Every time we saw lights behind us, he tensed. It must have been contagious, because my own jaw was hard with flexed muscle by the time we dropped Taylor off at her place. I didn't walk her to the door, didn't try for a good night kiss. I didn't want to leave my brother alone.

Three days later, he was gone. One night he went out and never came home. A deputy found his car pulled onto the berm with the driver's door open and the engine still running. That was seven years ago, and Victor's body ain't ever been found.

• • •

Chilton County is a weird place. You've got flatlands, and you've got the very last little rolling hills that form the bottom of the Appalachians. But more than that, you've got rivers and creeks and swamps and bogs. There's a million places to hide a body where no one will discover it.

My brother Victor is out there somewhere.

For the first year that Victor was considered missing, Caleb White played it cool. He didn't say or do anything to arouse suspicion. He'd been questioned by the county sheriff, but his mushmouth family lied him an alibi so he walked out of the sheriff's office a free man.

They dragged the creek and brought out cadaver dogs. But there was never any sign of Victor's body. He was considered missing until this year, when a judge finally declared him dead. Seven years in the hell of knowing what had happened, but not knowing it for sure, either.

Everyone knew that Caleb had killed my brother. We didn't have a body, so we couldn't have a funeral. We held a vigil instead, an earthbound constellation of candles glowing in the dark like they would guide Victor's wayward soul home. It broke Mama, the uncertainty of what had happened to her younger boy. She died six months later, a shell of the vivacious and funny woman she'd once been. At least we had a funeral for Mama.

Another body to add to Caleb White's ledger.

Taylor came to the vigil for Victor and held a candle high for my brother. But the torch that I'd carried in my heart for her since we were little had seemed to burn itself out. I didn't speak to her that night, even though she hung around after everyone else had gone, trying to catch my eyes with hers. I didn't want to talk, though. I didn't care right then if I never talked to another person.

I became a ghost myself, haunting the Buxahatchee. I fished

sometimes, even in that evil and poisoned water, but what I mostly did was pole up and down the banks of the creek all the way to the mouth of the Coosa River. I'd convinced myself that Caleb had put Victor's body in the water, and that if I got close enough to it, I'd feel my brother's presence.

I let my beard and hair grow long. Went weeks without washing sometimes. My face was lined with exposure to the elements and ground-in dirt. I forgot to eat, and my clothes began to look like unfurled limp sails on a broken mast. I looked twenty years older than I was, and felt older than that. Nobody ever saw me around the Skate Shack anymore. I didn't grow peaches, and I didn't make meth. All I did was look for my brother's body, keep my guns clean and my knife sharp.

When I saw Caleb White again, I would have to kill him. I didn't want to do that, was afraid of him in fact. That was the secret truth that I could never say out loud. If he could kill my brother Victor, who was so special, so strong-willed and so full of life, what hope did I have?

Willow Mosses, one of the older ladies who went to church with my mother, found me one day when she was out gathering wild herbs for a poultice, and at first she didn't know who I was.

"I ken you now," she said when she finally recognized me through the hair and filth. "Michael Fagan, ain't it? Lost your brother and your sweet ma last year."

I nodded. I didn't trust myself to speak. Hearing someone else acknowledge my loss felt like a dagger through my soul. Her voice was full of pity and something else.

"I heard that fella Caleb White talkin' about it, you know. Bragging when they thought no one could hear 'em. Him and his cousin Willard laid for your brother, Willard hunched over on the side of the highway like he was hurt. When Victor came along, he stopped to help."

I waited.

"You know how he was. He would help anyone. But there were two of them then, and they took him."

I took off my hat and wiped a skinny forearm across my brow.

"Do you know what they did with the body?"

Those were the first words that I'd spoken to another person in weeks, maybe months, and my voice sounded like a rusty hinge on a door that's been long disused.

Willow couldn't answer me. She didn't know that part. But she had given me something important. She had given me certainty. Where before there had been an overwhelming sense of suspicion that Caleb White had killed my brother, now I knew for sure.

I felt rage ignite like a hungry fire in the pit of my belly, and that fire illuminated the fear I felt. At last I understood that I was wrong. I was not afraid of Caleb White. I had been, until this moment, afraid that I would make a mistake, afraid that I would kill a man based on suspicion and dislike and nothing else.

Not anymore.

Caleb had moved out of the family trailer to a slapdash wooden cabin fifty yards off of a meander of the creek where he lived alone. Willow Mosses told me that his family had finally gotten tired of him and kicked him out. Or maybe it was the other way around. It's been so long that it's hard to remember now. But I do remember that the bank of the creek below his place was high, maybe ten feet above the placid surface of the Buxahatchee. I floated down every night for a week, but I couldn't see his shack. One night when the moon was high and bright like a beacon above me, I tied my jon boat to the root of a cypress tree and climbed, using exposed roots as handholds and finally hauling myself over the lip of the little cliff onto the spongy green grass of what passed for Caleb's yard.

I just meant to look around. The place was ugly and old with a couple of broken-down vehicles parked haphazardly like soldiers left on the battlefield where they'd fallen. The trees looked like they had never been pruned, and the limbs hung heavy, some broken off from the gravity of their own weight, others with their leaves dragging the ground. The cat-piss smell of methamphetamine cooking was heavy in the air. A generator sat inert alongside a couple of uncapped five-gallon gas cans that appeared to be empty.

A small, narrow building squatted behind Caleb's shack. I knew what it was, and I made my way to it, my steps silent in the soft black loam. As I got closer, my nose confirmed that this was the outhouse. Sooner or later, Caleb would make a trip. It would be the last one.

I don't remember taking my gun out. I carried the gun all the time, reassured by the comfortable weight of it in my back pocket. I flicked the safety off and waited. My palm grew sweaty, and I switched the gun to my left and wiped my right hand on the dirty thigh of my jeans.

The wind whispered in the leaves, and I thought I could hear my brother's voice coming to me from somewhere far away, a whisper forgotten almost as soon as it reached my ears. But I knew Victor, and I knew that he wouldn't want me to let his killer go free.

I don't know how long I waited there in the dark. Long enough that Caleb's staggering, drunken steps toward the outhouse startled me. He had a flashlight with him, and its beam cut through the dark and swept the yard. I stayed hidden behind the outhouse. My hand tightened on the gun and it was only through sheer panic that I was able to stop myself from squeezing off a shot as he approached. Instead, I stayed still and silent. Heard the shithouse door open and close. Felt the creak of the board as he settled in to take care of his business.

Every step then was careful, every stretch of my foot fraught with the danger of breaking a twig or rolling on a stone hidden by rich dirt or dark shadow as I moved to the side of the little building. But Caleb was too drunk and too busy to notice anything that might be amiss.

He finished. The outhouse door swung open and he headed for his shack. One long step put me directly behind him. I didn't hesitate, didn't even think about it, just put a bullet in his head.

He fell. The boogeyman was dead.

It wasn't enough.

I dragged his body to the bank. More work than it sounds like. Caleb wasn't a big man by any stretch, but a hundred and seventy pounds of dead weight is heavy. And that soft loamy dirt that helped me silently creep up on Caleb's shack? It was the enemy now, bogging his body down, slowing me. Every night sound that I heard — every cricket, every cicada, every hooting owl — reminded me that I was not alone out here. Someone could be creeping up on me the same way that I had sneaked up on Caleb.

Once I even whirled around, dropping Caleb's feet with a soft thud, convinced that someone was behind me, between me and the salvation of the Buxahatchee.

There was no one. When I got to the edge of the bank, I lowered Caleb's body as far as I could toward the jon boat and dropped him. The carcass made a muffled gonging sound when it hit the boat, half over the side and nearly capsizing the damned thing. I worked my way down the drop, again using exposed roots for hand- and foot-holds.

I made two more stops that night, stealing the logging chain and anvil from a guy I used to know.

We floated down to the train trestle, and you know what happened next. They've never found his body either. And they never will.

The trouble is that Caleb's ghost won't leave me alone. He's nearly more irritating in the next world than he was in this one. He killed my brother seven years ago, and it's been five years since I took Caleb's life — or whatever passed for it — in revenge.

People have their suspicions, I suppose. But I've never told a soul about what I did, and I'll keep it inside me until I find my own grave. The Whites give me the eyeball sometimes if I see them around, but I stay away. I did what I had to do. And I don't regret it.

I started coming around people again a couple of years ago. Shaved my beard, got a haircut. Started eating again. I look almost like the boy I was, except for the deep-grooved lines that bracket my face and the gray hair that makes me look older than twenty-eight. Or maybe it's the look in my eyes that I see in the mirror. My eyes are gray, intense. Taylor says they're intimidating. I don't look in the mirror often. When I do, my reflected eyes look cold and brutal and unfeeling. Predator eyes. Shark eyes.

Caleb's ghost has been with me every step of the way, though. And I think I know why.

Earlier today, I ran into Willow Mosses again. She was in town buying what she called her "necessaries," and I was on my way to see Taylor, my hands full of flowers for the occasion. Willow and I were in line together at the Piggly Wiggly, the supermarket my Mama used to call the Hoggly Woggly.

She told me that I looked good. That my mama would be proud, and Victor would, too. Then she leaned toward me and I canted my head to hear her better

"I guess you heard about Caleb's cousin," she said, her voice pitched low so only the two of us could hear. "Got married, he did. Got a baby, fat little happy thing that squirms and laughs fit to bust."

The thought of Caleb's cousin getting off scot-free made me go cold inside. I felt like the ground after the first hard freeze. I had held Caleb White to account, settled his check for good. But he wasn't the only one, was he?

I left the flowers on Taylor's doorstep and left without knocking.

Then I went and got my gun, loaded it carefully, and put the boat in the water. I floated down the creek with my mind clear and the understanding that my work wasn't finished. In the prow of my boat, shimmering in the gentle breeze, Caleb White's ghost stared at me and didn't say anything. Maybe it was my imagination, a trick of the light and the dancing shadows that dappled the brown water, but I thought I saw him nod once in satisfaction.

I don't want Caleb to be lonely in the afterlife anymore. It's time to give him some company.

LOVE SEAT

HOUSTON IS MADE UP OF CONCENTRIC RINGS, suburbs and exurbs surrounding the compacted central hell of the city. My hotel was somewhere in the middle of this vast Inferno, two-and-a-half million people living around, underneath, and on top of one another, a sexless orgy of humanity.

Here on the twenty-fourth floor and suitably anonymous, where the view is nothing but the jagged teeth of other high-rise buildings against the deep velvet blue of the darkening summer sky, nothing can touch me. And thank God—or whomever—for that. The room is technically a suite, I guess, with a separate sitting area and a little burlap-covered love seat along one beige-painted wall. The bed is maybe ten feet away, but neither Chris nor I can look at it. Not yet. Maybe not ever.

Chris is perched on some cheap Ikea reproduction of an Eames chair, her nearly empty lowball glass dangling from the elegant long fingers of one hand. I'm alone on the love seat, my own drink untouched on the narrow glass-topped coffee table in front of me. My wedding ring feels heavy and prominent, like it's weighing down my left hand. Maybe it is.

Chris is Chris, same as she ever was: dark hair and piercing eyes, thick well-defined eyebrows. Her mouth is full but not too much so, and her teeth are white and even. She's put on a few pounds since we were together, but so have I. Besides, back then she was too thin; now her dancer's body has had a chance to slow down and let the rest of the world catch up with her. She doesn't wear glasses anymore.

"Something I always liked about you," she says in the deepening gloom. "You take me to the weirdest places."

We've just returned from a wedding at the Natural History Museum out in Sugar Land, maybe forty minutes from the hotel, a straight shot down I-69 in Chris's light blue two-seater BMW convertible. Out there in the middle of the fossils and the displays and a bunch of people neither one of us had ever met before, we watched my friend Callie get married, ate the rubber-chicken dinner, and again meandered through the museum to look at everything. We could walk around, together but never touching, and laugh with one another and cast sidelong glances, grinning like little kids when one of us catches the other looking.

"It's a hard-won skill," I answer. My voice sounds normal. Calm.

I lean forward and pick up my glass, sipping a little of the single-malt scotch and feeling the fire bloom inside my chest down close to my heart. I put the glass back down onto the table carefully, placing it exactly where it had been.

"It's—god, has it really been ten years?"

A little more. The last time I'd seen her, she had come to see me during a layover at Denver International. I was flying out to take a job with a newspaper somewhere in the wilds of Wyoming and had a couple of hours to kill. She was living in Colorado Springs. We'd decided that we'd meet for dinner at one of those awful airport restaurants. The food wasn't the point, of course. My point, as it had always been since the day I met Chris, was to see her and be in her orbit, a fading planet finding warmth from an increasingly distant star.

But Chris was always more complicated than me. She showed up, like she always did, running a little late and a little breathless. Her boyfriend came with her, and I understood then why she had agreed to see me: She needed me to see that it was over, that the separation was real, and that she wasn't coming back. None of that was ever said, not out loud. When she introduced me to Perry, I shook his hand gravely and thought of those relay runners who hand a baton off to another racer once their lap is done.

But that was then and this was now. Perry's lap around the track was over, just like mine had been finished before his. She was married to someone else now, some guy who had conned his way into the Trump administration and then had to resign because of all the lies on his resume. The thought made me smile, but the darkness in the room hid my satisfaction.

Chris moved on and on serially, always finding another relationship to leap toward just as the last one struck the iceberg. I knew that as well as anyone. She had leapt from a helicopter pilot named Josh to me, with hardly any hesitation whatsoever, and I was good enough until someone else came along. These days she was with an Indian national while he was in the country, and with whomever else she felt like when he left the country on business trips.

I knew all of this about her, knew that faithfulness was not a part of her being, that monogamy—even serial monogamy—was not in her makeup. She had cheated on me whenever the occasion presented itself, whenever the desire struck her, and still I stayed within her orbit. When we were together, the other men she had been with did not matter; when we were apart, the other men were only obstacles.

Nothing had mattered to me. Only her.

And now here we sat together in a darkened hotel room again. Not touching. Fully dressed.

I could tell her how many years it had been. Hell, I could tell her the number of days since the last time we'd slept together. I could count the hours down from the time I had carefully and gently kissed her lips goodbye before she drove away to start a new life in a new place, far away from me. I could remember the taste of her lips, the way her mouth opened to mine like a flower toward the Sun. I could feel our sex and how I could never get enough of it, how being with her was like giving oxygen to a drowning man. I couldn't show her the scars on my soul, but she knew they were there. I could feel them throb.

I rose and took my glass over to the sink, rinsed it out, and poured a couple more fingers of scotch. I raised the bottle and looked at Chris perched there in that chair, her black skirt slid slightly up her thighs, the royal blue silk button-down blouse. She shook her head.

I went back to the love seat and sat, leaning forward this time. Control, Hank. Control.

"What are you smiling about?"

"I don't know," I said. "I guess it's funny."

"What?"

"This is the longest we've ever spent together in a hotel room with our clothes on."

Chris nodded as if I'd said something very wise. Or very foolish. She took a long drink from her glass, then looked over its rim at me. As always, her gaze was direct and nearly unsettling. In the dim room, her eyes looked black.

"A new world record."

Between the sitting area and the bar was a sliding-glass door that led out to a small concrete balcony with an iron railing about waist height. You could stand out there on the balcony and smoke a cigarette, let the updraft carry the ashes away somewhere so that you would never have to deal with the consequences of dropping hot gray ash from twenty-some stories up. It was too bad I didn't smoke.

I step out to the balcony anyway, letting the vertical blinds that hang in the doorway slither past me like harmless hanging snakes.

At the railing, I can look out on the ugly city. My hands grip the railing, and in the failing gray light I can see that my knuckles are so tight that they are white. A moment later, Chris joins me. She puts one soft and elegant hand on my back, between my shoulder blades, and the weight of it there calms me.

A couple of years ago, I went to the Kentucky Derby. I got to prowl around the paddock and look at some of the horses up close, big chestnut-colored beasts with streaming manes and tails, their hides fairly glowing under the Bluegrass sky. One of the horses had become restless, and so his jockey put one hand on the horse's shoulder, up near the neck, and it gentled right down.

That's what she's doing to me, I thought. Hundred-pound jockeys control thousand-pound horses with a nudge. It's about control.

Every time Chris and I made love, it was about control, being careful. Like carrying a cup filled right up the brim with hot liquid and keeping it from spilling over and burning your hand or making a mess on the carpet. The first time had been in her bed, on top of the covers, barely room for the two of us, the springs beneath us squeaking and crying out desperately. There were no words, or at least none I can remember. What I still remember, as if it had just happened yesterday, is the way she tasted, the way she smelled, the way she looked afterward, how those intense eyes softened as she held me close.

And I remember, as I always did, my sense of wonder that she had chosen me to make love with, chosen me to fill her and move with her and simply be with her in that way. The only thing I have seen in the twenty years since that first moment afterward, when the silence lay upon us and we swam back to the surface like divers from a deep blue sea, that filled me with more awe was the birth of my sons.

"Come back inside," she says, and slides her hand down to my waist to take hold of one of my belt loops. It's hot as hell outside, swampy and wet even up here away from the streets. I can feel my shirt cling to my back where she's pressed it down.

I turn to her there on the balcony, my hands finding the familiar territory of her waist, then her hips. She moves in closer to me, and our lips brush against one another, almost as if by accident. And then there is no space at all between us as we lose ourselves, lips and tongues made for nothing other than this singular moment.

Four years. That's how long it took us from first kiss to last. I didn't know the pain that would come afterward, did not understand the hurt. I was twenty-nine years old the first time I knew what it was like to really be in love, and thirty-three when she killed me the first time.

The first time she cheated on me was with a guy named Patrick. After she told me, I lay in bed and devised ways to kill him. He and I knew one another slightly in that way that you know who a person is when you've grown up in the same town with them and gone to the same high school. He'd always been a nice guy, not a friend, but someone I knew. He was bigger than me, and even though he wasn't known as a particularly tough kid, I was pretty sure he could handle me in any kind of fair fight.

I couldn't get out of bed for days. I devised plans to keep them apart. I would talk with Chris on the phone, pathetic in my need for her, and I could feel the distance in the sound of her curt replies to me. Couldn't she see I needed her?

Patrick was a recovering drug addict and open about it. I could buy a sizable amount of weed and hide it in his car. Then call the cops. That could work. But I had never done drugs, not at all, and I had always hung around a kind of churchy crowd when I was younger, so even though I might have a workable idea, the plan seemed stalled, with no way to put it into motion. I didn't have a hookup, not even as a thirty-year-old adult.

I needed a way to drive a wedge between them, so I did the next-best thing: I told Chris that Patrick had begun doing drugs again. It was a lousy thing to do. But my need for her outweighed everything else. I was an addict myself, but it was her that I was addicted to. When they broke up—when Chris couldn't or wouldn't believe Patrick's denials—she came back to me.

Now, moving on the balcony together, fitting like long-lost pieces of a jigsaw puzzle, it felt different. I don't know which of us pulled away first, so that means it was probably her.

"I'd forgotten how ... intense ... you could be," she said. Her lips were swollen, her chin reddened from my five-o'clock shadow. How do we leave so many words unspoken and still understand one another?

We go back inside, and now she kicks her shoes off and joins me on the love seat, sitting turned toward me with her feet tucked under her admirable little butt. We're both sweating now, and the air-conditioner in the hotel room is working hard. I left the door of the balcony open, and we can hear distant sounds of city streets, human noises that will wake us eventually from this small isolated dream and drown us back to reality.

"We've always been different," I say. "You're the practical one. I'm the hopeless romantic."

Chris rises from the love seat and goes to the sink. She pours us new drinks in the old glasses, pads back across the room and hands me one. My arm is draped across the back of the little couch, forming a perfect little nook for her to cuddle in against me. But she sits again as she had before, our knees nearly touching. She is very like a cat, my Chris. If you want her to come to you too badly, she will not.

"I wouldn't say hopeless," she says, and uses those elegant fingers to reach out along the back of the love seat to find my hand and stroke my wedding ring. She's wearing one, too. It doesn't match mine, of course.

The second time she cheated on me was with Kevin. He was a flyboy at the local Army post, stationed there for flight school, learning to fly attack helicopters in one endless war or another. I'm sure he was handsome in his flight suit. They all are, and they all seem to land townie girlfriends for the three- to six-month courses they take out at the base. I never met Kevin, but I saw him from a distance a few times.

Just as with Patrick, I didn't know how to get rid of Kevin, either. He lived on the Army post, so I had no access to him. I took to driving around my hometown at all hours of the night. I knew what he drove, and I'd see the car around town. One night when he was at Chris's place, I sneaked up to the passenger side of his car and scratched a gay slur in huge block letters in the paint with a flat-tipped screwdriver. His Army buddies got blamed for it. Chris told me he wasn't well-liked by them, either.

It took her a while, but Chris came back to me again. Kevin had grown distant (of course he had—he was only there to fly, and to get a little piece on the side). She told me that he had a huge cock, and I was dumb enough to ask "How big?" At least twice as long as yours, she said. "But yours is thicker, I think."

The night she told me that, I fucked her five times.

We had made love countless times, but that was the first time that it felt well and truly like fucking, like I was using her as an object just to get myself off. I could feel when she orgasmed beneath me, but I didn't care if she came. Her pleasure was incidental to my own, and yet she kept encouraging me. *Keep going, keep going, keep going.* My head was a red haze of anger, my hips nothing but a piston-driving machine. And when I was at last done, exhausted and slick with fever-sweat, I rolled away from her and off the bed toward the shower. I couldn't stand feeling wrong about what we had just done.

But that was a long time ago. Tonight, I caressed her cheek, and she tilted her warm face into the palm of my hand. Her hair fell over my wrist, soft and full. I could remember how it felt in my fingers, how lovely it looked splayed across the pillow on her bed. There was a moment, so many years ago, when she'd cut her hair from its long tresses down into a pixie cut. She'd given me a lock of her hair then. I still have it somewhere.

"I don't know what's wrong with me," she said finally, and stood up. She ran her fingers through her hair and let out a loud sigh. "I don't think we should do this."

I laughed, a mostly silent little chuff of sound. But she caught it. She knew me so well, even after all these years. I tended to forget that she knew me almost as well as I knew her. And if she didn't know all of my secrets that was simply because I had more secrets to keep than she did.

"I know, I know. I'm impossible. I can't—"

"Hush," I say. "I get it."

"Do you?"

"I think so," I say. "We've been doing this dance for how long? I get on a plane to come see you—"

"I thought you wanted to go to your friend's wedding."

"Do I have to spell everything out for you?" I ask. "You know why I came. Why I'm really here, charging at the football like Charlie Brown. You wouldn't be Lucy if you didn't snatch it away at the last second. Every time."

She folded her arms across her chest, a hard frown pulling down the corners of her mouth. In the glowering dark, she looked ancient and unknowable, an Easter Island head with a shroud of hair.

"That's what you really think?"

"It's not what I think. It's how it is."

"You fucking bastard," she says. "I don't know why I thought maybe you'd changed after all this time."

"I could say the same."

"Everything that's not a *yes* is a rejection to you," she says. "Maybe I can't always say yes, Hank. Did you ever think of that? It's not always about you and what you want."

"When has it ever been?"

Chris sits down in the faux Eames chair and begins putting her shoes back on. In the darkness, she feels around like a blind person, patting the floor for her other shoe and not breaking eye contact with me. When she finds the shoe, she slides it on and stands back up. She's in my face now.

"It is *always* about you," she says. "It's about you and why in the hell I can't give you what you want, why I can't ever be what you want me to be. How can you not see that?"

I don't know what to say to that. This is the most anger I've ever seen from her. Even when we were on the rocks, when we were fighting over Patrick or Kevin or whomever else she let into her bed, she was never this angry. I don't know what to do with this anger, a fury that matches my own in its intensity and pain. Chris takes a deep breath, steadies herself, and lunges forward with her next salvo.

"You and I, God, this is why we can't be together. You know the DNA strand, the double-helix thing? That's what I think about when I think about you and me. We're constantly pulling apart and coming back together. We're part of the same thing, but we can't always be together. I thought you knew that. I thought you understood."

"I love you," I say. "I always have."

The smile that breaks on Chris's face is irrevocably sad, like an orphan on Christmas morning.

"I know," she says. "And I love you, too. But it's not enough. It never was. I'm sorry."

And now she's at the door. Why is she the one who always leaves? Why am I the one left behind, always left behind. Charlie Brown watching the football being pulled away and away and away, kicking hopelessly and praying that this time--by God, *this time*--it will be different.

But it's not. I watch her go, hear the final click in the hotel room door as she closes it softly behind her. I cross to the sink, pour myself a little more of the scotch, and step out through the open door onto the balcony. The heat, after the air-conditioning in the room, is like a warm, damp blanket pressed down on a baby's

face and held there against the inevitable thrash and wail of a
dying infant.

She's killed me again, and I think again about how very like
a cat Chris is. But maybe I am, too. I drink a little scotch and
watch it disappear as the night grows deeper and the traffic and
the people in the city center disappear. My watch tells me it's past
midnight, and all of the scotch in the glass is gone. I hold the glass
out over the balcony and see the light refract and sparkle with the
dim fury of the city lights.

And then I let it go. The empty glass tumbles from my fingers and falls down, down, down, a streak of quicksilver against
the black velvet of the night. Twenty-four stories to the black and
waiting Styx of the pavement. It's so far away that I don't even hear
the glass shatter when it hits the street.

GENERAL EXCELLENCE

THEY GAVE ME THE AWARD on a Monday, and it fucked up my whole week. I had to stand there grinning, shaking hands with the publisher and holding the small bronze plaque with the words *General Excellence* etched in the metal while one of our photographers shot pictures. Underneath those words, in smaller letters, the newspaper's name was written in a similarly flowing script. In even smaller letters, on the third line, my name was misspelled.

Some award.

All I could think about was where I was going to sleep that night.

I was still accepting congratulations on the award when Kate, a trim blonde verging into her late 30s and specializing in local business news, nudged me in the ribs with her elbow. She leaned in and whispered, "They misspelled your name."

I nodded and lowered my voice to match hers. "It seemed impolite to mention it."

Kate rolled her eyes. She had won her own award, and her name wasn't misspelled. We followed the crowd to the break room, where the paper had sprung for a catered lunch to celebrate its triumph. We each fixed a plate and moved off to one side of the noisy room so that we could talk between bites of finger foods and sips of sweet tea. Kate and I weren't friends, exactly—our schedules were too different from one another to do much more than say 'hi' in the newsroom—but we always found things to chat about when our paths crossed.

"The plaques will look nice on the wall," she said. "Too bad it doesn't come with any money."

No kidding. The awards didn't do a hell of a lot for you, except maybe add another line to your resume, but the paper would publish a big front-page story listing all of our accomplishments as a way to bolster its own reputation. Meanwhile, I was still four days away from payday and had to borrow gas money from the woman who thought she was my girlfriend to make the trip down.

I swallowed a little sweet tea and looked at the crowd of reporters and editors devouring the free food. "Any idea when mileage checks are coming out?"

The newspaper paid us twenty-five cents a mile for the wear and tear we put on our vehicles as we ran down stories and covered events. Sometimes, even if I did interviews over the phone, I'd write down mileage so my reimbursement check would be a tiny bit more. When I was breaking into the newspaper business a lifetime ago, a veteran reporter had told me that if I wasn't cheating on my expense report, I was only cheating myself. I took that advice to heart.

Kate chewed some overcooked chicken breast and shook her head.

"No, but I could use it."

Why should she be different? The joke around the office was that everyone in the newsroom eventually developed a drinking problem, because alcohol made the long hours and the low pay easier to bear. But the truth was that I couldn't afford to drink. I wouldn't even let myself splurge on the dollar draft beer nights down at the local dive. Instead I drank water and, when I could afford it, Faygo soft drinks. Fifty-nine cents for a twenty-ounce bottle.

I got a second plate of food—I'd had to skip breakfast—and went back to my cubicle, munching on pimento cheese sandwiches cut into neat triangles with the crusts removed. I checked my email and made small adjustments to the day's budget, a list of stories we anticipated for the next day's news, and filled out photo request forms for our photographers. A presence hovered at my shoulder, and I turned around to find Alex, our Georgia Southern beat reporter, glowering at me.

"Nice to see you're working for once," she said. Alex had the premier beat on the staff. She was young and sure of herself and a star waiting to happen. She was a good reporter, and it was obvious she wouldn't be in Statesboro more than a year or two. But we'd never gotten along. She thought I was lazy and shiftless, and I thought she was a private-school snob who thought she was better than she actually was. We were probably both right. She almost always had to lay out the sports section on one of my days off, and it chafed her. As a journalist, I understood that. Laying out pages was tedious and time-consuming, and it kept us shackled to a desk in the office. The problem, of course, was that the better you got at laying out pages, the more the management wanted you to do it. God help me, but I rue the day I ever learned to use design software.

"Just happy to be here," I said. "You gonna have the coaching hire? I'll check the wire for art."

Alex said she would, and we talked for a couple of minutes about the direction of her story.

The powers that be at the local university had fired their championship-winning football coach after a couple of down seasons and hired a journeyman NFL coach, and nearly everyone in the community could tell he'd only taken the job as a stepping stone to something better. The problem was that he wasn't a very good coach, and Alex was highlighting several of his missteps at other programs. The clock was already ticking on his departure, and he hadn't even begun work yet. The only question was whether he'd leave on his own at the end of the season or if the booster club would run him out of town on a rail.

When Alex finally moved off to her cubicle, I changed the slugline in the budget to reflect the probable angle of the story and its potential word count. From there, I worked the phones for a while, checking in with the area high school coaches. I'd visit practice at Statesboro High School and file a story on whatever struck my fancy there, and there was a varsity girls' softball game that I could shoot for wild art, the stand-alone photos that populated the interior pages of the sports section. I still wasn't used to how Georgia high schools played softball as a fall sport, but I'd get used to it. Basketball season hadn't started yet, but practice was in full swing, so I'd talk to the coach there, too, and write a preview about what he expected from the season.

The newspaper is a beast that demands to be fed. If you're a reporter, it eats your words every day and wants a second helping. You learn early on that your best is never quite good enough, that your editors will demand something more, no matter what you give them. Bring them a thousand-word feature on the daughter of a high school coach who attends a rival school and how she's torn between loyalty to her dad and her friends? Your editor will read it, correct some grammar, and ask "Got a sidebar?"

The day went smoothly and I got the section done by deadline. I also managed a couple of trips past the buffet table and scrounged enough from the detritus of lunch to feed myself dinner and breakfast. Maybe I had to feed the beast, but I had to feed myself, too. When I was done, I sat outside in the parking lot, legs dangling from the cargo compartment of my Nissan, the big door raised to let in the warm October breeze while I chomped a thrown-together sandwich of chicken and pimento cheese, washing it down with warm sweet tea.

General Excellence. Hot damn.

Good thing they didn't count your personal life against you. I was living part time with a woman I hated—and couldn't

leave—and sometimes dating three others. I was physically ragged, and my mental state was worse. My finances could have been
declared a natural disaster, and even if I hid it well most of the
time, I knew down deep that I was a walking wreck, a ship that
should have been scuttled long ago. I don't know if that autumn in
Statesboro was my low point, but it had to be close.

A car bumped into the lot and cut its high beams. It glided over
and came to rest right in front of me. It was a late-model Volvo,
dark blue, and when the window slid noiselessly down, Kate was
at the wheel.

"I figured you were putting it to bed," she said. Her smile in the
gloomy dark of the warm fall night was bright. "We're all having
drinks at the Hat. Get in."

I thought about it for a second, then hopped down from the
Nissan and brushed my hands against the backside of my khaki
pants. I slammed the cargo door closed and beeped the lock to
make sure my stuff was secure.

El Sombrero was the go-to Mexican restaurant in the 'Boro,
but hardly anyone ever called it that. It was simply *The Hat*, and
it was only ten minutes from the office by car. Kate was already a
couple of drinks in by this time, telling me about her divorce —
"Thank God we didn't have kids," — and informing me that she
was being considered for the city editor slot. If that happened,
we'd be seeing a lot more of one another, because the city editor
worked nights. She sounded excited about it.

Even with some alcohol in her bloodstream, Kate drove well.
Her movements were languid, relaxed. In contrast, my grip on
the Oh Shit handle was iron. When she parked at the outer edge
of the lot, I nearly had to pry my fingers free with my other hand.

The bar area was crowded. Familiar faces were abundant. James,
the editor; Edward, his right hand; Lanie, the fat crime reporter
who'd fool you. She may not have been good-looking, but she was
a bulldog on a story; Luke, who worked days as a reporter and

would have rather been doing anything else; and Alex, of course. James smiled when he saw me and waved me over.

"Hey," he yelled at the bartender, then pointed to me once he had her attention. "His first drink's on me!"

James, of course, didn't know that it would likely be my only one. I ordered a tequila sunrise because I hate tequila. That way I wouldn't drink it quickly. Luke and Lanie made room for Kate and me at the bar, and we stood there talking. The whole time I was aware of how close Kate's slim body was to mine. We were packed so tightly at the bar that she stood sideways; one of my thighs was between hers. In the dimly lit bar, Kate radiated heat. Or maybe that was wishful thinking on my part. Either way, it was nice.

The bar was loud. Music spilled out of speakers placed near the high ceiling, and the clatter of silver- and glassware added their own notes. But the conversations were loud enough that Kate and I had to turn and place our lips to one another's ear as we talked. At one point when we each tried to talk at the same time, our lips brushed against one another with a softness that reminded me of the warm and gentle breeze from earlier in the night.

It wasn't quite a kiss. It also wasn't quite *not* a kiss, either. We pulled back from one another as much as we could. It wasn't far. The press of bodies around us kept us close. Our eyes were wide with surprise. Around us, the noise and the crowd fell away, and we might as well have been the only two people in the place. For all I noticed, we were the only two people in the entire world at that moment.

"What was that?" She asked, her head tilted sideways a little, as if judging me as an unknown quantity for the first time.

"I have no idea," I said, and grinned at her. I think in the end it was the grin that did it, that go-to-hell smile that got me into—and sometimes out of—so much trouble in my life. Kate took my chin in her hands and deliberately turned my ear toward her and leaned her lips ever so close, so that I could feel the heat of her words as well as hear the sound.

"We should get out of here."

I laughed and leaned toward her.

"You're drunk," I said.

"Not even close," she said, and staggered against my arm. "Okay, fine. Maybe a little tipsy."

My drink—barely touched—sat in a watery ring on the bar. Overhead, a dozen ceiling fans muddled the warm air and hidden speakers played Jimmy Buffett. Wastin' away again in Statesboro. The place was dim but not dark. Kate's cheeks were flushed. She grabbed my drink and downed it before I could object. Hooked her fingers into the front pockets of my pants.

"Come on," she said. "Let's go to your place."

That wasn't going to happen. I shook my head, then lied into her ear. "My roommate's there. What about your place?"

"No," she said. "That's ... not a good idea. Let's find a room."

Easy enough.

As sports editor, I usually took Monday and Tuesday off so that I could stay with my sort-of (and sort-of-not) girlfriend for a couple of days. At her place, I did laundry and tried to catch up on the sleep I never seemed to get during the rest of the week. I'd leave the Atlanta suburb where Ann lived on Tuesday afternoon and make the three-hour trek down I-75 to Statesboro so that I could get started early the next day.

That evening and the next I usually spent at a thirty-dollar-a-night roach motel about three blocks from the newspaper office.

That's where I took Kate. We were kissing by the time I got the door unlocked, her hands running underneath my shirt, her soft, warm palms brushing against my nipples. My own hands were busy under her shirt, fighting with her bra. She tasted like sweet dark rum and salt. We found the bed more by accident than design, and flopped onto it.

Making love is rarely elegant. Even less so when you can't get your belt unbuckled. We lay there kissing for a few moments until I finally had to rise and strip the whole thing off. My pants followed suit, and then I kissed down to Kate's navel, brushing the soft shallow chalice of it with my lips and tongue. I felt her relax, and then I undid her jeans, slipping them off and tossing them across the room.

I slipped back down on top of her, kissing the line of muscle along her thigh. Kate was easily the best-looking woman I'd ever gone to bed with, and I was ready—so ready—to make it a memorable night.

That's when I heard her snore.

I sat up and looked at her in the dim light of the cheap motel room. She did it again, a soft buzz that told me in no uncertain terms that she was asleep.

Son of a bitch.

I turned on the bedside light. She was naked except for a pair of tiny black panties. In the dim quiet of the room, my own breath sounded ragged and harsh. Desire raged white-hot in the pit of my stomach—and further south as well—and it took me a moment to get control of myself.

I went to the bathroom, stepping lightly around our mutually shed clothes. After a few minutes, I was able to rejoin Kate, this time in a much more stable frame of mind. I lay down next to her and rolled onto my side, facing away. At some point during the night, I slept.

I wasn't sure what I would do for the rest of the week. The awards ceremony had thrown everything off. On the nights I couldn't afford a motel room, I bathed and brushed my teeth in the sink at the office and kept a Dopp kit with shaving necessities and deodorant in an otherwise empty bottom drawer in my desk. Thursdays, I usually slept in the office, sprawled out in the back cubicle no one used. Friday nights, after I'd covered local high school football and put the sports section to bed, I'd wait until around 3 a.m. and watch the papers roll off the web press, folded neatly and warm to the touch, like freshly baked bread.

Janitors cleaned the buildings on Friday. If they were done by the time I finished, I'd sleep in the office again. If not, I would spend that night in my silver SUV, parked in the back lot of a local bookstore. The rear seats of my Nissan folded nearly flat, and if I cracked the windows, it was almost bearable in the sweltering south Georgia heat. Even in October, it was hot, and sweat would run freely down my body all night long.

Saturdays, I didn't do much writing. But it was college football season, and that's the time of year that matters most to Southern sports fans. I'd push deadline as late as I dared, waiting on West Coast games like Oregon-Washington or USC-UCLA while filling the front page with news from Georgia Southern, UGA, and Tech, usually in that order. When the last page was done, I'd sleep in the SUV again.

But now I wasn't sure what to do. I'd planned to sleep that night in my vehicle, but Kate and I had blown up that idea. At some point during the night, she had rolled toward me and wrapped her arms around my torso. Her hands felt like fire against my skin, and I tried to ignore frustration bordering on pain.

Kate woke up around 7 a.m. She shifted in the bed and pulled away from me. I won't say that she recoiled in horror, but she was surprised.

"Oh, God," she said. "Did we—"

"No," I said. "You fell asleep on me. Well, under me."

She covered her face and laughed.

"That can't be good for your ego."

"Almost fatal," I said, and slid out of bed. At some point I'd put my underwear back on, and now I was glad.

"I'm sorry. I just … I don't do things like that."

"Like what?"

"Like pick up co-workers when I'm drunk."

"I didn't realize that you were actually impaired," I said. "Not until we were, you know, already in bed."

"And you didn't—"

"You started snoring. As mood-killers go, it's pretty effective."

She stifled a laugh and put her hand on my arm. "I'm so sorry."

Kate slipped out of bed, clutching the covers close to her body.

"I know you've already seen everything," she said. "I just ... I guess I'm embarrassed."

"It's okay."

I turned the TV on and sat in an ancient wingback chair to watch SportsCenter while Kate gathered her clothes and went into the bathroom to dress. Once the door closed, I put my own clothes back on, so that she would be more comfortable when she came back.

"I've gotta go change," she said once she reappeared. "I can't go into the office wearing yesterday's clothes."

Of course she couldn't. I understood.

Kate came over and kissed me on the corner of the mouth.

"You're a very dear man," she said. "Thank you."

"For what? I didn't do anything."

"Exactly," she said, and left.

I stayed in the motel room until checkout time, enjoying the air-conditioning and watching the morning editions of SportsCenter that played back-to-back-to-back. I took mental notes of stories that would likely be on the AP wire and then used the motel room phone to call around to some of my sources for stories later in the week. At 11 a.m., I turned in the room key at the front desk and walked the three blocks to the newspaper office.

Kate was at her desk when I walked by. We nodded politely to each other and didn't say anything.

VISITATION AT NINE

KELLY STOOD ALONE greeting mourners, covertly casting glances down the line as people moved on. Fifty yards away, in the sanctuary of this cavernous city block of a church, her father lay in his casket while Kelly was stuck with the macabre duty of receiving visitors before they laid him to rest. She recognized me during one of those long gray looks, and I wanted to crawl away. The weight gain and the hair loss, two decades of physical erosion, didn't matter. She knew it was me.

According to his obituary, Conrad Gilpin was eighty-four when he died, although he'd been an old man as long as I could remember. Mr. Gilpin didn't walk the halls of the high school where he taught AP English. He shuffled. White-haired and stoop-shouldered, he never raised his voice; he didn't have to. His quiet sarcasm cut down a classroom troublemaker more viciously than a shout.

His daughter had once been my closest friend, back when I was a half-formed human being in the primordial ooze of public school, the unreliable narrator of my own life. As my friend, Kelly was long-suffering. She made apologies for my behavior when I didn't know how to make them myself.

The mourners trudged forward one slow step at a time. Andrew Snodgrass, who had sent me the obit two days before, elbowed me in the ribs and put his lips to my ear.

"I don't see her husband," he said. "Do you?"

I looked around and shook my head.

"I don't," I whispered back. "But I only met the guy once. How would I know?"

Andrew shrugged, and we moved up a space as Kelly finished with one well-wisher and the endless conveyor belt of mourners rolled forward.

Ice-cold air conditioning prickled my skin while the Alabama summer boiled away uselessly outside the car. Ten minutes until nine a.m., already eighty-seven degrees, and climbing. If I shut the car off, I'd have to go in. I'd see people that I'd known a long time ago, but they wouldn't know me. They would know the boy I'd been, half-formed but full of certainties; they wouldn't know the man who had replaced that boy, who had traded the cockiness and surety of a teenager for the doubts and insecurities of middle age.

I texted Andrew: "Made it. Sitting in the side lot." The church was huge, with multiple parking lots, so I had to specify where I parked.

"Want to wait for me?" He wrote back. Andrew was a son-of-a-bitch in high school, but--like me--he'd become something different as an adult, something kinder and fuller than who he used to be.

"We'll see," I texted back, knowing full well that I'd wait. It would be easier to go inside behind a shield. When Andrew wheeled into the lot, I stepped out of the rental car, beeped the locks, and ambled over. We faced each other across ten feet of soft asphalt and a wellspring of long years. He still had all of his hair, the bastard. I stuck out my hand for him to shake.

"The hell with that," he said. "I'm gonna hug your neck."

So we hugged, a curious thing for grown men who only know each other through social media. But it was comforting, too. Inside the church, the sanctuary was high-ceilinged with a pair of chandeliers--one above the pulpit and one above the long middle pews--hung like burned-out constellations in the empty cavernous space. Stained-glass windows illuminated the room with refracted light. I'd spent many Sundays there, and the weight of the memories made me feel small and compacted.

The casket lay in front of the altar, the lid propped open. I didn't want to go near the coffin, didn't want to see the grotesquerie of Conrad Gilpin's body lying there. But Andrew spotted Jennifer Sanders, a girl we'd both known--and sometimes lusted after-- when we were young, and he drifted down toward the coffin with her. I trailed along in their wake like a piece of flotsam in the tide.

Close up, the body didn't look like the man I'd known. I'd been to enough funerals by then to know that it never does. When I was young, people would look down at the body in the box and say things like "He looks like he could get up and talk, don't he?" But it wasn't true then, and it isn't true now. A dead body looks like a dead body, and whatever makeup and skills the morticians use can never erase the fact that the spark of life is simply gone from the husk we leave behind.

For a long moment we said nothing, because there was nothing to say. Conrad Gilpin had been a good man, had taught us the basic rules of English grammar and encouraged us to read and write--and think, never forget that part--critically. His influence on me was reason enough to make the three-hour trip from Birmingham.

We retreated from the body, and then Jennifer left us. She was helping Kelly's family, of course. In times of need, Jennifer would pitch in for just about anyone. It was a defining part of her character. Andrew and I found a place to sit on one of the cushioned

pews in the middle of the sanctuary, not too far back and certainly not too close to the front where the family would be seated.

"We did some terrible things in this building," Andrew said,
his voice low so as not to disturb the folks sitting around us. It
made me smile.

"I won't talk about it if you don't," I said, and that made him
snicker quietly.

An usher came forward with the solicitous manner of funeral
directors everywhere, asking if we were members of the family.
Yes, I could have said, a lifetime ago. Instead, Andrew and I shook
our heads. We weren't family. After all this time without contact, without even any kind of word from Kelly, we weren't really
friends, either. The best I could have told the man was that we
were witnesses. We'd witnessed Kelly growing up, witnessed her
wedding. And now we were here to witness her father's funeral.

By the time those words occurred to me, Andrew had already
replied that we were former students of Mr. Gilpin. The usher told
us where the family was receiving visitors, and added that he was
sure they'd be happy to see us. He was much more positive about
it than me. But after a moment, Andrew and I rose and walked
out of the sanctuary, down a long hall that had not existed when
we'd gone to church here, and found ourselves at the back of a line
of well-wishers, mourners, and witnesses like ourselves.

It was Andrew's turn in line. I had stepped back deliberately,
letting him go before me, putting his body between Kelly and me.
Stalling. What could I say to someone I'd once known so well?
Someone who, once she got married, cut me--and nearly all of
her friends--out of her life as neatly as clipping a coupon from a
newspaper. A few warm comments passed between Andrew and
Kelly, and then he moved on down the line to share his condolences with others in the family. Kelly turned her cornflower-col-
ored eyes to me and smiled.

"Paul," she said, and reached forward and hugged me with no
hesitation at all. "It's so good of you to come."

Up close, it was easier to read the passage of time upon her face. Little crow's feet peeked shyly out at the corners of her eyes, and small lines drew down at the corners of her mouth. Her eyes were pink and puffy where she'd been crying. We looked at each other without saying all of the things that needed to be said.

"I'm sorry for your loss," I managed. My throat felt close and hot. "Your dad was such a good man."

What else was there to say? We locked eyes, and our joined silence spun out a beat too long.

We didn't know each other anymore. I'd been out of her life far longer than I'd ever been in it, and whatever had passed in those intervening years had made us strangers. In one world, the one in which we both lived and breathed, the awkward moment lasted only a couple of seconds. Anyone witnessing it wouldn't have given it a second thought. But somewhere else--in some universe where time has no meaning, where an hour or a day or a second or a year is all the same thing--I could sense that she knew everything that I wanted to say. In that place without time, we would go on speaking without words for eternity.

"Well," Kelly said at last. "It's ... good to see you."

"Yes," I said. "It's good to see you, too. I'm sorry it wasn't under happier circumstances. Take care of yourself."

And with that, I moved on down the line.

I caught up to Andrew at the far end of the room. He was standing with a bearded guy and a pair of tall young men who were fighting the good fight against acne and losing. I stuck out my hand to the man with the beard.

"I'm Paul," I said.

"Pleased to meet you," he said. "I'm Will."

"Oh." I hadn't meant to say anything, but he'd startled the word out of me. Will, of course. Kelly's husband. He'd put on pounds around the middle--hadn't we all?--and lost some hair on top. His bushy black beard that made him look more fierce than I remembered. And then before I could rein in my tongue: "We met before one time, actually, at Kelly's wedding."

I paused. Andrew paused. So did Will and the two tall young men beside him. And into the silence, I blurted, "Of course, I guess it was your wedding, too."

Andrew's glib smoothness was no help at all. There was no hand-hold anywhere, no crack in the rock of this mountain of mortification where I could jam my hand into the crease all the way up to the wrist like a piton of bone and stop this hurtling plunge. This was worse than the time I'd confused the anatomical term "philtrum"—that divider space under the human nose--for another anatomical term, "frenulum," the underside of the head of a penis. I drew in a breath. If I could survive that embarrassment, I could survive this one.

"Yeah," Will said drily. "It was my wedding, too." He introduced me to the tall young men beside him. Kelly's sons. And his, too. Naturally. They had his height and her complexion, so that they looked slightly wind-chapped even though we were in the apotheosis of summer. I shook their hands and smiled my empty smile at them. I learned there was a third boy, but he had enlisted in the Marines and was unable to attend the funeral. He was just as unreal to me as the two boys who were present.

When she moved to Clarksville, things changed. The phone calls—near daily rituals between us—dried up. She had finally been hired as a kindergarten teacher and worked long hours in the classroom, getting things just right. At night I would call and the phone would ring. And ring. And ring. I thought about driving up. I *should* have driven up. But north Tennessee is a long way from south Alabama. The phone was easier. The phone was enough.

A few weeks later when I finally connected with her, she told me that she'd met a guy. He was in the construction business. No college, just a blue-collar roofer with plans to open his own business one day. I was happy for her.

"What will you do if you get married?" I asked her one time, my voice light and teasing. "Will we still be friends?"

"He'll have to understand," she said. "You're my best friend. We're kind of, you know, a package deal."

But within two months, Will started answering the phone at Kelly's apartment. When I was able to talk to her, things were strained. We couldn't say things we might have wanted to say. A third person in any kind of relationship changes the dynamic. I stopped calling.

I didn't get an invitation to the wedding. In those days the only mail I got was overdue notices from the credit card companies and the student loan people. I looked for an invitation every day as the year went on. None ever came. I read the engagement announcement in the paper. *Mr. and Mrs. Conrad Gilpin announce the engagement of their daughter, Kelly, to Will Whatever-his-name-was.* I stared at their picture for a long time before I read the announcement. It gave the date and place and time for the wedding. Would I go? Of course I would. Invitation or no, Kelly had meant too much to me to miss it.

"I don't know," Jacob Reeser told me before the ceremony. "I don't think it's a good idea." I'd known Jacob just as long as I'd known Kelly. Jacob's father had money, and so he'd been able to go to the tony private college along with her. While she'd gotten a degree in early childhood education, Jacob had majored in Bible. I was majoring, off and on, in getting laid. Occasionally with a helping of journalism on the side.

"You're probably right," I said. We sat on the tailgate of his pickup truck in the parking lot of the town's library, about three blocks from the church. Jacob was wearing a summer-weight suit, which is about the only formal outfit a man should wear in the Alabama heat. I had on navy blue slacks and a rust-colored tweed jacket. Sweat pooled at my armpits and the small of my back. My hair hung wet and limp over my forehead.

"I heard he's a real jerk," Jacob said. "Jen said Kelly wanted to lose weight for the wedding, but the guy wouldn't even let her go to a coed gym. He got her a membership at an all-women's gym."

"Huh," I said.

"And I was driving through there on my way back up to Wilmore, gonna visit some friends. I asked her if I could sleep on her couch if I got tired on the road, and that was a no-go, let me tell you. A complete non-starter. 'Will wouldn't <u>like</u> it.' Well, I wasn't planning on forcing myself on her. I just wanted to use the couch for a night."

In the sanctuary, we found our seats. The sweat on my forehead dried while the organist played. Will and a few groomsmen slipped into the sanctuary from a side door and stood near the altar while the pastor took center stage. Jennifer Sanders was the first bridesmaid to enter, her slim figure clad in a pale peach dress, hair pulled back in an intricate chignon. When she turned to come down the center aisle of the church, everyone gasped at how visibly pregnant she was.

Jacob's ex-girlfriend, Cindy, was next. Raven-haired and doe-eyed, she was a perfect counterpoint to Kelly's Irish prettiness. I was the one who had introduced Cindy to Kelly and Jennifer--not to mention Jacob--and even though I keenly felt the sense of loss of my dearest friend, I was still happy to be near people that I loved and who loved me back.

More bridesmaids came out, but they were insignificant. I didn't know them, and didn't care to. The music halted for the space of a moment, and we all rose to our feet as the first strains of the bridal march played.

Kelly was beautiful. Her blonde hair had been further highlighted and piled atop her head in a convoluted tower held together with a combination of bobby pins and Aqua Net. Baby's breath blossoms shone in her hair like a tiara. She wore a lace veil that did nothing to hide her beauty but instead magnified it. Her milky white shoulders were bare and toned. Whatever gym she had gone to had worked its magic. Her figure was a perfect hourglass sheathed in white. The train of her dress spread out behind her, and two small children held it at either corner. Mr. Gilpin was beside her, and the force of his happiness and pride was warm and radiant. Kelly had to step carefully in her dress, so her slow pace matched the shuffle of her father's walk.

A lump formed in my throat as she approached the altar, and I didn't understand why. When the music ended, I sat down and was glad that Jacob sat beside me. The preacher began to talk, and I tuned out until I heard the phrase "If anyone here objects to this couple being joined in holy matrimony, speak now or forever hold your peace." Kelly picked that moment to make eye contact with me. There was a pleading in her eyes that I couldn't read. Did she want me to stand up? Had she been waiting for me all this time, for all these years that we had known and cared for each other? Or was it askance of a different sort? She had made her choice, so maybe the pleading was simply that I stay put and not make a damned fool out of myself nor a farce out of her wedding.

Beside me, Jacob gripped my arm so tightly that his knuckles were white. I tried to shrug away, but he kept his hold. We looked at each other, and I shook my head at him. I wasn't going to do anything. He dropped his hand and the still quiet silence of that moment for an objection spun on like the elastic and perfectly sad moment after a child's heart drops on Christmas morning when all the toys have been opened.

Later on at the reception, Will made a big production of lifting Kelly's skirt and sliding a white garter down her thigh, standing up afterward and twirling the it around his index finger while the guests laughed. Tradition called for the uncoupled young men to try to catch the garter, so we gathered in the foyer of the fellowship hall. Jacob and I found ourselves pushed toward the front of a rowdy, laughing group of overgrown boys. On the second-floor landing, Will held Kelly's garter taut on his left index finger and pulled it back, hard, with his right hand. He snapped the garter right at me, and I plucked it from the air. It was decorated with white and pink roses. Around us the party whooped with delight. Will nodded curtly at me, and I returned the gesture.

I still don't understand why he shot Kelly's garter directly at me. Was it so that I would have a memento from a day that meant so much to her? Was it just another way to remind me that he had won and that I had lost, that my time in Kelly's life--as her friend--was now over? I'll never ask him, so I guess I'll never know for sure. But I kept the garter.

I saved my tears for the ride home. I was driving a little Ford Ranger that year, its body was as dented and scarred and ugly as I felt when I left the church. My eyes brimmed by the time I put the transmission in gear, and I was full-on bawling by the time I pulled onto the street. I parked in an empty lot a couple of blocks away where no one could hear me, and I screamed my loss in great, huge gulping sobs. I sounded like an animal writhing in pain, and in some ways I guess I was.

In the sanctuary, Andrew found some of our old high school friends, but I couldn't remain still. I kept thinking about the stranger in Kelly's eyes. The years had erased the days and nights we'd spent together, and the secrets we once shared were now arti-facts lost to memory.

I looked down the center aisle of the church to where Mr. Gilpin's coffin lay. My duty was discharged. I made apologetic noises to Andrew and the people around him, who were planning to go to lunch with one another once the funeral was done. Then I stood and walked away. On the way to the car, I could feel the lump in my throat rise like the tide.

I pulled the car over before I got very far. The frigid AC prick-led the unsprung tears that stood in my eyes and made my cheeks burn. But not one tear spilled, and no cries of sorrow escaped my lips. Not this time. I was older, and the feelings that had once burned so hot in my heart and soul were muted now, like water-colors faded in the sun.

CATERPILLAR

HE STARTED OFF EASY, a simple trick to relax his muscles and his mind. The coin, glinting in the early morning sunlight, slipped easily from the thumb and forefinger of his left hand into his right palm. From there he let the silver dollar slide down his wrist into the cuff of his slightly bagged sleeve, a movement so quick and delicate that no one caught it. He opened his palms wide for the small, scattered group of onlookers. Nothing in either hand. The little crowd clapped. A couple of the girls laughed. And almost all of them dropped money into the battered black tuba case that lay on the grass near his feet. Some of the money was bills. Some of it was coins. And some was seed money he put in there himself.

Logan Carson never talked to the people who passed by the quad on their way to classes at the university. His voice was too high, too nasal to be a pitchman. Instead he relied on the performance itself to draw the people in. The tricks weren't magic — or at least not all of them were. Some little sleight-of-hand he had picked up in his travels, but he would never have the audacity to call himself a magician. He couldn't produce a dove from a wand, or make a rabbit disappear from a hat. But getting a coin to disappear? That was easy. Money always tried to vanish anyway. To make it disappear was natural.

From the coin, he moved on to the tennis balls. He started by juggling two in one hand, then added a third. When all the balls — six of them — were in the air and everything was simply muscle memory and reflex, Logan sized up the crowd. Some were clapping, and some were laughing. But more and more he began to notice a look in the faces of the people who walked past: boredom. They might toss a quarter into the tuba case, but they kept on going. Didn't even stop to notice him. He snatched the balls out of the air. Each catch was deftly timed to keep from disrupting the rhythm of the rest of the balls in the air.

The onlookers — it was too generous to call them a crowd — couldn't see that, of course. They didn't see the hours of practice. They saw effortless tricks that amused them. And then the amusement faded, and they walked on to their classes, to their friends, to the lives waiting on ahead for them. Logan remained behind on the quad with his tricks and his act and his welcoming smile — just another amusement in a culture that offered thousands of them. Logan shook his head to clear the image of himself alone and left behind and nearly dropped one of the balls. Catching that one threw his rhythm off for the others, and it was only by reflex that no balls hit the ground.

He moved on to the basketball, spinning it on the middle finger of his right hand, letting it roll over the back of his hand, back into his palm and finally onto the tip of his finger again. When the spin wound down, he transitioned into his free-throw shooting stance, as if there were an invisible orange hoop and white nylon net 15 feet away. He put the shot up with a lot of backspin on it, just as he would if he were on the court. String music, baby. But instead of arcing the ball toward the imaginary goal, Logan sent it straight up. There was a collective tension in the crowd as the ball reached its apex and came back down. There always was. But now it was less than on previous days. Logan held his shooter's stance, with his right hand extended nearly ninety degrees. He caught the ball on its downward path, using the back of his right hand, and let the ball roll down his right arm. Logan dipped his head slightly to let the ball pass over his neck and down his left shoulder. He extended his left arm and let the ball roll up it, then began to pass the ball from arm to arm as it rolled across his chest.

The move was stunning, something right out of the Harlem Globetrotters' playbook. Those who hadn't seen it before stopped and stared. It was a good trick. Logan knew it, and the people who passed on the sidewalk knew it too. A fresh shower of money spattered into the tuba case. But still they walked on. It went that way for the rest of the morning and on through the afternoon, no matter which trick he tried. When Logan packed up all his props after a long afternoon sweating in the sun, he had made more than two hundred dollars. But the attention he once commanded on the quad had never materialized. So many of them walked around in their own world, ear buds canceling out any noise that they didn't want to hear, eyes cast downward and glued to their phones, pedestrians on autopilot and blissfully unaware of the world around them. Head hanging, at the end of the day he dragged his tuba case behind him along the sidewalk like a disobedient dog.

At home Logan kicked off his shoes, grabbed a beer from the fridge and collapsed onto the living-room couch. Bradley, his roommate, was already there, surrounded by his laptop, the latest smartphone, open textbooks, and spiral-bound notebooks. In a week, the college had its spring semester finals. Then there would be no work, not for a while at least. The summer mini-term would help. But Logan could expect a dip — a significant one — in money. Some students stayed for summer, but most went on vacation. The money they could have left with Logan would go to someone else, in Cancun or Miami or Panama City. He and Bradley sat in silence for a while. There was no noise in the apartment aside from the small creaks and ticks of the run-down building settling into its old age. There was no TV. Logan couldn't afford one, and Bradley was too studious, too serious, to care about TV. He was so engrossed in cramming for finals that Logan wasn't sure Bradley had heard him come in.

"I've been doing this too long," Logan said.

"What?" Until Bradley answered, Logan hadn't realized he had spoken aloud.

"Performing," Logan said. "I've been doing it too long. They've seen everything I can do. Now they're not even watching anymore. They just toss me a couple of coins, maybe a buck, and walk on by."

"So what? You're still getting their money."

"The money isn't the point," Logan said. "It's the principle of the thing."

Bradley took off his glasses and cleaned the lenses with the tail of his shirt.

"Anytime someone says that, what they really mean is that it's the money. Bad day?"

"Nope. It was OK." He thought of the two hundred bucks in bills and change. Better than OK, really. "But nobody was watching. They didn't care. Had other places to be or better things to do, I don't know."

Logan swallowed some beer and thought about it for a little while.

"See, if they're watching my show, I'm earning their money," he said. "It's a trade-off, no matter if they give me a dollar or a nickel. I'm still being paid for my work. But now a lot of them don't even look, not even a pause to ask themselves for a second, 'How did he do that?'"

"I don't see where it matters," Bradley said. "You're still making money. Why worry about it?"

"If they're not watching, I might as well be panhandling out there. Maybe I should get a little sign that says 'Will work for food." I'm a performer, Brad. I don't just want their money. I want their hearts."

"Settle for the money. Maybe it makes a difference to you, but most people don't see any difference between you and some guy with a cardboard sign around his neck."

Leave it to Bradley to shove it in his face like that. Bradley, who never had to worry about his half of the rent because his parents always paid it. Logan was sure that Bradley — who had the 4.0 GPA and a path to graduate summa cum laude, who had a job waiting with his father's company when he finished his degree — fell somewhere on the autism spectrum, because he was so direct and seemingly unaware of social niceties. But he also wasn't wrong.

I've got to show them the difference, Logan thought.

The next day it rained, so he couldn't perform. Instead, he paced around the apartment and tried to think of a new trick, something that would really stand out to the meandering crowds that passed him daily. There were ordinances against fire. He had learned that the first day on the quad, nearly three years ago. The university wasn't pleased to have him on campus, but they were loath to throw him out as long as he obeyed the rules. And no fire was one of the biggies.

Besides, fire was unpredictable. He needed a situation where he could be in complete control. Catching an arrow was out. He knew how, but the trick required an assistant who was as skilled as he was. He could snap the cigarette out of someone's mouth with a bullwhip, but one mistake and he would be done. No more performing on university grounds, and probably criminal charges on top of that. Certainly a lawsuit.

Logan had learned his craft and showmanship in Paris, where he had stood out among the buskers and the con men. His tricks were smooth and funny, engaging and performed with a knowing wink, as though he were performing in some sort of campy 1980s comedy film. His hands were deft, and he never made the mistake that so many of his fellows did: he never took his performances to the Metro. It was a common thing to see a street performer hustle into a crowded metro car with a portable karaoke machine and a musical instrument in tow. Once the doors closed, the performer put on his show, crooning or dancing while his partner passed a hat throughout the car. But there wasn't much money in it, Logan could see that from the first. People — especially people in a hurry to get somewhere — didn't appreciate being a captive audience, and whatever money the hat contained, it never seemed to be full.

There was always a collective sigh of relief when those guys left the train car to go annoy someone else.

And then there were guys like Francois, the always smiling Frenchman who had helped Logan from the start. Francois was a former acrobat, injured in a fall while working with Cirque du Soleil. He could no longer tumble, but his body remained supple, and he could play at anything and still make money.

"The thing is to always be one step ahead of your mark," Francois said one day as they nursed tiny cups of bitter coffee in front of the Baille de Suffren near the base of the Eiffel Tower. "They expect something, but you change the direction of the dance. You have to wow them, give them some reason to stop and open their purses."

They were eating badly cooked steak and *pommes frites* – the restaurant had a great location but its food wasn't fit for *un chien*, as Francois said on more than one occasion. They called it the Belly of Suffering, and felt badly for the tourists, who could afford finer food but didn't know any better. They thought everything in Paris was wonderful.

In the shadow of the tower they plied their trade until the ministry of tourism ran them off, moving them further and further away from the tourists each day until there was no money to be made. Finally, they said the hell with it and went up to Montmartre. The money was better there for a while, and Logan learned some more tricks from Francois: handstands and head-stands, walkovers, spinning plates on top of broomsticks, even some comedic fencing. They worked and played until one day Francois performed a trick he didn't know quite as well as he thought – he picked a mark's pocket on the way down the stairs from the mountain.

The man was Maxim, an artist of some note who did carica-tures of the tourists that frequented the square near Sacre Couer. Maxim caught Francois by the hand — the hand that still held the artist's wallet — and bent it back behind his shoulder blade. Even six meters away, Logan could hear the bone when it snapped above the elbow.

Francois screamed, and Maxim let him go. The little man fell forward, tried to break his fall with his hands, and screamed again. Logan ran to him, careful of the Frenchman's broken arm. Maxim squatted nearby and picked up the wallet. After he stood and slipped the wallet back into his coat, Maxim looked calmly at the two street performers.

"No trouble, no trouble," Logan said in his broken French. He had one arm around Francois and was trying to help him to his feet. "My friend is sorry. It's just been a bad day."

"It can get worse," Maxim said. He stood calmly in the wan-ing afternoon light, his long hair waving gently in the small polite breeze. Behind him Paris was a glorious blur against a slate-gray sky.

"We will go," Logan said. "My friend needs a hospital."

Maxim nodded.

"Don't come back to Montmartre," he said, turning away from them like a dismissive teacher scolding unruly pupils. And they hadn't. In fact, it was a long time before Logan had seen Francois again. He had gone by his friend's small studio apartment only to find it empty. Neither of them had a telephone. They met in the mornings at a prearranged location, and at night they went their own way.

One day Francois was there. The next, he wasn't.

Six months later, Logan boarded the Metro at Chemin Vert, he walked onto the subway car and heard the music. He nearly turned around and got off, but the damned singers — beggars, he and Francois had called them — seemed to be everywhere these days. The singer was awful, belting out some Euro-trash pop song. He couldn't hold his voice in tune with the music, and the subway patrons were rolling their eyes. When the singer slithered through the car with a paper cup, asking for change, Logan finally recognized him. It was Francois. He was noticeably thinner, as if he hadn't eaten in weeks, and his right arm still hung at an odd angle, the way it had before the emergency room doctor put it in a cast.

When Francois saw Logan's face, his eyes dropped away in shame. Logan tried to put a Euro in Francois's empty cup, but the little Frenchman turned away. At the next stop, he got off the metro and hurried for the sortie, dragging his karaoke machine like his own private albatross. Logan was only a couple of steps behind him.

"Wait!" He said. "Francois! Why are you doing this?"

Francois wouldn't turn around, but Logan's legs were longer. He caught his friend before they reached the first set of stairs leading to the exit. Logan grabbed his friend by the arm – the wrong arm. Francois hissed as he turned around. He tried to slap Logan's hand away, but Logan had already released him.

"What do you want?" Francois said, massaging his injured arm above the elbow. He wouldn't look Logan in the eye. Up close, his clothes were more ragged than usual. He hadn't shaved, and his breath smelled of cheap cigarettes.

"Why are you doing this?" Logan said. "Where have you been?"

Francois pursed his lips in a wry smile.

"I can't go near the tower, can't go back to Montmartre," he said. "The Arc is too dangerous to work because of the traffic, and the priests ran me away from Notre Dame. What else can I do?"

"What about your arm?"

"The cast lasted about three weeks. When you perform for a living, you can't miss work. You know that. I took it off with a hammer."

Logan shook his head. Of course Francois had to work. Why hadn't Logan thought of that? He had been making money — a lot of it, in fact more than ever — since Francois hadn't been coming around. He took a fifty Euro note from his wallet and pressed it into Francois's hand. It left him short on ready cash, but he would be performing again tonight. Francois would not.

"Get something to eat," he said in his stilted French. "Go somewhere warm. Drink some wine. Rethink this silly thing. Tomorrow we will go to Maxim and talk to him together. Meet me at the Bastille station at eight tomorrow night. It will all work out."

Francois took the money. But he didn't meet Logan the next night. Nor the night after that. In the weeks that followed, Logan thought often about his friend. He should have ridden the Metro at every opportunity, searched Francois out and helped him as the man had helped Logan in the old days. But the tourists were thick like the clouds of summer flies. Logan was having fun performing for the crowds, and most importantly he was making nearly three hundred Euros a day. And then it happened by accident, months after Logan had stopped looking.

Francois, looking older and thinner than ever, came onto the crowded subway car with his karaoke machine in tow. The car was hot and stifling with the press of bodies and the heat turned up in the vents along the subway car's walls. Before Francois could turn his microphone on, a short burly man with a badly trimmed van dyke said "Oh hell no" in American-accented English and grabbed the machine and launched it out the open door of the subway car. People applauded. Some whistled. Nearly everyone laughed. Francois scrambled out of the car barely before the doors swished closed and fell to his knees by the machine, which had shattered. Logan caught one last glimpse of his friend: head down, crying, trying hopelessly to pull the cheap plastic machine back into some semblance of order.

After that, Logan was finished with Paris. It felt soured the way that old milk tastes. All the old hangouts seemed lonely and haunted, as if the lights in the city were dimmer than they should be. The money was still good, but any small bit of success tasted like ashes in his mouth. Spring was gray, rainy and cold, and the city itself seemed that way, too. He saved enough money to pack his duffle and hop a flight back to the states. By the time the plane left the ground, he was already asleep. Ten hours later he was back on American soil. Two days after that, he was asked by airport police to leave Atlanta's Hartsfield International Airport. He didn't go. The third time they asked, they'd thrown him in jail for ten days on a vagrancy charge. Logan moved on. He finally ended up in Tuscaloosa, playing to a college crowd that could afford to be generous. After all, so many of them were paying for school with Daddy's money.

There were occasional problems — drunk frat boys, mostly, trying to look cool in front of their even drunker friends. But those problems were few and far between. Logan handled them with humor that deflected their attempts to belittle or scare him, and soon they left him alone except for the occasional flutter of money into his case. Even the street preacher who stood at the other end of the quad and shouted scripture at the top of his lungs treated him decently, although the preacher had never once dropped anything into the tuba case except a tract explaining why Logan — and everyone else, apparently — was going to hell. The administration ignored Logan, and would do so until someone complained. He was generally accepted as just another fixture around campus.

And that was where the problem lay. Logan no longer stood out. His first year in Tuscaloosa, the smiles on the faces of the passing crowd were genuine — happy and surprised. Logan was something new and interesting. A few girls even lingered awhile and flirted. Sometimes he went home with one of the artsy-looking girls who lived off-campus and thought they were being daring by bringing the busker back to their place. A couple of times, sorority girls flashed him while he was juggling or balancing plates, just to see if he would lose his concentration. He didn't, but he did appreciate the view.

Nothing like that had happened for a long time. Logan was still pacing the length of the shabby little apartment when Bradley returned from one of his finals.

"Aced it, man!" Bradley said. He tossed his book bag onto the floor beside the threshold. It landed with a massive thump, and Bradley stood for a moment with his hands on his hips, leaning backwards to stretch. Logan could see the man Bradley would become at forty, at fifty. He would be something or someone else than he was right now when he had blossomed into the fullness of adulthood. Looking at his roommate, Logan caught a glimmer — not an idea, but the shape of an idea — something that showed itself for just a moment and then slipped back into the mists of his mind.

"I swear, I thought Welch was going to be tough, but that thing was a tit." Bradley seemed to expand as he came into the apartment, his presence filling more and more of the space until Logan could barely stand it anymore. He rubbed his eyes. Been thinking too hard all day. Too many memories. Too much. Too much. And still he kept staring at this new Bradley shining as if with some interior light, fresh with life, bursting with joy.

Logan watched his roommate strip off his jacket and tie. Bradley went to the fridge and got a beer, then plopped down on the sprung couch. But it wasn't until he took off his glasses and leaned back with his head toward the ceiling that things finally clicked for Logan. Bradley didn't look like himself. With a tough exam past, with time to relax, Bradley was something or someone new and different. Without pressure, his features looked fresher. The lines that pinched his face while he studied were gone. His posture was different.

And there was the idea. Logan clapped his hand to his forehead hard enough to hurt. Charlie Chaplin had done something like it. Francois had told him about it one time. Logan wasn't sure he could do it. But he knew he had to try.

• • •

Everyone felt sorry for the little old lady on the quad. She stood alone, her back humped from years of carrying heavy burdens. A few wisps of gray hair peeked out from under the kerchief she wore over her head, and she had little round spectacles like John Lennon used to wear. A little oak bucket sat next to her on the ground. Some just assumed she was a beggar. And maybe she was. Money would occasionally clink into the bucket. Some passersby — students and professors — tried to ask her if they could help. The woman wouldn't say anything. She wasn't rude about it, just shook her head.

They weren't sure when it happened, but sometime during the morning, the woman began to change. She stood a little taller. Her manner seemed less matronly. Inch by inch, she began to slowly morph into something different. As this change went on, word began to spread around campus that something odd, something strange, was happening down on the quad.

Students and faculty paused for a second on their way to or from class. They meant to stay for only a moment, but as the changes — little slips of personality or clothing sliding away to reveal something else entirely — began to pile up, they stayed, fascinated like a bird standing before a cobra. Administration officials arrived, as did security. An officer made a move toward the old woman, but he was shouted down violently by the crowd. His path to the woman was blocked, almost as if by accident. The officials conferred and decided it was best to let whatever was happening, happen. No one seemed to be in any danger. And the crowd grew. People elbowed to the front to catch a glimpse of what was going on and then were elbowed back themselves as even more people arrived. Students held their smartphones high into the air to take photos, uploading live video to social media. A reporter and photographer from the student newspaper showed up. A local TV crew, helmed by a bored-looking videographer and a thin, dark-haired young woman whose hair was too perfect to be anything but an on-camera reporter, got out of their mini-van and began unloading equipment for a live shot.

The air quivered with excitement and no small sense of confusion.

The woman seemed to grow, to change, then to be simply her-self again, with some bit of her outfit or posture changed. Maybe it was the time of day, maybe it was some trick of the eye, but she seemed to be lit with a glow that struck the onlookers as inexpli-cable. The movements were slow and mesmerizing, and onlook-ers were left with the impression of a butterfly worming its way free of a cocoon. A caterpillar had gone in, and no one knew what would come out the other side.

It was well past lunch when it finally ended, when the woman finally straightened and was no longer a woman. She whipped off the kerchief and the last wisps of her gray hair slipped harmlessly away in the spring breeze. Before them stood a man – a man none of them had really seen before. He stood tall and straight, with his arms extended from his sides. Did the crowd gasp? No, but they stared, unsure of just what they were seeing, uncertain that the show was over.

Logan took a bow.

The applause started slowly, somewhere in the back. By then there were hundreds of students and faculty gathered. They shook their heads as if waking from some drowning dream, blinked rap-idly, coming back to their senses from the hypnotic moment that had captured them all like a spider snaring its prey in an unseen web. Someone grabbed the old woman's bucket — Logan's bucket

— and began to pass it around. The applause grew until it filled Logan's ears, filled his heart, filled his world. He had them, every last one of them. He could look at their faces and recognize the joy of seeing something new. Logan bowed again.

Security eventually dispersed the crowd and escorted Logan away from the quad to scattered boos. He understood, without being told, that he would no longer be welcome. But he didn't care. He had them. Had their hearts. Had their minds. It was time to move on anyway. It couldn't get any better.

ROOM FOR AN HOUR

HE LAY STILL ON THE BED while the woman molded herself to him, her head on his shoulder. One of her arms was draped across his chest. The room had been drab and cramped with the lights on, and the weight of what they were there to do had lain heavily upon him. With the lights off, it was easier. The shades were drawn tight across the windows. He had turned on the bathroom light and left the door open a crack. There was just enough light that he could make out the slim length of her thigh pressed against him.

It shouldn't have been that difficult. He reached for the bedside table, groping past the remnants of the condom package and found the remote control. A smiling desk clerk had issued the clicker with the same efficiency she'd used to present his key. He would have to turn in the remote and the room key when he checked out, she said. The smiling desk clerk hadn't seen the woman waiting in the car.

He turned on the TV. Automatically, he began to scroll through the channels again. Halfway through, the woman began to move restlessly beside him. It annoyed her when he did that. That was the reason he did it.

"Why don't we watch the news?" She said. Her voice didn't betray her irritation, but she held her body rigid until he settled on a channel.

"All right?"

"It's fine," she said. Meaning, of course, that it wasn't.

On the screen, a group of well-dressed men and women were discussing the election. They escalated, going from squabbling to screaming, then full-on shouting at one another. It was like watching spoiled children who weren't their way. He had never understood why politics was so personal to some people.

Of course that had changed. He understood now. All too well.

The woman took the remote from his hand and pointed it at the TV. The screen went black.

"They can't help themselves, can they?" She asked. "Do you understand it?"

"No."

"I don't either. You would think after a while that they'd get tired. They *won*, for God's sake. It makes me exhausted just watching."

"Me too."

"You don't want to talk, do you?" She said. He shrugged. She sat up and looked at him in the gloomy darkness. "You never want to talk anymore afterward. It's enough for you to bring me to a place like this."

"It was all we had time for," he said. "You know how things are."

"Yes," she said. "I know. You're too busy now for anything else. We used to talk about art and books and people we know. Now you just say you don't know. We can't even have a conversation."

"Yes we can," he said. He sat up too. "What do you want to talk about?"

"I don't know." She chewed her lower lip. "Let's talk about the election. Why do you think they keep going on like they are?"

"I guess it's because you fight for so long for something. You want it so badly. But then in the end it turns out you can't have it. It's hard to let go of the things you really want."

"That makes sense," she said.

"It should," he said. He hadn't meant to sound so waspish. He put his arm around her and pulled her close. His lips brushed hers.

"I'm sorry," she said, then laughed bitterly. "I don't even know why I'm apologizing."

"Me either," he said.

He lay back down on the thin mattress, and she pressed herself against him. It was very warm in the room, and their bodies wore a thin coat of sweat like a second frictionless skin. She held him tightly, as if she were afraid she would lose him in the dark. He stayed comfortably still in her embrace. After a while, she could no longer stand the quiet.

"I love you," she said.

He said it back, and after a minute, she sat up.

"We'd better go. It's getting late."

The digital clock on the bedside table glowed 8:37. Not late at all. He turned on the wall lamp above the bed. The top sheet was bunched in her lap, exposing her breasts. She saw him looking at her and smiled.

"Will you hand me my underwear?" She asked.

Their clothes were strewn around the room as if thrown by a cyclone. He giggled once, and then covered his mouth. He didn't remember it being that passionate. He dutifully brought her underwear and sat on the edge of the bed while she put it on. She dressed quickly, then went into the bathroom and closed the door.

He dressed while she was in the bathroom. It was always that way. He could be naked with her, but he never dressed or undressed in front of her.

When she came out of the bathroom, he had already put on his jacket. His car keys were in his hand. She went to the bedside table and picked up the condom wrapper with two fingers. She disappeared back into the bathroom. He heard the toilet flush, and then she came back out.

"There now," she said. "I think we're ready."

He opened the door of the room and looked out. There was no one outside. He let her go first, head ducked down deep into her coat. He opened the car door for her, and then got in on the driver's side. They drove away without stopping by the front desk to check out, just left the room key on the bureau beside the TV. The remote control stayed hidden in the right front pocket of his jacket.

A LITTLE PUSH

WE WERE FIVE MILES OUT to sea when Lindley cut the engine and let the boat drift. Occasionally a sea-bird would pierce the cobalt sky like an arrow shot toward nowhere, but other than that we were alone with the quiet sound of green waves lapping gently at the boat's white hull.

"Now we can talk," he said, "and not worry about curious ears listening in."

Lindley was around fifty, maybe a couple of years on either side, tan and trim, but other than the hard knots of muscle that bunched in his forearms while he guided the boat out into the Gulf of Mexico, he looked perfectly ordinary. His hair was hair-colored, his eyes a forgettable brown. A couple of inches shorter than six feet. No dimples deepened when he smiled. No scars left an indelible mark for the eye to fall upon. He wore khaki cargo shorts, a white polo, deck shoes, and a long-billed boating cap.

In other words, he looked like ninety percent of the other boat owners at the marina from where we'd set off.

That was, I supposed, one reason for his success. Brian Lindley was a nearly forgettable human presence. But if my information was right, Lindley had killed more than sixty people, none of them for love or hate or any other human emotion. Instead, he killed for one reason and one only: the good old American dollar.

The boat rocked us gently back and forth to the rhythm of a lullaby only Mother Earth could hear, causing me to shake my head. I was sitting at a little built-in table on the rear deck (would they still call it a poop deck?) of Lindley's forty-foot Hatteras convertible. He dropped into the seat opposite me and waited.

I took my phone out of my purse, and he laughed.

"Won't work here," he said. "We're a bit too far out for signal."

"I'm just going to record this, if that's all right."

He shrugged, but then leaned forward, and in the unrelenting sunlight I saw how stone-cold those eyes were. He looked at me as if I weren't human, as if I were a thing that he could--and would--destroy if he saw fit.

"You're sure no one will be able to make a voice-print?"

"Yes," I said. "There's an app that lets me scramble your voice as it records. I'll have it on for our whole conversation. Listeners will be able to understand your words, but there's no way to identify your voice."

"Won't that sound weird," he asked, "with your voice digitized, too?"

He was sharp, give him that, and wary as a fox. It had taken me nearly a year of coaxing, wheedling, and begging to get Brian Lindley to talk with me. And then, of course, he wouldn't talk to me on the phone. It had to be in person. I didn't mind, though. I thought things would work out better that way, too.

"I'll cut my part out and re-record my questions, make everything seem just a little more dramatic, a little breathless, you know?"

I recorded thirty seconds of my own voice through the app and played it back for him. I sounded like an old man trapped deep in a well, nothing at all like my normal voice.

He nodded in satisfaction, his eyes narrowed.

"Okay, let's get to it," I said, and clicked the app. "This is April Daley with the Just Plain Murder podcast, and our guest today is someone that I've been wanting to talk with for a very long time ..."

That part would never make broadcast, obviously. But going through the motions made me feel better, made me feel like I was a little bit in control out here alone with a hit man that no one else had ever been able to catch.

I had taken precautions. I'm not an idiot. Two people, my producer and my sound mixer, both knew where I was. Earlier in the week, we'd taken turns using a camera with a telephoto lens to get shots of Lindley aboard his boat. Ava Buchanan, my producer, had gotten what I considered the best one, with Lindley standing at the back of the boat, its name--The Wildflower--written in deep blue cursive on the hull.

If for some reason I didn't show up at the marina by midnight, Brian Lindley's photo would be plastered everywhere, and whatever camouflage his perfect ordinariness lent him would be completely blown.

But out here on the boat, alone, just me and him, I felt like a tightrope walker who feels the rope beginning to separate under his feet: you know the rope is going to snap, but you hope you've made it safely across before it finally does. If Lindley decided that I was a liability, things could turn bad in a hurry if I didn't take charge of this interview.

"First question: How did you get started as a hit man? It's not exactly something you can go to college for, is it?"

Lindley looked away over the calm green water of the Gulf. Somewhere to the North was Panama City Beach and the run-down yacht basin from where we'd set sail. Westward was Baton Rouge and New Orleans and Galveston. The boat was blindingly white, and I had to squint through my sunglasses to watch him. For a while, I thought he hadn't heard me, but he finally shrugged--more to himself than to me, I think--and answered my question.

"I grew up poor, so there was never a real shot at college anyway.

But no, there's no prep course for this kind of work. I can't speak for everyone, but it's just something I fell into."

I let the silence spill out between us. It's a great interview technique, because the person you're talking with often feels the need to push that silence away, to fill the void with something. But Lindley didn't seem to mind at all. He was perfectly fine talking; not talking didn't bother him, either. I took a breath.

"How did you start?"

"I pushed a little boy off the roof of the six-story building where we were playing."

The answer was so straightforward, so naked, that I was taken aback. My impartial journalist mask slipped and fell away.

"You what?"

"This was the kind of kid, he wouldn't take your lunch money," Lindley said. "That would be the cliche, wouldn't it? No, he'd wait until you had your lunch tray in your hands, then he'd walk past you--sneak up on you if he could, so you wouldn't see it coming--and slap his hand down on the tray, knock it on the floor. It wasn't ... he wasn't even greedy. He didn't want the money. He was just mean."

"What happened?"

"I told him we could see a girl, a high school girl we all knew, changing clothes in her room. The best place to get a good look into her window was from the roof of the building next door. We went in through the fire door, because it was broken, and the kids in the neighborhood played on the roof. At least the boys did. The whole time we're walking up the stairwell, I'm telling him about the view, if you know what I mean. By the time we were up on the roof, he was raring to go. When he leaned over the edge to get a look at the girl, I gave him a little push. That's all it took."

"How old were you?"

"Nine."

Holy shit.

"And how old was he?"

"Same age, I think. We were in the same class. I stayed up on the roof, of course, looking down as he fell, watching him hit the street."

He shook his head, lost in the memory of it, and I took a look down at my phone to make sure the app was still recording. It was. At the same time, I noticed the service bars on my phone- -they were nonexistent, just like Brian said they would be. For a little while, I didn't say anything, and this time the silence seemed to work.

"I think about that kid from time to time. I did so much wrong there. We were seen together in public, but we were just kids, right? I stayed up on that roof, looking down at the body. People looked up, saw me. I didn't run. Didn't try to hide."

"Were you arrested?"

"No. The cops questioned me, but I didn't have a whole lot to say. They thought I was in shock; by the time they got to me up on the roof, they thought the kid had fallen. An accident. It--it doesn't take much, if they're off-balance anyway. Just a little push."

"What happened after the cops questioned you?"

"The principal at my school thought it would be good for me to take a few days off from school, and everyone seemed to agree. About a week after the funeral, I came back to class, and the kids who asked me to do it finally paid me."

"The--wait, the kids in your class hired you?"

He blinked a grin like a caution light--on-and-off--and said, "Yeah, of course."

"How much?"

"They pooled their money and came up with twenty-five dollars."

I didn't know what to say to that, but it was just as well. Now that I'd gotten him started, Lindley opened up like a broken faucet. We talked for nearly four hours--long enough for the sun to sink low in the sky, not quite touching the water, but close enough for the reflected light to reflect and sparkle off the waves. Long enough for my phone battery to run completely down and force me to rely on my memory.

He told me that his rates had gone up significantly, told me about offshore accounts and how he used cutouts in the form of dead drops and legitimate businesspeople as go-betweens in order to screen himself from scrutiny. He told me he rarely used a gun.

"A gun is traceable, and it's almost always a mistake to shoot someone," he said. "If I use one now, I break into a house--never in the city where I'm going to do the hit--and steal one. And when I'm done, the gun is done, too. I take it apart, and then put the parts in different places. In a random garbage bin, in a lake, in a sewer."

I got the idea that this kind of conversation--essentially shop-talk--was something he craved very badly.

As the interview wound down, Lindley began to act restless. A few times, I touched him, bare slender fingers on the steel cables in his forearms. When I did that, he would be still for a little while. The conversation and the setting were intimate, and I was pretty sure he was going to make a pass at me before we went back. And pretty sure I'd let him.

"We'd probably better head in soon," he said, finally. We'd been drifting for hours out in the calm sea. He wasn't quite sure where we were, and I had no idea. Every now and then, we had seen a boat trawl near the horizon. But no one had come near us.

Lindley disappeared belowdecks, and I followed. I had to use the bathroom--on a boat they call it the head--but I also had another reason: I wanted to get a better look at how the hit man lived. I found that I wasn't afraid of him, not really. I was mostly fascinated.

I'd waited so long to get to this point, this face-to-face meeting with one of the most secretive, sought-after hit men in the world. I wanted to prolong the experience.

Everything underneath was gleaming teak, from the floor to the walls (they call them bulkheads, April). The salon--that's

kind of a sitting room in miniature--had seating for six or seven
people, and there was a built-in dining nook that I saw could be
easily converted into a bunk. The cunning little bathroom in the
stern was a tight squeeze for me. Everyone says I'm "tall for a girl"
but Lindley and I were the same height, and I wondered if the
cramped space aggravated him as much as it did me.

When I was done, I washed my hands and dried them on a
clean white towel I was pretty sure Lindley had put out especially
for my visit. I opened the door, and there he was, standing--okay,
more like looming--in the doorway.

I'm not proud of what happened next, okay? But when I started
writing this down, I said I'd tell everything.

We went to bed. Well, I guess we went to bunk. Lindley stepped
to me and put his arms around my waist, pulling me to him. I
came willingly enough. We kissed, hesitantly at first, and then
more firmly as his passion grew.

He was surprisingly gentle. We made it to the bunk, and then
my simple A-line dress was above my waist and my underwear
was an afterthought. I want to be flowery here and talk about
making love and all that stuff that a 26-year-old girl is supposed to
believe in. But it was sex, that's all. I'd known it was going to happen from the moment I stepped on the boat, and even if I wasn't
totally engaged, I was a willing participant. I *wanted* to have sex
with him, to be with someone who had held the power of life or
death in his hands.

Afterward, I went back to the head and cleaned myself up as
much as I could in that tiny space, and we went up to the deck.
There was a difference in him now, a kind of courtesy and ease of
manner that I hadn't expected. Was it just because we'd been to
bed--to bunk--together? Men are weird.

The sun was down now, and I could see a sliver of moon in the
cloudless night sky. Venus was there, too, big and bright in the
black sea sky. Now there were no birds wheeling overhead, and it
seemed to me that the waves had changed at some point while we

were belowdecks. I could hear the water now, loud and rumbling, like a constant beat of low thunder.

"What will you do now?" I asked. It was my last question.

He thought for a minute, his physical body seated there comfortably with me, his mind somewhere else completely. I liked seeing the easy way he held himself now, after we had sex. He was more relaxed than he'd been all day.

"Brian Lindley won't be here anymore," he said. "This identity was about used up anyway. I held onto it for a little too long. Probably one of the ways you caught onto me."

And then his demeanor changed, became more serious. Not threatening, exactly. But it was frightening nonetheless.

"That won't happen again," he said. "I can't let it. If an amateur, even a talented one like you" --he paused here to wink at me, to maybe let me know that I'd been talented in more ways than just one-- "can find me, then it's time to burn this identity and move on. After I drop you ashore tonight, I'll be gone."

I wasn't taking notes now.

"How will you do it?"

Here's where I find out if I'm really going to make it back to shore.

"No," Lindley said. "I won't tell you."

I exhaled. Thank God. If he had told me how he was planning to change identities, I would have likely ended the night down at the bottom of the Gulf. He would have felt that he had to kill me to keep his secrets. So far the lion-tamer was still in charge of the lion.

But I knew that could change at any time. I had to keep my guard up.

Lindley rose, and I was startled by the lithe way he moved. I'll admit it now: I jumped a little in my seat. He saw it, and grinned a shark's grin at me. I could feel my heart hammer in my chest.

"I'm going up to the pulpit to get a bearing," he said. "We'll get you back to shore safe and sound. Don't worry."

"What do you mean? Does that mean we're lost?"

His grin this time was far softer, and I liked it better.

"No, but we've been drifting for hours. I want to get a bearing, check the charts, and then we'll head back."

Right. The charts. I'd seen them on the desk belowdecks.

The Hatteras convertible has a long, narrow prow that projects out over the water like an insect's proboscis. It's called the pulpit. There's a metal railing along the front, a little less than hip-high on a tall girl like me. I followed Brian Lindley to it, watching him concentrate on the little compass in his hand.

I stepped up on the pulpit with him and immediately regretted it. The wind was stronger up there, and there was nothing but deep green sea under it, and the pulpit swayed and rolled with the motion of the waves. If I stayed out there long, I'd be seasick, and I'd never been seasick a day in my life.

"There," he said finally, and pointed. "We should be able to hit the--"

He was right. All it took was a little push.

Brian Lindley windmilled his arms and went overboard so fast that he didn't even get a chance to scream. I saw his head pop up out of the water and then the drifting boat struck him hard. The hollow thud could be heard over the noise of the night ocean.

He went down then, I think. All I know is that I never saw him again.

I went to the bridge of the big boat and turned the engine on. It was an old boat, without an updated GPS system, but that didn't matter. Lindley had pointed me toward shore. I kept the boat steady--not quite like driving a car, but not too dissimilar, either--and made it back to Panama City Beach.

I didn't go back to the second-rate marina we'd launched from. Instead, I ran the boat aground at the jetty, the big finger of black rocks at Saint Andrews State Park. The park was closed for the night, so there was no one around to hear the crash as the boat rammed onto the rocks.

I was careful when I went ashore. A broken leg out here would ruin everything. I left my purse with the April Daley ID in it. Left the phone, too. I couldn't help smiling as I picked my way over the rocks. The past year had been perfect. Starting a podcast with the express purpose of finding Brian Lindley, coaxing him out of hiding, getting him out on that big boat in the middle of the Gulf of Mexico.

Now my producer and sound engineer would find the boat; they'd find my ID and phone. And they'd think Brian Lindley murdered me. It was sad, in a way. I'd come up with the podcast as a legitimate way to hunt down Brian Lindley, building an audience, working with legitimate people, pushing Just Plain Murder into one of the top ten podcasts in the world--don't forget to subscribe on iTunes or Spotify.

Of course, I couldn't revel in that success. I was gone, lost at sea. No one would look for April Daley, but they'd try like hell to find Lindley.

Good luck with that.

The car was waiting for me in a gravel lot, right where my cutout said it would be. I found the key buried under the rear driver's side tire. I got in and drove away.

Brian Lindley was dead. The person who hired me had gotten his revenge, even if it had taken me a year-and-a-half to do it. Now I had to fly to Venezuela and start putting the pieces of a new identity together. But for that amount of cash? It was worth it. So worth it.

Who says you have to hire a hit *man*?

THE BIG GAMBLE

WHEN JOHN MIDDLETON OPENED his hotel suite door, I shot him. The little .22 revolver popped twice, and a hole appeared in his right shoulder. I meant to kill the squirmy little sonofabitch, but he twisted away at the last second. My other shot imploded the big-screen LCD television behind him. I walked in and kicked the door shut with my foot. Middleton scrambled behind the white leather couch in the sitting room. The gun hadn't been any louder than, say, a couple of firecrackers. Up here on the penthouse floor, most people wouldn't have even heard it. Middleton didn't say anything at first, just little "huh, huh, huh" sounds in the back of his throat.

I went over the couch like a swimmer diving into the surf, grabbed Middleton by the lapels and thumped him twice with the butt of the gun. The second time I thumped him, he lay still. I wanted to keep hitting him, but instead I got up and walked to the other end of the room. There was champagne chilling in a silver bucket. I grabbed the bottle by the neck and swigged down a couple of big swallows. I'm not a violent guy – not by nature. Then I set the bottle down on a glass-topped coffee table and took the ice bucket back to Middleton. He was trying to sit up, so I helped him. The carpet was thick burgundy pile and had probably cushioned his head a little. I put a couple of ice cubes in his palm and pressed his hand against his temple where the skin had split open.

He looked up, dazed recognition in his eyes. He tried to scramble away from me, but I was right there on top of him, tapping the muzzle of the little .22 against the bridge of his nose every time he squirmed. He was already woozy from the gunshot and the beating. Pretty soon he settled down.

"You?" He said.

"You stole my money," I said.

"Like hell," he said. "I won it. You don't own that damn machine."

"My name's not on the papers, but that was my machine. That was my payout you stole."

"Go to hell," he said. "You're not getting anything from me."

"I already got something," I said. "Screwed."

I hit him with the butt of the gun again, and this time he stayed out for a while.

I knew that machine was going to pay off big. Progressive slots always do. You know the kind I'm talking about – a row of slot machines with a big board across the top showing the big jackpot in blinking LED numbers. Go into Harrah's on Canal Street, walk past the roulette, the craps tables, the blackjack and poker tables, past the penny-ante stuff that I can't make sense of anyway, and there's a row of six slots. The big board above them read $6 million and change when I started playing. That was one year, six days, three hours and eleven minutes ago. I play the second machine from the right. It's a dollar machine, and if you bet the maximum – that's three bucks a whirl – you could win it all.

In the year-plus I've been playing, nobody hit on the progressive machines. No big winners. I watched the numbers climb. On the progressive, every spin adds a few more cents to the pot. My first day in New Orleans, I won five hundred at the machine, and it had been paying out in dribs and drabs ever since. I hate to admit it, but I fell in love with that machine. It was like the girl in high school who led you on but never put out. I was determined that the machine was going to put out for me.

I got a room in a fleabag motel two blocks from Harrah's on Decatur. The room was grim and gray, but the towels were clean and there was cable television. I played that machine five days a week, eight hours a day. Sometimes I'd hit a hundred dollar spin, and that money would go into my pocket. One time I hit for two grand. But mostly what I won was walking-around money. It was easier than a real job. I could make five hundred a week, but that big board with its neon numbers had gotten into my head.

When I was away from the casino, all I could think about was getting back to it. I tried to work it from 10 a.m. until 7 p.m., Wednesday through Sunday. I took Monday and Tuesday off, but I had to be there on the weekends, because that was when the tourists came over from Mississippi or Alabama. I didn't want some toothless hick getting his hands on my machine. It would be like finding out your girl was cheating on you. And when I went home at night to my little grungy room, I could hear that machine calling to me.

What happened was this: I was late. No two ways about it. I was late, and that was my fault. I stopped into the motel office to pay the weekly rent. Should have done it the night before, but I'd had a little too much of the watered-down firewater they serve at the casino. I had hit the machine for a grand and decided I owed myself a good dinner. The result was that I slept for about twelve hours, only to be awakened by the manager's knock.

"You going to pay or get out," he said. I'm assuming it was a question, but it didn't sound like one. The sun was bright outside, and I knew I had overslept. I just didn't know how badly.

"I'll pay," I said, blinking at the bright sun. "Where the hell else could I go?"

The manager didn't know what to say to that, but he went away. I could tell I'd overslept, but I needed a shower and my mouth felt like the Chinese army had camped there on a two-week bivouac. When I was done in the bathroom, I stopped by the office and paid for the next week.

By the time I got to the casino, that little twerp Middleton was at my machine. Of course, I didn't know his name at the time. That came later, after he got his picture in the paper. It made me nervous, looking at his narrow shoulders and balding head underneath the big jackpot readout. I knew it was going to happen. Don't ask me how. Maybe it's the fatalist in me. I ordered Jack and Coke from the waitress, drank it and watched that louse spin. In the months since I had begun playing, the jackpot grew. It stood at $17 million and change that morning.

So you know how the story goes: The four diamonds rolled over, the bells went off, Middleton leaped up from his chair and screamed, and the LED over the bank of dollar slots exploded into one word, over and over: WINNER! WINNER! WINNER!

Security hustled over and confirmed that the machine hadn't been tampered with. Kilkenny, the head of security, saw me watching the show and shook his head at me, as if in apology. We'd sat in the casino bar a couple of times and had a few drinks together. Now he was escorting this little guy up to the manager's office. I ordered another drink and wondered what in the hell to do now. Around me, the neon glowed and the people played. I just stared at that backstabbing machine.

About half an hour later, Kilkenny tapped me on the arm. He sat down next to me. I was on my sixth drink by then.

"You were right," he said. "That baby finally paid off."

I didn't say anything.

"They'll be coming down in a minute to do the check presentation," he said. I knew what he meant. The casino manager and the big winner would stand behind a huge fake check. The winner would be grinning from ear to ear. The casino manager's smile would be much more cramped. Casinos are supposed to take money, not give it back. Some kid fresh out of college would come and take a picture for the Times-Picayune and ask a couple of dumb questions. The winner wouldn't know what to say. I would have known. I had rehearsed it in my head a thousand times.

"It should have been me," I told Kilkenny. He looked at me funny.

"I knew you'd see it that way. That's why I'm here. Supposed to make sure you don't do anything stupid." He opened his right hand, big and square and hard like a stonemason's. There was a roll of quarters in it.

"If you try to do anything stupid, I'm going to slug you in the kidneys with this before you can get out of your chair," he said. "You'll piss blood for a week. And as many drinks as you've had, you'll ralph all over the floor."

I nodded.

"Been keeping tabs, have you?" I took another pull of my drink.

"That's the job," Kilkenny said. "Just stay steady. You've won some good money here. No reason to get blackballed because you think somebody owes you something."

"Sure," I said and ordered another drink.

So I didn't think I was going to do anything. Have you ever been hit by a guy holding a roll of quarters in his fist? It hurts like hell. But when the casino manager and John Middleton came out with that check, I couldn't help myself. I wandered over to watch, just like nearly everyone else in the casino. I was conscious of Kilkenny off to my left and a little behind me. But when the newspaper guy told them to hold up the check and smile, I shouted.

"That's my money! You were playing my machine, you little weasel!"

I was moving toward the little platform where the two of them were standing. People were turning to stare at me by the time Kilkenny got to me. When I felt his fist drive into my back, a wave of nausea gripped me and I folded like a card table. I hit the floor on my knees, and the drinks I'd had for breakfast came back up, burning and hot. Kilkenny was right there to pull me up. My eyes locked with Middleton's for just a moment, and as they dragged me toward the Canal St. exit, I kept my eyes on him the whole time.

Outside, Kilkenny shoved me toward the steps. When I turned around, he moved in front of me. The hand with the roll of quarters in it came up about chest high, and I knew he was going to level me if I took another step.

"Am I blackballed?" I said.

He grinned.

"Stay gone for a month. Come back after that, we'll let bygones be bygones."

I turned around and went down the steps and back to my motel. There was a gun in the safe in my room, and I knew what I was going to do.

Harrah's puts the big winners up in the Westin Hotel. It's right by the casino and close to the River Walk. I knew some of the staff there – had met them, and even gone to bed with a couple of the cleaning ladies. Hey, sex is easy when you're not picky. Of course, maybe they weren't that picky, either. But I was on good terms with a few of them, and I used a five-hundred-dollar chip to bribe myself one of the magnetic cards that accessed the elevator to the penthouse.

So here we were, Middleton and me. He was in his boxers and robe, bleeding quietly on the floor from the gunshot wound to his shoulder and the gun butt to the temple. I pinched him a couple of times on the inside of his skinny, pale thigh to try to bring him around. When that didn't work, I stepped hard on the bleeding shoulder.

He groaned and tried to move. I dug my foot in a little harder, and Middleton opened his eyes. I took him by the hair and yanked him up into a sitting position. He began to slump over, and it took both of us working to get him positioned against the couch so that he could sit up and talk to me.

"What do you want?" He said. His voice was slow and thick,

like it cost him a great deal to dredge it up from the bottom of his throat.

"My money."

"Not ... yours," he said, and passed out again.

It had seemed so simple. Go up to his suite and get my money. But on the way up I had gotten so worked up, so angry, that I'd tried to kill Middleton the moment he opened the door. The winner's suite was nice. Two floors, and the smoked glass walls on the second story let you see the city in 360 degrees. The Mississippi River and the big bridge that spanned it (I had never learned its proper name) were beautiful from this distance. But that was illusion. Any city looks beautiful from a distance. But the very nature of a city makes promises it can't afford to keep. Up close, a city is messy and filled with problems – just like life.

I didn't really want to kill Middleton. I wanted my money. All I could see in my head were those flashing lights shouting WINNER! And if Middleton was the winner, what did that make me? I thought about it for a long time, and then I thought about going back down to my machine and putting my money in. Spinning slots for another year or maybe more? With no guarantee that it would pay out again? I couldn't do it. No, I was committed. Couldn't back out if I wanted to.

I went back to Middleton, and snapped my fingers along the underside of his nose. He came out of it slowly, and I remember thinking he either had a concussion or maybe a cracked skull.

"Please," he said. "I have a family."

"And my money," I said. "Are you ready to make your wife a rich widow?"

He shook his head slowly.

"Good. Are you ready to pay me the money?"

He shook his head slowly again.

"Here is the plan. You pay me, I go away. You get your head checked, get the bullet taken out of your shoulder. I go to some deserted beach in South America, someplace they don't have an extradition treaty."

This time he paused to think about it.

"How much?" He said. I laughed. This was good. This wasn't robbery. This was a negotiation.

"All of it," I said.

"Two million," he said.

"Is that all your life is worth to you?" I said. "I'll tell you what. You insult me again, and I'm going to shoot you in the head, right behind the ear. Little bullets like these bounce around in your skull. And then I'll get your wallet and go find your rich widow."

I let the threat hang in the air for a minute.

"I want it all," I said.

"I won that money," he said. "It was your machine, sure. You played it a lot?"

"Quit stalling," I said.

"I'll give you four mil," he said. "That's nearly a quarter of the money."

I cocked the revolver. I didn't need to because it was a double-action, but cocking it is a hell of a dramatic move. Middleton's eyes widened.

"Half," he said. "I'll give you half."

Hell of a deal. I took it. We spent the rest of the afternoon together – part of the time with him on the phone to his bank. Eight million in cash is heavy, too heavy for one man to carry. So we arranged nine bearer bonds to be sent to the penthouse. By the time the bank courier was there, I had Middleton up and dressed. We plugged the gunshot wound with a thick, small bath cloth and I bandaged his head with supplies from the hotel-issued first aid kit under the kitchenette sink.

The courier checked Middleton's ID while I stood out of sight behind the penthouse door. When he closed the door, I took the bonds from him and examined them closely. Eight million dollars.

"You really think you're going to get away with this?"

Middleton's mouth was pulled down in a grimace. It wasn't pain—not the physical kind, anyway. I'd have frowned like hell if eight mil of my money was walking out the door, too.

"I already have," I said. "You got a nice life somewhere, and this way you get to keep it. The way I look at it, you got half of my money. You're getting off easy."

Middleton didn't say anything. He just stared at me with an intensity that built and built. I knew if I didn't get out of there soon, he'd make a jump for the gun. If I really wanted to kill him, that was my chance. I took the gun by the barrel and slugged Middleton with it again. But I was nice about it – I hit the other temple this time. He was out before he hit the floor, and that was the last I thought about the guy.

I spent seven months in Brazil, keeping a low profile and renting local girls by the hour. It was a routine license check on the way out of Sao Paulo that got me. They ran me through the computer, and I didn't come up. Out came the handcuffs, and into custody I went. I don't feel bad about it. ID is harder and harder to fake, even when you have millions. But I had enough money for a good lawyer. I figured I would be okay. But something had gone wrong somewhere. I'd been in the can three days and no lawyer – not even a mention of one. Every day the cops would question me. It would start off easy and then get more and more tense. At the end of the first day, I had been sweating and trembling like a used-up racehorse. The next day, more of the same. Today, they'd been questioning me for an hour or so, with my hands locked to a metal ring in the center of a drab steel table in the middle of a drab, cramped interrogation room.

That's when John Middleton came through the door. He had thinned down in the months that had passed. Before, he had looked well-fed and happy, probably like any other middle class American citizen.

Now he looked hungry.

Middleton held out his hand to one of the officers in the room.

The cop unsnapped his holster and handed his big 9-millimeter automatic to Middleton. Middleton reversed the gun and took it by the barrel.

I could see it coming, but I couldn't move. I was locked down to the table, and I guess I knew it was payback. He swung, and stars exploded in my skull. The big bang. I could feel blood trickling down my face as my temple started to swell. From somewhere in another galaxy, Middleton spoke.

"You stole my money."

ALL DEBTS PAID

THE GAS TANK WAS ALMOST EMPTY, so they peeled off the relentless ribbon of Interstate at the next exit. There were four of them in the late-model Ford. Chelsea and her boyfriend sat in front. The other two, hulking men in dark suits and ties, crowded the back.

Jeff, her boyfriend, was in his best gray suit and slouched comfortably behind the wheel. He pulled up to a pump and everyone crawled out, knees popping like miniature firecrackers. Chelsea pushed her hands against the small of her back and leaned her hips forward, trying to soothe muscles sat too long in one position.

Around her, the men were doing the same. The two bruisers from the back of the car walked a little ways away to pass gas. Jeff didn't care. He'd lift a leg and let one rip, and the rest of them would let their windows down. The old-highway smell of burnt gas and diesel exhaust was better than what Jeff left in the car.

One of the big guys—Paul was his name—went inside to pay for the fuel. The other one opened the lid to the tank and stood there with the gas nozzle ready until the pump clicked on. They were paying cash. No credit card records, no receipts. Paul came back out with a plastic bag full of soft drinks and snacks. He handed Chelsea a bottle of water.

She smiled at him. "Thank you."

The big guy grinned back at her.

"Hey, it don't take me long to learn." He cocked his head at Jeff. "Just like I know better than to bring that one any more beef jerky. Jesus."

Jeff stepped over, still stretching. He looked in the bag. "Yeah? What'd you bring me instead?"

"Some Tums, I hope," Chelsea said. Paul and his friend—she couldn't remember his name—laughed. She cracked the seal on the water and took a sip.

Paul's friend looked around. There were four gas pumps, and the store was glass all the way across the front. The cashier inside was a vague shape behind a tall counter. The four people from the Ford were the only customers in the lot at the moment. He folded his arms on top of the car and said, "You know what this reminds me of?"

"Canarsie," Paul said.

"That's right," he said. "You never forget your first time, you know."

"I've heard that," Chelsea said. Jeff smirked, but stayed silent.

"We could have a little fun here," the anonymous one said, but Paul was already shaking his head.

"We are not knocking over a gas station in the middle of Bumfuck, Arkansas."

"I think we're in Oklahoma now."

"I don't give a shit," Paul said.

"Did you catch where the bathrooms are?" Chelsea said. She needed to pee, but her question was also intentional, designed to derail the pissing match that she could see was brewing. The bruisers from the backseat had known each other a long time, and the long ride had given them time to revisit old stories and open new wounds. Chelsea found herself more and more in the role of, not exactly a peacemaker, but a distraction.

"Yeah," Paul said. "They're around on the right side of the building."

"Perfect." Chelsea grabbed her purse off the passenger floorboard and tucked it under her arm. Her flats sounded hollow as they thocked across the tarmac. Jeff trailed along after her, catching up just as she opened the bathroom door.

"Hey," he said, leaning against the doorjamb and grinning at her like a kid who's gotten away with skipping class. "You know what might be fun?"

"No, I can't. Not in a public bathroom," she said, and gently pushed him away. He stiffened for a moment, but when he saw the serious look on her face, he stepped back on his own.

"Come on, babe. We haven't had any alone time in a couple days."

"I can't think of anything less sexy than this. I think you'll live."

"Such a ballbuster."

"That's what you love about me."

Chelsea flashed him her widest, fakest smile, shut the door, and locked it. The bathroom was clean, as far as gas station bathrooms went, and she was pleased to see the toilet seat was dry. When she was done, she washed her hands and opened the door. Jeff hadn't waited for her. Of course not. There he was, ten yards ahead of her, heading back to the Ford. She tucked her purse under her arm again and marched back to the car.

Paul and his buddy were leaning against the car, looking toward the Interstate and watching the cars zoom past. The sky was low and overcast, full of clouds that looked heavy and foreboding.

"We'll take our turn now," Paul said. "Do not leave the car."

"You don't have to tell us that," Jeff said. "It's not like we're amateurs."

Paul got right in Jeff's face.

"I don't care what you are. We're all here because you fucked up. You fucked up, and it made me look like a fuckup. It made

Reese over there look like one, too. And we are not fuckups. You understand?"

Jeff looked away, and so did Chelsea. Another car pulled into the station parking lot and glided up to the pumps. The air of tension didn't quite dissipate, but it lessened. Paul jerked his head at Reese.

"Come on," he said. "Let's make this quick. We gotta get back on the road."

Jeff opened the back door of the Ford and climbed in. After a second, Chelsea joined him.

"Tired of driving?"

"Tired of everything."

Jeff looked at the corner of the building where Paul and Reese had disappeared.

"We could leave right now," he said. "Just take off. I'd love to see the look on their bozo faces."

"Dandy wouldn't like that."

Jeff ran his hands through his fine brown hair.

"I know, I know. We got our orders, right?"

"Yes."

Paul came around the corner of the building. His tie was wrapped around one hand, and blood trickled from one nostril. He paused when he saw Jeff and Chelsea in the backseat, shrugged, and reached for the driver's door. The car rocked when he settled behind the wheel.

He cranked the car and drove away. Chelsea cast a nervous look through the rear windshield.

"Don't bother," Paul said. Chelsea settled back into her seat and closed her eyes. Paul turned the AC on high, and she moved her face to catch the breeze a little better.

"I didn't hear a shot," Jeff said.

Paul glanced back in the rear-view mirror. "No. You didn't."

Chelsea tried to tune them out. She didn't want to know the details. Knowing the details—being involved in them—was how she'd gotten into this mess to begin with. Dandy never forgot and only rarely forgave. Jeff and the others were in his debt. This cross-country trek, moving product from one place to another, was a way for them to earn a second chance. And Chelsea wanted that second chance. She didn't care about working for Dandy. She cared about living.

Somewhere along the way, Chelsea fell asleep. It was late when they woke her, a hundred miles past Albuquerque.

"Your turn to drive for a while, babe."

Jeff reached down and took her hand, helped her sit upright. Every muscle in Chelsea's back was screaming, but she tried not to pay attention. She got out of the car and went around to the driver's seat. Jeff and Paul got into the backseat. The road was straight, traffic was light, and she had to blink several times to adjust to the darkness. The headlights cut through the black, and she put the hammer down. They were making good time, but eventually her bladder caught up with her.

"I guess I missed the rest stop, huh?"

"Yep." Paul was looking out the window, watching the miles pass. The bags under his eyes were huge now. He shuffled one huge hand across his face, yawned, and closed his eyes. Jeff, his eyes closed and head tilted back, was more slender and not as rumpled-looking in the low, pale light. He didn't move at all. She could almost convince herself he was dead.

Almost.

"Sorry, fellas. I have got to pee."

Chelsea pulled the car over to the breakdown lane and parked. She pulled the keys out of the ignition and took them with her. She walked out into the empty desert until she was fairly sure they couldn't see her, and then she walked a little farther. Then she pulled her pants down and squatted behind a short clump of Manzanita.

Above, the night sky was a riot of stars. Chelsea finished and stood, yanking her pants up and wishing she'd brought a wipe from her purse. Oh well. If the boys could stand it, so could she. She took another look up at the stars, tracing the line of the Big Dipper with her eyes and finding the Little Dipper and Cassiopeia.

She didn't turn around when she heard the shot.

Chelsea silently counted down two minutes before turning back toward the car. The headlights were easy to see alongside the mostly empty road. She stepped carefully around the sparse cactus and sagebrush. She tried not to look at the car, unsure of what—or who—was waiting for her. When she got closer, Chelsea blew out a long breath she didn't know she'd been holding. The smell of gunpowder hung in the air. Jeff was sitting on the front bumper of the car.

"Come on," he said when he saw her. "We gotta go before someone comes along."

Chelsea looked at the dark and deserted road, then back to Jeff. She moved to the driver's door, maybe a little slower than she had to. No hurry. No rush. She took her time getting the key in the slot and turned over the ignition. Then she put on her seatbelt and adjusted the mirrors.

"Would you get on with it? You don't have to show off."

Well, maybe not. But it didn't hurt. Chelsea was calm about things. They were four days on this ridiculous road trip. Boston to Miami, Miami to Memphis. Memphis to LA. At each point they made a delivery, and a pick-up. And, of course, Dandy had given them a task to complete. Reese was the first to go. He was the lookout on that last job, the one that went so far South it might have hit the Equator. Paul took care of him. And now Jeff had done for Paul.

That left the two of them home free.

But it was bothering him. Chelsea could tell by the way he wouldn't look at her, the way he kept his hands to himself. Jeff stared out the window, consumed with his own thoughts. He pulled the gun, a snub-nosed .38-caliber revolver, out of his waistband and slipped it between his seat and the console between them.

"Do you want to talk about it?"

He turned toward her at last. "No."

"You can if you want, you know."

Jeff shook his head. "I wouldn't even know where to start."

"You hadn't ever done it before, have you?"

The silence that spun out between them was crystalline, as fragile as glass.

"No," Jeff said finally. "I hadn't."

"And now you have. How does that make you feel?"

"I really don't know. I—he went out to take a leak, told me to stay with the car. Like usual. You know Paul. He's gotta think he's in charge. So he walked out there, I guess a little bit away from you. And, well, I snuck up behind him. He never knew it was coming."

"You're sure he's dead?"

"Yeah. I'm sure."

Chelsea's knuckles tightened on the steering wheel.

"How do you know?"

Jeff blew out a long, hard breath. The air in the Ford felt stale. Too many bodies for too many hours. He ran his hands through his hair, touched his moustache with his fingertips.

"The shot blew the top of his head off." He gagged. "I saw—I saw his—pull over. Pull over, dammit."

Chelsea hit the brakes, swerving over as far as she could. Jeff popped his seat belt free and leaned far over toward the cracked and peeling asphalt. His body spasmed as he vomited. She grimaced when she heard the splash.

It wasn't supposed to be like this. It wasn't the right time. But Chelsea wasn't sure when she'd get another chance. Her hand slipped down beside the console and came up with the gun. She leaned forward until the tip of the barrel was nearly touching Jeff's hair, and pulled the trigger.

She wasn't prepared for the kick, the way the gun bounced back and up in her hand. It fell onto the seat as Jeff tumbled out, his hair on fire. Panicked, Chelsea hit the gas, but one of Jeff's feet caught in the seat belt and the car dragged his body for several yards. The sound it made bumping along the uneven blacktop made Chelsea cringe. She hoped Jeff never knew what hit him. He was the final piece of business, a little something to clean up, Dandy had said when he called her. Kill Jeff, or I'll give you to Paul and the boys—and I'll make your boyfriend watch. Only one of you is coming out of this trip alive. Who do you want it to be?

It wasn't even a contest. Tears rolled down Chelsea's cheeks, and her hands shook uncontrollably. She got out of the car and freed Jeff's foot from the seat belt, then closed the passenger door. There wasn't really much blood at all on the car door, and she could wipe it down at her next rest stop. But there wasn't going to be any more driving through the night. Chelsea was tired, and Los Angeles was a long way away.

Two weeks later, she was sitting on a plastic chair on a mostly empty Malibu beach. It was late in the season, but far away she could still see people running or walking their dogs. She kept a tartan comforter on her lap against the chill breeze coming in from the ocean and listened to the gulls squawk and cry as they wheeled above the sand. The waves crashed the shore, and Chelsea let her mind be consumed by the constant, peaceful sound. When a shadow blocked the late afternoon sun and didn't move, she opened her eyes.

Dandy. Tall and lithe, in linen shorts and a guayabera shirt. His dark curly hair was held tight to his skull. It didn't move in the soft breeze at all. He held his leather sandals in one hand and a thick cigar in the other. His teeth were even and white, and there were pleasant little laugh lines at the corners of his eyes. He looked kind. Chelsea knew he wasn't.

"So it's done," he said, staring out at the deep iron-colored ocean. Chelsea didn't say anything because there was nothing to say. Of course it was done. She was the only one left.

"Where's the car?"

This time Chelsea did speak. No matter how afraid she was of Dandy, she hated to have her professionalism questioned. "I left it on the street in East L.A., the keys in the ignition. It's gone by now. If you ask me if I remembered to wipe the prints clean, I'm going to make you eat that cigar."

Dandy laughed. It was like watching a tiger play with its food. Dandy could laugh and laugh, and then turn on a moment's notice. There was no way to tell when the danger would come, but Chelsea knew it was there. Her stomach tightened and her calves knotted in tension. If he made a move toward her on this lonely strand of beach, she wouldn't have much of a chance.

"You take a risk, speaking to me like that."

He drew deep on his cigar, held the smoke in his mouth for a moment, then opened his mouth. Creamy smoke drifted out and away, carried by the soft touch of the wind.

"Tell me how it went down."

So Chelsea did. It didn't take long. By the time she was done, Dandy was squatting next to her chair, his hand on her thigh. His palm felt rough and warm, and Chelsea thought again of a tiger in the jungle. The big cats prey on the weak. And right now she looked weak. The cross-country jaunt had cost her something. It was most obvious at night when she rolled in bed for hours before finally drifting off to sleep, but she could tell it in the way she walked, the way she held her head. She felt like an old woman now, coming at last to the end of her days.

It wasn't true. Chelsea was only twenty-nine. But her soul felt the weight of countless eons. When she got in that car, she knew that she'd be the only one to come out alive. What kind of woman—hell, what kind of person—did that make her? She didn't sleep because she kept seeing Jeff's hair on fire, kept smelling that burning odor.

At last, Dandy moved his hand, and Chelsea felt that she could breathe again.

"It couldn't have gone better," he said.

"Does our deal still hold?"

Dandy clamped the cigar between his teeth and smiled. "Of course. I told you at the end of the ride all debts would be paid, didn't I?"

"And I get to keep the baby." Chelsea wished that her voice hadn't broken. She'd meant to sound strong, to sound confident. Instead, she came off as a supplicant seeking one more favor.

"I have no desire to separate you from your child," Dandy said. He took the cigar from his mouth and blew a wide smoke ring into the clear evening air. He watched it break apart and dissipate. "We meet here, we talk, all debts paid, yes?"

"Yes," Chelsea said, and relaxed into her chair.

It was the opening Dandy had been looking for. He pushed the hot end of the cigar toward Chelsea's eye, but she flinched away and toppled backward, shrieking in surprise and pain as the burning ember touched her cheek and pressed hard into her skin. The beach chair seemed to turn on her as well, folding up and trapping her feet so that she had no chance at all to run, to get away. On the empty stretch of sand, there was no one to hear her scream. Chelsea flailed with her hands under the tartan blanket and came up with the gun that she'd hidden there. She'd kept it in her lap every day, waiting for Dandy, knowing that he would come. Knowing he couldn't be trusted.

Dandy's eyes widened in surprise and he tried to raise his hands, tried to back away from the black dead-eyed barrel of the revolver looking into his soul. He had time to say "No, wait," but by then it didn't matter. The gun roared once, twice, and then Dandy was falling, falling down into a dark and hazy red place that finally faded to black and blinked out.

Chelsea kicked free of the beach chair, losing one of her sandals in the process, and scrambled to her feet. One hand covered her badly burned cheek as the pain pulsed steadily, pain beyond anything she had ever endured before.

He went for my eyes. The bastard. She could feel the freshly burned flesh of her cheek, the tightness of flesh that had puckered and blistered almost immediately, and thought that it was a small price to pay to be free. Dandy lay on the loosely packed beach, his blood soaking into the sand. His eyes were open and his mouth gasped like a fish out of water. She watched him until he stopped moving. The gun in her hand never wavered.

Chelsea walked away from the limp and ungainly body that had been her husband. She cupped her free hand over her gently growing belly while the gun hung loosely from the other. She didn't look back.

DANCE THE
NIGHT AWAY

IT WAS THE KIND OF NIGHT on Bourbon Street when the heat comes down and smothers you like a jealous sibling holding a feather pillow. The shot girls were busy in their Daisy Dukes and bikini tops, hawking cheap liquor from expensive bottles. Drink the bottom-shelf tequila someone funneled into a Patron bottle and wander down the block past the strippers and the three-card monte dealers, past the fortune tellers and street prophets. Behind it all is the endless cacophony of sound, jazz and jizz in New Orleans.

Your kind of town.

Or at least it had been until they threw you out of Marie LeVeau's on Decatur Street. The hotel offers a voucher for two free cocktails at a minuscule saloon with room for three at the bar and a single two-top near the door. The walls are covered in mirrors to make the place look bigger than it really is, but after a while you've drunk too much and it gets tiring as hell to look at your own damned reflection for so long. At the Cigar Factory where old Honduran men hand-roll wet leaves and bind them in the big wooden molds to hold their shape, the young white kid behind the counter will sell you a mediocre cigar at a premium price.

So you walk out of there with the cigar lit and smoke billowing around you like you're the steam engine that pulls the world, feeling almost fine. But after half a block the humidity has set in and your smoke won't stay lit no matter how hard you puff. Walking around just a stone's throw from the Gulf feels like you're wading shoulder-deep in water so warm someone else must have already pissed in it.

That's how you end up on Bourbon Street in the first place, you know. You walk away from the water, flee the smell of the salt carried on the incoming breeze like rancid cologne sprayed over the body of a decaying corpse. The Gulf has no love for the Big Easy, and the big water has already tried to murder this town on multiple occasions. The last time, it nearly succeeded.

For some reason, Bourbon Street feels safer. Maybe it's because you can't see the Gulf from here. Maybe it's because of the endless tide of humanity that flows back and forth along the street, pulled not by the moon but by the drink specials.

It's always a party down here, but it's never clear whether the festivities are a celebration or a wake. Bourbon Street smells like warm piss and stale beer—maybe the same thing, right?—and you find a darkened doorway so that you can add a little of your own special brand to the glittering stream that runs through the gutter.

That's when you see her. You're trying to zip it up, got your gun in your hand right there, and not a weapon in sight. But this girl isn't a danger to you, not a danger to anybody. She's curled in the fetal position, with jeans that would be skin-tight if they weren't puddled around her ankles. Her green tank top is dark with sweat, and as far as you can tell, she's wearing neither bra nor panties, and row upon row of garish plastic beads weighs down her slender, delicate neck.

Never mind that it's the height of summer and Fat Tuesday won't waddle its way around again until after the new year, the cheap and tawdry beads have become synonymous with the decadence of the French Quarter. If you don't see a nipple on Bourbon

Street, you're not looking very hard. They're more common than chicory coffee, and less expensive, to boot.

You try not to look at the girl too closely, just a peek out of the corner of your eye. You don't want to know if she's gone, another poor child who went looking for some fun and found something else entirely. It's the Big Easy, right? And there ain't a thing in this old world that's easier than murder. Like breathing and sex, it just comes naturally for some people.

Oh, you know that's a generalization of course. Most folks won't ever *really* kill someone, but there's lots of folks out there with murder on their minds. Hell, you're one of them tonight.

Then the girl's arm twitches, and you let out a breath you didn't know you'd been holding. She's alive, at least for now. That means you can go your own way if you want to. Just keep that burned-out stogie in the corner of your mouth, wander back into the anonymous flow of humanity as it slides by, let the current take you on to the next drink, to the next bar, let it wash you ashore at the next saloon and hope you can live with the memory of a girl you left alone and helpless in the gutter.

But you're just kidding yourself, and you know it. Think about the Good Samaritan, the things they taught you in Sunday school when you were just a boy. A long time ago, you think, but some lessons stick more than others.

Kneel beside the girl, put your hand on her bare shoulder. There's grit and muck down there; feel it through the dirty knees of your faded blue jeans, and you try not to think about what kind of filth you're getting into. Her skin is warm under your palm, and you try not to look at her tit hanging out the side of her shirt.

She looks up at you, eyes bleary and unfocused. There's vomit in her hair. You take your hand away quickly as she tries to sit up. The girl doesn't make it, and you wrap your arm around her so that she doesn't fall onto the concrete and bust her head.

"Oh God," she says, her voice almost unintelligible, a croak. She rolls over onto her knees, gives you—and anyone who cares to look—a glimpse of a full moon on an otherwise overcast night. Then she straightens up, struggling to get her jeans over scabby knees, jerking the waistband over her butt and nearly to her navel.

She's wearing cork-soled espadrilles, but she's been so far down in the muck that the bottoms of her feet are black like the soul of a witchy woman from the swamps.

"You okay?" You ask, because you've got to say something. She's on her feet now, unsteady, like a toddler taking her first steps. But she's obviously better off than she was. She runs her hands through her dirty wet hair, and you can see by the way she casually flicks her fingers toward the gutter, slinging chunks of vomit and who knows what else, that she's had some experience waking up like this.

She wobbles toward you, arms spread wide, lipstick-smeared mouth open for a good night kiss. Catch her wrists with your hands, fingers tight, and turn your cheek just in time so that she only shares a little lipstick—god, you hope it's just lipstick—on the side of your face.

"Nice time," she slurs in your ear. "Had a nice time."

You're glad one of you did. You watch her as she toddles off, wondering if she found what she was looking for down here in the Quarter. So many people looking, most of them drunk or high out of their minds, sometimes both. For the tourists, Bourbon Street is a pilgrimage, a trip they make once in their lives just so they can say they did it. Like a Las Vegas of the Deep South, what happens in New Orleans is supposed to stay there.

But you're no tourist. The hotel room on Decatur was supposed to be a place for you to crash so that you don't try to drive home drunk, so that you don't see Mary Alice while the booze is in you and you say too much. Or worse. So you drink a little more and you watch the people. It's a carnival without Carnival. And you end up down near the end of the street where no one goes, where the music can't reach you and the partners who come to dance the night away will never visit.

The end of the street is where the serious drinkers come. This is the place where the bartenders don't talk, because they got their own problems, Jack, you better believe it. This is the kind of place where every other man at the bar is over fifty, overweight, and nearly overcome by some heavy burden he'll never talk about. It's the kind of bar where a sleeping drunk can be ignored, and where the regulars wear the burst capillaries in their cheeks as a badge of honor.

There's no shame down on Bourbon Street, not anywhere, but there's even less here, where the juke is broken and the sawdust on the floor hasn't been changed in so long that it's turned gray. Order a whiskey, whatever they've got in the well. Gotta keep drinking, because if you don't, the headache and the heartache will catch up to you. Ask for water back, because somebody once told you that the reason hangovers last so long is that drunks get dehydrated easily. Nod at the lush on the next stool, and he takes it as an opening.

"Them Saints," he says, "how 'bout 'em, ey?"

"They gonna be any good this year?"

He drains off his whiskey. Like you, he's drinking it neat, or trying to. A little dribble runs down his chin and drips onto the bar top.

"Cain't never tell, can you?"

"No," you say. It's true. You can never really tell about anything. Just take it as it comes.

"Death and taxes and the Carnival," he says, "and damn if Fat Tuesday ain't too far away to worry about right now. The hell with it. Who dat, am I right?"

He's right, of course he is. Who dat and all. But you'd agree with anything at this point. There's no use in two drunks arguing with one another. High up in one corner of the bar, there's a flat-screen TV tuned to the weather channel. There are storms in the Gulf, just like there are every summer, but this year they're all headed toward Mexico or the East coast. Still, folks down here keep an eye on the storms. They can turn at any time, like an angry drunk looking for his next victim.

The guy next to you slides off his stool and heads to the rear of the saloon. There's a sign on the wall that reads RESTROOMS, with an arrow pointing helpfully in the correct direction. You mind your own business, thoughts about Mary Alice circling in your head. You don't know the guy, pretty sure you'd never seen him before, carrying a leather bomber jacket—in this heat no less—and most of his clothes in his arms as he scrambled over the privacy fence in the back yard. And of course you want to take it out on the woman. That's your first instinct. My God, she's right there. Twenty-three years with Mary Alice, and today's the first day you ever came home early and unannounced. Guess who won the pony, boy, did you ever.

So now you've got a quiet place to drink, and after the second one you realize that it's not what you want. Not what you need, either. No, what you need is down there at the other end of the street with the lights and the music and the girls who don't wear any underwear.

Shit.

You leave some cash on the bar, enough to cover your drinks and a little leftover for a barkeep who doesn't ask questions, just pours 'em real strong. And then you're outside in the air again, thick and salty enough to be the soup left at the bottom of a bowl of gumbo. This end of the street is dark, the lights few and far between, and you walk it with your head up and your shoulders back, daring some young punk to come out of the shadows. Oh, you're drunk enough to roll, sure, but there are easier pickings in this town. There always are. You're a big man, six-foot five-inches in your sock feet, a might taller in the cowboy boots you always wear.

A big man. But not big enough for Mary Alice, the whore. You shake your head, try to clear it. You know she's not a whore, know that she'd yell at you for shaming sex workers with the word. But you don't know what in the hell she was missing, why she'd turn to another man. And she didn't get time to tell you.

That's because your dumb ass got into your Ford F-250 and drove off before she could say anything. Left her at the end of that dirt road in the doublewide y'all are still paying for. Let her explain why you left, why you put two plumes of red dust in the air like rooster tails and got on down the road. You made two phone calls on the way from shit-ass Slidell into the city, and then you threw your damned phone off the bridge and into Lake Ponchartrain. Did you know you were throwing your life away, too? You must have.

It's an easy three blocks back to the noise and back to the bustle. Bourbon Street and one last hooray, one last night with the music and the girls and the booze and everything that goes with it. One last time to watch the sun come up, one last chance to dance the night away.

It wasn't supposed to be like this.

Two phone calls was all it took to end a life. The first call was to the hotel, where you got a room for two nights; that second call, though, that's the one that seals the deal. That's the call that brings the scrawny little man with the ill-fitting suit and the pencil mustache. He was an oily little man, and there was something about the way he kept patting his slicked down hair that you really didn't like.

He's got brown eyes, big and deep like the waters of Lake Ponch. Like Mary Alice's eyes.

For five thousand dollars, he'll kill your wife and take her body off into the swamp where the gators and the snakes and the bobcats will take care of the rest, and nobody will ever find out what happened to her. The price is right, and you give him half up-front. Never mind why you have that much cash on hand. That's nobody's business but your own.

"Don't worry about a thing," the oily little man says. "I got just the thing for her. You ain't gotta deal with that bitch ever again."

What is it about that word? What made it strike a nerve? God knows you've called her that over and over for the last three hours. You still don't understand why it set you off the way it did, but you lean back as if you've just been struck by a blow.

"Don't call her that," you say. Were you already drunk? You don't think so, but maybe. Hell, probably. You stopped at a liquor store on the way in, and you can remember what the pint of Old Forester tasted like when you uncapped it and guzzled it down in the parking lot. It was just a pint, but how much does a man need to get drunk? Even a big man like you.

Now he's looking at you with a wrinkle between his eyebrows and a question on his lips that he'll never get to ask, because now your fingers are around his throat. Your hands are big, like the rest of you, big as dinner plates, and this scrawny chicken wing of a man is small, no bigger than Mary Alice.

He looks up at you with her eyes, and his fingers dig into your forearms. You can feel the dull bite of his nails on your skin. But you've already used your weight to bear him down, push him onto his back on the floor. Even if he's got a weapon, he can't think well enough to get to it. It doesn't matter anyway. What's he gonna do other than put you out of your misery?

You read somewhere that it takes eight minutes to strangle a man to death. You're not sure how long you keep hold of his throat, but it could have been hours. The big tendons in your forearms hurt like hell, and your hands feel useless. You can't straighten your fingers. You don't look at the would-be killer. You can't bring yourself to do it. Out of the corner of your eye, you can see that his face is purple.

And Mary Alice's eyes are in his face, and they're wide open and staring at you.

You run water in the bathroom sink, cold first to help your hands. When they feel halfway normal again, switch the water over to hot and scrub your face. When you're done everything feels raw and painful, but the tears that left dirty trail-marks down your face aren't there anymore, and that's a relief.

Step around the corpse on the floor, a dead man whose eyes remind you so much of your wife, and go downstairs. Take a left out of the hotel, and there you are at Marie LeVeau's. You've got drink tickets in your pocket and no reason not to use them.

So the night goes on, and you lose yourself in the darkness and the music, in the flow of humanity that never stops on Bourbon Street. And sometime around four a.m., you're enough and horny enough to ask a girl to dance. She's too young for you by a good fifteen years, but she's drunk too, so you dance while the band plays, and you talk while the musicians go out to smoke their cigarettes and toke their joints.

It's a good time. You drink and you smoke and you dance the night away, just the way you ought to.

Because you know the sun will come up eventually, and some poor, underpaid hotel maid will find that body, the little man with Mary Alice's eyes, and then they'll come for you.

If you're lucky, maybe you'll still be drunk when they do.

TRAP HOUSE

THEY CAME SWARMING IN THE FRONT like blue-jacketed ants, 'POLICE' scrawled across their ballistic vests in reflective white letters that looked three feet high in the gloom, so I broke a window out the back of the trap house and went through it with a little more than my share of the cash.

The shattered glass hitting the cracked and patchy blacktop wasn't too loud. Besides, nobody in this part of Birmingham was gonna notice another window gone, and that's a fact. The houses are mostly empty, but they're close together here on the west side, creating a warren of alleys with lots of corners to dodge past. This neighborhood used to be a town of its own, but the so-called Magic City annexed the place back in the 1980s, and then ignored it ever since. I made two turns before I felt them behind me running in heavy jump-laced boots that kept them from turning an ankle on the buckled and warped sidewalks out here.

I didn't have that kind of protection, so I had to pick my way along while I listened to the bastards gaining on me. It wasn't fair. Any kind of fair race and I'da been half a mile ahead and lost inside a labyrinth of deserted streets and shadows where even someone with a badge would hesitate to go.

Fingers flicked the back of my collar, grasping. I put on a burst of speed, a last ditch effort to get some distance and fade into the night. The cops could sit at the bar and tell tall tales about me, like old fishermen talking about the one that got away. They were yelling at me, but their words were lost to the rush of wind in my ears. I gained a step, and then another. A half-block ahead, the black and yawning mouth of an access road beckoned with a promise of dark salvation. My legs and arms pumped harder, my head leaning forward tucking away from those grasping hands.

I hit that pothole at the speed of light. That's what it felt like, at least, while I was tumbling through the air with no idea what body part would hit the ground first. The blacktop took skin off my elbows and shoulders, bit and bloodied my knees and shins. I rolled forward and up to my feet automatically, wondering how badly I'd been hurt.

I didn't have time to figure it out. The cops were on me by then, and they drove me back down to the asphalt, putting my face in the ashy, salty, smudgy surface. My breath exploded out in a long and ugly groan, and I instinctively tried to get back to my feet.

"Stay down," one of the cops said. He put a knee in the middle of my back while he twisted my arms behind me to put the cuffs on. I could see his partner, wearing tactical gear -- hard knee-pads, a riot helmet, heavy black leather gloves. The partner had one hand to the radio unit on his shoulder. It partially covered his mouth, so I couldn't hear what he was saying, but I had been arrested enough times by then to know that he was probably calling in our location so one of those big-ass white BPD Expeditions could swoop in and transport us back to the trap house.

And then to the jail.

"You're holding," the cop said. It wasn't a question. I tried to shake my head, tell him no, I wasn't down like that.

"No," I finally managed, but by that time he was already patting me down. He pulled my genuine imitation leather wallet from my back pocket, found the ID badge the jail gave me on the day I got my release. There wasn't much else in there: Arende's expired EBT card, a couple faded pictures, an appointment card with a date and time scribbled on it that I'd probably never get to keep.

The cop rolled me over, and the hard steel cuffs bit into my wrists and lower back. I put my shoulders on the pavement to try to arch my back a little and take some of the pressure off of my spine. My lungs were still working to get back most of the breath that I'd lost, and the weird position left me uncomfortable and exposed. The other cop saw what I was doing, chuffed a little laugh like it was the funniest thing he'd ever seen. He took one long diagonal step toward me, like a field-goal kicker on a six-ty-yard try, and booted me right below the ribs.

I puked. I couldn't even remember the last thing I'd eaten, but whatever it was came up like a geyser. Old unfaithful, that's me. Some of it came back down in my mouth and went down my throat. I tried to spit it out, but couldn't. No breath, no nothing. Just blind panic. Spots swam in front of my eyes and a rising black sea threatened to take me down into darkness deeper than midnight. From far above me, I could hear the cops yelling.

"... aspirated, get him turned ..."

Rough hands rolled me onto my side and held me fast, but my chest and throat felt locked tight, suctioned closed.

"Goddamn it," one of the cops said. "Hold him still."

Another jackbooted toe found my abdomen, this time about two inches above my navel. This time, everything I'd eaten over the last decade came out and splashed against the wavy, uneven pavement, and suddenly fresh air whooshed in and burned its way down into my lungs. Snot and drool trailed from my face to the ground, and I could feel tears hot and fresh on my face. I hated myself for crying, hated hearing the sound of my sobs echo against the ugly siding walls of the houses that loomed close over us like giants spying on the games of children.

The cop who kicked me the first time stood back from me, his face turned away. I couldn't tell if it made any difference to him that he'd nearly killed me just to get his jollies. I probably wasn't the first defenseless arrest he'd kicked or punched or otherwise taken advantage of. That's how the police play the game.

"Hey."

The cop squatting next to me snapped his fingers in front of my face to get my attention. I turned bleary, red eyes toward him.

"You okay now? Breathing all right?"

I breathed in and out a couple of times, gingerly, like I was testing it out. Then I nodded at him.

"I'm gonna stand you up, go through the rest of your pockets. You got anything sharp in your pockets? Anything that's gonna stick me?"

"No," I said. "I got a Swiss Army knife. Right front pocket."

With him supporting me by one shoulder, we managed to lever my body into a sitting position. The kicking bastard cop came over, ran his hand under my other shoulder and helped his partner pull me to my feet.

"I get stuck by a needle, you ain't making it to jail."

I didn't even acknowledge the words, just stood still. The frisk was fast, professional. He found the knife I'd promised, and the wad of money I hadn't said a word about. He undid the rubber band I'd wound around the cash to keep it tight and fanned the green out in his hands. It was a lot of money.

"Hey hey," he said. "What's this? Mark, shine a light over here."

I didn't say anything. I knew better. It was the best part of five grand, enough to pay off what I owed. And now it was going away from me like water disappearing down a drain. The first cop, the one who wanted to act like a nice guy, shook the money in my face.

"How much were you there to buy? Too much for just you, am I right?"

He had his mind on that money, and not on me. If I'd had my hands free, maybe I could have done something. But they had me cuffed good, and I was still shaking and exhausted from the boots to the belly.

"You owe me, you know," Mr. I'm-an-Alright-Guy Cop said. "How much you wanna give me for saving your life? All of it? That's very kind of you." He paused, staring me down, as if he were waiting for me to say something. He wasn't, though. He was acting. Just playing around. I knew he was gonna keep my money. He knew he was gonna keep it. We all knew. I knew better--I've always known better--than to talk to the cops, but this time I couldn't help myself.

"That's my money," I said. "You can't just take it."

Officer Nice Guy laughed in my face, fanned himself with all my money.

"We can confiscate drug money any fucking time we please, kid."

"That's not drug money," I said. "Come on, man. It's for my kid."

That didn't even move him, not that I thought it would. Cops want to think they're the good guys. They'll go right on thinking that while they smile and smile and put you in the fucking ground, man.

"Please," I said. "I gotta put it back. It's college fund money. My boy, he's six. You saw the picture in my wallet, right? I took it out to help a buddy. I just got it back tonight. I wasn't even supposed to be there."

"Right," Officer Alright Guy said.

He divided the money, took half of it and gave it to his partner. The guy looked at the stack of green in his hand, grinned so hard I could see the cavities in his back molars, and stuffed the cash in his own pocket. Maybe he could use some of my kid's money to fix his teeth.

Now he came forward, and I flinched away. I'd had enough of him already. But the truth is that I preferred him to the alright guy. At least this one knew he was a piece of shit. The guy who frisked me and took my money would never think about it again.

He'd think he deserved a medal for saving my life after his shit-kicker buddy nearly ended it.

"You could be a help with this other thing," the cop who first kicked me said. His partner had called him Mark. He fished in his pants pocket for a minute and I tensed. I knew he was going to bring up a throwdown piece and start shooting, and there was nothing I could do about it. The idea was so visceral that I could see it happening in my mind. I tensed and started moving away, ready to break into a run no matter how useless it might be, until the Alright Guy grabbed my arm and held me still.

Officer Mark held a burner phone in one black-gloved hand. He pushed a button on the side of the phone and it lit up, illuminating his face like he was the man behind the curtain. Oz the great and powerful.

Yeah, right.

He tapped the contacts on the phone. Of course there weren't any. No voicemails or texts, either. But there were five numbers on the recent calls. I didn't recognize any of them.

"Who do these numbers belong to?"

I lifted whatever part of my eyebrows hadn't been sanded off by my spills on the blacktop. If my arms had been free, I would have shrugged.

"How am I supposed to know? I've never seen them before."

Officer Mark grinned at me like a hyena stalking helpless prey. He held the phone up to my face so that its brightly lit screen made me squint.

"Those numbers, you know who those guys are, right? If you don't know now, you could find out. You're a bright guy, got a kid you wanna put in college, right?"

I closed my eyes, shook my head.

"Hey," I said. "Don't fuck with me about my kid."

I never saw the slap coming. Mark probably didn't hit me as hard as he could, but it was close. I rocked back on my heels, would have fallen down and busted up what was left of my head, but Officer Alright Guy was there holding me up. Constellations that no other person could see in the night sky were wandering around in my vision.

"Uncuff him," Officer Mark said.

"You sure?"

"Yeah," he said. "I think we can work something out here."

The cuffs clicked free. Warily, I brought my hands around in front of me, chafed my wrists to restore some circulation.

"Wrong place, wrong time tonight, huh?" Officer Mark said. "I get it, I get it--you're a good guy, just trying to protect your family. Just trying to do right by your kid. Right?"

Now that my hands were free, I was getting pissed. It didn't matter, though. Officer Alright Guy was close by, his hand on his Taser. I wasn't going anywhere, even with the cuffs off. And the sooner I recognized that, the sooner I could maybe get myself out of this. As soon as those words went through my head, I shook them off. I knew that I was going to jail. To think anything else would just be believing in fairy tales, and I gave those up a long time ago.

"What do you want," I said. Maybe it was supposed to be a question. I don't know.

"You're gonna know those numbers," Officer Mark said. "Nick's gonna turn his body cam on, and then we're gonna find the phone when we search you. Got it? Eventually, we're gonna tell you who the digits belong to, and you're gonna pass that to the detectives who interview you. When it comes to trial, you're gonna stand up and point the finger at the guys we tell you. Get me?"

I got him. What I didn't know yet was what I was going to get outta the deal. So I didn't say anything for a while. Officer Mark's radio squawked a couple of times, and he radioed in that he'd found a suspect and what our position was.

"Quick now," he said, "before they get here."

"Why should I?"

Officer Nick, the Alright Guy, slapped me hard across the back of the head.

"We'll make sure your kid gets the money, you dumbass. Now choose. You gonna be helpful or not?"

I thought about Rodney, six years old and living with his grandma. Thought about what that money would mean to him one day. He could get away, get up and out of Birmingham. Out of Alabama. He could go somewhere better. God, I hoped he could at any rate. So I said yeah, I'd help them out. Shrugged my heavy shoulders and said, "Of course I know those numbers. I know all about it."

They handcuffed me again, only this time it was looser. When that bright white BPD ride rolled up on us, I slid into the back seat, behind the chicken wire that separated me from the driver, closed my eyes, and tried to get some rest.

I didn't want to think about what came next.

WHIPPING POST

SUNNY HAD HER HAND IN ERIC'S LAP when I dropped into the other side of the sticky vinyl booth, her arm moving slow and rhythmic, inevitable. She stopped when she saw it was me, the muscles in her shoulders and upper arms taut with anger. No shame, though. She was caught; she knew it, and she was pissed. Eric was an afterthought. He was so glassy-eyed from getting his joint greased that it took him a full thirty seconds to pull himself together. I coulda shot them both right then.

Maybe I should have.

The saloon wasn't nothing but a neon smear. Miller Time and Bud Light, PBR in cold longneck bottles. Smoke so thick you could almost stand on it, the juke playing low-down hurting cheating songs and the sound of billiard balls clicking hard and falling home. The ceiling was brown with tobacco stains and the paint on the walls had been unevenly applied so that it bubbled up and peeled away from the sheetrock. Framed Alabama jerseys hung askew on the walls alongside posters for the Allman Brothers and Molly Hatchet and the Drive-By Truckers. Schooners of cheap draft beer stood half-drunk in front of Sunny and Eric, and the liquid sloshed from where I banged the table with my hip when I sat down. The well whiskey was just like the juke, low-down and mean, and I ordered a double shot of it when the waitress hustled past.

"What are you doing here?" Sunny said. Her hands were empty now. Eric fixed himself while she reached for the paper napkin dispenser that sat on the table between us. Sunny wiped her hands, wadded the napkin into a ball, and threw it at me. I swatted it away, trying not to think about what she'd wiped on it. "Aren't you supposed to be at your mother's?"

"That's all you got to say? You empty the bank account, you wreck the car. You think I'm that stupid?"

Sunny flashed her teeth at me. She was long and lean, predatory. A cheetah ready to pounce.

"You really want me to answer that?" She asked.

I ignored her.

"You're out with him?" I pointed a thumb at Eric. "With *him*?"

"Hey," Eric said, and sat up straighter. "Come on, man. None of us expected this. It just, you know, it happened."

The waitress dropped off my double shot and I pounded it down, the alcohol burning away my indecision and leaving me with nothing but a good clean hate. It tasted like all of the shit that I'd taken from Sunny over the past four years, all the times she told me that she was going out with the girls and instead was face down and ass up with some stranger at the Skyway Inn or the Rodeway or the Trailhead Motor Lodge, rooms where you pay by the hour and the walls look like something Pollock might have painted if you look at 'em under a black light.

I shook my head to clear it, stared Eric down with a bulldog gaze. He tried to hold my eyes but finally looked away. Muttered "Sorry" under his breath, but I knew that was a lie because I knew what Sunny was like. Every moment with her was enthralling. When it had been my turn with her, everything felt new and fresh, like soft-bladed grass in the spring and I would have done anything at all to prolong those sweet and happy moments when we were together and nothing else could ever matter.

"Shut your mouth," I told him. "You'll live longer."

I met her when I was twenty-seven. That's a great age to meet the woman of your dreams unless your first date is on the same day your grandfather dies. I got the news as I was leaving to pick Sunny up that first time, and I didn't know what to do. My grandfather had been an anchor in my life, a sharecropping farmer who chewed Red Man tobacco and drank warm Schlitz beer when granny wouldn't let him bring alcohol into their house. He had always been there for me, and I had thought in my naive young brain that in some way he always would. But then he was gone and I was unmoored.

I rang Sunny's bell and she answered the door in a yellow backless sundress that made me believe there could be a God. She took one look at my face and knew something was wrong. She did the only thing she knew that would fix it. The sundress puddled itself on the floor and spread out like the dying light of day, and we went to her bed and stayed there for three days. We left the apartment to buy wine or weed, had Chinese food delivered, and the rest of the time we spent naked.

By the time my grandfather's funeral came around, I knew her body like it was a road map to buried treasure. I had traveled the curve of her back and tasted the tiny red blossom of a dilated vein or a broken capillary between her shoulder blades, read the braille of her breasts, and drank from the chalice of her navel. She wasn't perfect but she was perfect to me. She was mine and I was hers and I knew with the certainty of a fool that I would never want anything else and that we would be intertwined like this forever.

Ronnie Locke was the first one of my friends to tell me that Sunny was cheating on me, and I punched him in the mouth so hard that it broke three of his teeth and two of my knuckles. There was no way, no way in hell, that she was cheating on me. She was with me every night except for the nights I was in class trying to finish my degree. I had ten credits to go and economics was kicking my ass so bad that I needed a night off. I stopped off at a supermarket and bought some flowers, a bright spray of yellow and pink and purple that I knew Sunny would love.

I knew something was wrong when I opened the door. The sounds from the bedroom were guttural, moans and panting gasps and strangled cries. I rushed in, worried that Sunny had somehow hurt herself and found her astride some guy I had never seen before, hips bucking hard and grinding down on him the same way that she had been with me just that morning. The flowers fell to the floor and scattered like ashes from an urn. My heart dropped in my chest and I screamed. I had heard people say that they felt their heart breaking and now I knew what they meant. I felt as though I'd been bound, struck hard over and over with something brutally sharp, my heart carved from my chest. But I couldn't move. I couldn't do anything but scream and wait for the next blow to land and pray that it would strike me dead.

The guy rolled away from me to the far side of the bed. He fell on his ass and scrambled around for his pants. He said something, words that were lost in the raging waves of blood pounding in my ears. I don't even remember what he looked like. The only way he mattered was as an obstacle between Sunny and me. Then he was out the door and gone, and it was just us -- just Sunny and me again -- and my soul re-entered my body.

I trembled when she touched me, and I held her while she cried and said she was sorry. And I believed her when she said that it would never happen again.

Sunny and I had different definitions of *never*. Over the next two years we fell into a pattern where she would find some new guy, grow infatuated, and begin sleeping with him. But it wasn't enough that she cheated. She wanted me to know, wanted to see me choke down her shit and take her back. She wanted to see my heart break, wanted to see my soul take another beating. It became a contest.

"I don't deserve you," she told me one night after I had taken her to a Shakespeare festival. Hamlet, We were drunk on the bard's words and a little high, kicking through the grass of a little park and looking up at the stars winking down on us from an impossibly clear sky. There was no one around. I had my fingers in the waistband of her skirt, my need to touch her, to possess her, overwhelming after the last time I had found her with another man. In bed she had become impassive. I could beat myself against her body like a ship against a rocky shore, hull breaking and everything good and safe spilling out into an angry sea.

She never denied me pleasure but took none of her own, and I considered that a bigger betrayal than any affair that she could ever have. Whenever she left the apartment, I followed at a distance, fearful of what I would find.

One night she drove to the Sun Inn by herself and got a room. I watched from the parking lot next door as she pulled her Jeep into the slot in front of Room 147 and parked. My phone rang on the seat next to me, and it was Sunny.

"Hey," I said when I answered her call. My voice wasn't shaking at all. "What's up, babe?"

"Not much," Sunny said. "I was just about to go into the gym. Wanted to let you know I'm about to hit my Zumba class and won't be able to answer the phone for a bit."

"Oh," I said. "OK."

A late-model Acura with windows tinted so dark they could have doubled as a Republican' heart pulled into the space next to Sunny's car, and a tall, thick-bodied man about my age got out. I knew him. Of course I knew him. Patrick and I had known each other since kindergarten, maybe even before that, a couple of goofy kids trying to learn how to swim at a YMCA summer camp. He played guitar and had substance abuse issues that I heard he'd overcome. I had always liked him and now I hated him.

I ended the call with Sunny, pushing myself to a dead run across the Sun Inn's cracked and buckled parking lot. Got there just before Patrick knocked, my face right up in his. We stared at one another without saying anything, and I knew what he knew. Sunny was his new drug, the thing that got him high. She did the same thing for me. Being in her presence was like blasting into orbit. Being without her could give a man the DTs. Patrick's hand hovered at the door until he dropped it to his side and turned away from me, shoulders slumped. He went back to his car, opened the door, and nodded at me. When he pulled away, I turned to the motel room and mashed my thumb over the peephole on the door to room 147.

My knock was soft, almost timid. Sunny opened the door wide and she was beautifully, wonderfully naked. Her jaw dropped open and her hands came up to ward me off and my arms went around her, the sound of my sobs cut off by her mouth. I bore her back into the room and down onto the bed.

Later, when we were done and the near-perfect darkness of the room had settled over us like a blanket, Sunny said "I'm sorry," and I knew she was sorry while at the same time knowing that she wasn't sorry. If I hadn't followed her, if I hadn't seen Patrick, she would have been as happy under his thick rutting body as she had been beneath me. I understood that it would happen again and again, that I was Sisyphus and she was the stone. And in my secret heart I thought that I could accept my fate, that being with her like this made all of the cheating and all of the pain worth it. I could survive being tied to this whipping post of a woman. I could endure until she loved and needed me the same way I loved and needed her.

The worst lies are the ones we tell ourselves.

I don't know when I started carrying the gun. Sometime in the last year. The comfortable weight of it in my pocket was a balm to my soul. And now as I sat across from Sunny and Eric in this derelict bar, I kept one hand in my jacket so that I could rest my fingers against the hard cold steel of the trigger. That Taurus .38 revolver with the stainless steel plating was my only anchor, the tenuous thread that connected me to whatever was left of the real world. With my other hand I waved down the server for another double shot. Pounded that one just like I did the first.

The rotgut tasted like hate, but I didn't know if it was hate for her or for me. Maybe it was hate for the world and for everything that had brought me here to a place where there was nothing but hurt and pain and blame. I don't know. Beat a dog and it still loves you with that kind of shaking whimpering crying love that breaks your heart. But you beat a dog long enough and one day it's gonna snap.

I had finally snapped. Across the booth Sunny had registered that there was something different about me this time, and she was trying to get back into her contrite polite sweet young Southern woman act. But I knew it was an act, had known that for years, and I was determined that I wasn't going to fall for it again.

"I'm sorry," Sunny said, but it all sounded rote. The rest of the words didn't matter. I closed her off in my mind. All that was left now was how many times she had made a fool of me. That was the part I couldn't take anymore. Eric looked from Sunny to me and back again, like a spectator watching a tennis match.

"I can't take it anymore," I told her. "You go off with somebody. I chase after you. I don't know what you get from it."

Sunny didn't say anything. She was studying the way the bubbles popped at the surface of her beer. Eric had an arm around Sunny. Protective. Possessive. As if there was anything he could do to keep Sunny somewhere that she didn't want to be.

"I want you to know that I see you," I told her then. "You're a goddamn succubus. You used me up and now that you're done you spit me out. I know what you are."

"Took you long enough," Sunny said. She didn't look up. She couldn't bring herself to meet my eyes anymore.

"Look, man --" Eric started in again, and I took my hand off of the gun just long enough to slap him hard across the face. His hands flew to his cheek, fingertips hovering over the bright red welt I left there. My hand went back to the gun. I almost pulled it then.

"You got something else to say, you can say it to me outside," I said. "Bring the cheating whore bitch with you."

I was feeling bold and inflated, full of anger and blood and bile. I stood up from the vinyl bench, hearing it squeak. I put a twenty down on the table to cover my bill and marched out the door.

The air in the parking lot smelled like soot and burned oil and baking asphalt, but the moon was bright and flat and hard looking down on us puny humans with neither resentment or judgment. I leaned against the wrecked front bumper of my car, the one that Sunny used to leave me that morning. I thought about Gary Cooper in High Noon, and John Wayne as Rooster Cogburn. A man's got to do what a man's got to do and all of that bullshit. When Eric hit the door, Sunny was right behind him.

He stood a few feet away from me, fingers curling and straightening like he couldn't wait to get his claws on me. Sunny stood off to the side a little ways behind him. I pulled the gun and brought it up.

Look what you made me do you bitch look what you made me do goddamn you look what you made me do look what you made —

THE HANDYMAN

I'M ONE OF THE LUCKY ONES. I come outta St. Clair Correctional with my life and most of my teeth. I oughta be grateful. Five years, straight up, armed robbery and assault on an unarmed person. Lots of guys go into St. Clair, and not all of us come out upright and breathing. But you try getting a job with a record like mine. Can't be done. Not in this town.

So I went into business for myself. You won't find me on Yelp, and if somebody ever leaves me a Google review, I'll hunt him down and make him eat it. But if you know where to look, you can find me. I don't have a set rate. I go from job to job, and so far it's worked out pretty good.

What I do, I fix things.

"I don't quite understand how this works," Melissa Talley said to me. She was pretty, a former high school cheerleader gone to seed. I was wearing my best shirt, a blue Oxford button-down--sixteen bucks at Wal-Mart--and a pair of clean and creased khaki pants. We were drinking overpriced coffee at Octane, a hipster-friendly coffee house in the flossy Uptown entertainment district just north of Interstate 20. The urban planners probably

called it the heart of Birmingham. That's how you get restaurants
nearby that sell "elevated pub grub" (at elevated prices, natch). I
didn't mind that the stuff was expensive. I wasn't the one paying.
I took a sip from the white china mug and grimaced at the dark
brown liquid. Bitter and over-roasted.

That could be the title of my memoir.

"Think of me as your personal handyman," I told her. "You got
a broken window, some frame damage. So you find a guy who
knows what he's doing to come and fix it. That's me."

Melissa smiled at me, dipping her chin in what I'm sure she
thought was a sexy way and said, "So you know what you're doing?"

"Sometimes," I said. "And what I don't know, I figure out as I
go along."

Melissa drank some of her coffee. She didn't seem to mind the
taste. Maybe it was just me. Around us, the din of the coffee house
clattered and banged away. It was a busy scene, but the movement
and the noise was why we'd settled on it when she reached out to
me. Big echoing spaces like this, with a lot of people around, make
it very hard to listen in on a conversation.

"I need something a little more complex than fixing a window,"
she said, and took an oversized brown leather purse from beside
her on the floor, reached in and brought out a small white envelope. I smiled. The only thing better could be a large envelope.

"That's okay," I said. "I don't do windows."

"I have twenty-five hundred here," she said. "Is that enough?"

I raised my eyebrows.

"It depends on the job."

She slid the envelope of cash toward me and I closed a cal-
loused palm over it, ready to make the cash disappear.

When she spoke again, her voice was harsh with fear and
need, and her face looked trapped, somewhere between hopeful
and panicked.

"I want you to kill my husband."

The coffee house was a wide-open space, with high ceilings

and concrete floors stained brown on purpose so that you can't tell if anything's been spilled. There were other people around us, all in their own conversations, but I swear that everything around me stopped for just a minute.

I'm not one of the good guys, and I've never even claimed to be. But neither am I a moron. I shoved the envelope back across the table, mournfully watching it skitter away like a cockroach when the lights come on. She looked down at the money and back up at me. Her eyes were wide.

"Not interested," I said, and got up to leave. It was early January, and I could walk a couple of blocks down to the Museum of Art. There was an exhibit I wanted to see. I put on my navy pea coat and a Birmingham Barons baseball cap to guard against the cold January air outside. The coat had fit me before I went to prison. Now it hung on me with room enough to fit another person inside.

"Good discussion," I said, and walked away. I left her there at the table, openmouthed and sputtering, like a fish that's just been hauled from deep water onto an open deck.

Twenty-five hundred dollars to kill her husband. I tried not to be insulted. Maybe she didn't have much money. But her coat had been good quality, and that was a Hermès scarf she was wearing. Her nails had been lacquered and her hair professionally done. Her teeth were so white and even that recent and ongoing dentistry were the only explanations. A woman like that's gonna offer me two-and-a-half to kill her husband?

I do work for hire. But I don't come cheap.

I went south and west, heading for the museum. Police headquarters was about a block away, and the snarl of a major highway interchange was not too distant to the east. Heavy equipment groaned and snorted in the distance where they were elevating and replacing major sections of the interstate. Traffic in Birmingham may not be as bad as Atlanta or Nashville, but the city's got ambitions.

Melissa Talley rushed to catch up with me. Her breath puffed white in the chilly air and she gasped.

"Wait," she said, the words half-whispered and urgent. "Please, I need help. I don't have anywhere else to go."

We were the only people on the street. This town ain't much for pedestrians.

"Fine," I said. "If you can keep up, you can tell me all about it." Abruptly, I changed directions and headed more directly south toward Linn Park. I didn't hurry, but I didn't wait around, either. She scurried after me and was soon matching me step for step, as much as her short legs could.

"Why won't you help me?"

Over to the east, the red rusted hump of the Sloss Furnaces water tank loomed over the city like something out of War of the Worlds. I could just barely see it, but every time I did, it kind of reoriented me in the city. I took a hard, cold breath, shoved my hands deep into the pockets of my pea coat, and stopped in front of the woman.

"You're cheap." I said. "And I can tell by your clothes and your purse and your face that you don't have to be. You go making that offer, and the next guy you approach is gonna be a cop."

Melissa Talley's smile was bitter.

"So what," she said. "Jail would be better."

Most of the time, that's bullshit. I've been to jail, and I could write a scholarly paper on the million little ways that it's bad, how every hour inside kills your soul just a little more. But Melissa was serious. And here in the natural light, I could see her more clearly. Underneath her makeup, her cheeks were lightly pock-marked. When I'd first seen her in the coffee shop, I'd chalked those scars up to chicken pox or a bad case of teenage acne. But out here where there wasn't soft and glowing light to help hide the damage, I could see more clearly.

The scars had tiny, square edges. And there were dozens of them, sprinkled from her hairline all the way down to her chin.

Shit.

"He hits you," I said. She didn't speak, instead settling for a small solemn nod. We walked together then, and I slowed my pace to match hers. Our breath hung around our heads like we were smoking the world's coldest cigars.

"Not every day," she said. "But it started early."

I didn't need the details—they were written all over her face—but she told me anyway. And then she did something that I wished she hadn't: Melissa Talley reached into her mouth and with a terrible slurping sound pulled out a complete set of false teeth. Uppers and lowers. They sat in her palm, gleaming in the thin winter sunlight.

I turned away.

"Put them back in," I said, and tried not to listen as she did.

"You think I've got money," she said after a moment. "But Frank is the one with the cash. We've got nice cars—a Bentley and a Mercedes—and a big house out in Mountain Brook. But I don't have anything."

"Nothing?"

"He controls everything. It took me nearly two years to scrape up this much. Meantime, that sonofabitch drops that much on a new set of golf clubs."

There was a park bench just ahead, and when we reached it, I sat down and motioned for her to join me. Linn Park was pretty, a small green square in a city caught up in growth and gentrification. I wondered how long it would stay the same in a place where everything changed almost daily.

"All right," I said. "Give me the envelope."

She passed it over, and I pocketed it. The money felt heavier than it should.

"Tell me everything."

That's how I found myself hanging around outside the Marble Ring, a real by-God speakeasy in the Avondale neighborhood a few nights later. Frank Talley was there on the second floor balcony, smoking a long cigar and flirting with his waitress. I'd been to the Ring before, sat at the horseshoe-shaped bar and admired the chrome-plated bathtub in the middle of the big room. The ceiling was stamped tin, and the bartenders wore white shirts, dark waistcoats, and bow ties.

Roaring twenties, baby.

I could go up there right now. But Frank was having a nice time, maybe his last good time. So instead I went down 41st street to Taco Morro Loco and got a couple of al pastor tacos and a Mexican Coke to go. On my way back to the speak, I stopped at a convenience store and bought a pint bottle of Sneaky Pete.

I ate the tacos and drank the Coke, ignoring the bottle in the brown paper bag next to me. Above, Frank Talley had smoked down most of his cigar. I could see the cherry-red end as he drew deeply on it. When he threw the cigar butt down and sparks scattered against the sidewalk below, I reached into the bag and unscrewed the cap on the bottle.

I swished a little Sneaky Pete around in my mouth and spit it out, then poured some into my palm like aftershave and patted it on the front of my gray tee shirt and faded jeans. I hadn't shaved in a couple of days, and my jeans and shirt were ripped. I was wearing a quilted black hoodie over the shirt, and I grabbed a couple handfuls of gritty dirt from the gutter and wiped it over my shirt and pants, then did the same with my face.

By the time Frank Talley came out, I looked like any other bum on the street. Frank was tall, taller than me, and thin as a whippet. He had a gold wedding ring on one hand, and on the other hand he wore a square, sharp-looking pinky ring that glinted silver in the dim streetlight.

I stumbled toward him with my half-empty bottle of port and took a swig.

"Howaya doin' champ, take a drink with me."

Talley muttered "Excuse me," and tried to go around, but I swayed toward him and leaned forward as if I was about to fall.

As I flailed, I tossed the bottle into the bushes that lined the side-walk. He tried to push me away, but I got an ankle in front of him and tripped him. He hit the sidewalk hard on his knees, tearing the fabric of his Armani suit. Oops.

"You sonofa—"

"Hol' on, hol' on," I slurred, stepping on his hand with a heavy steel-toed boot. Something snapped, and Frank howled in pain, yanking his hand free.

"Shorry, shorry," I said, "lemme he'p you up." While he was gripping his hand and flinching from the pain, I got hold of his collar with one hand and his belt with the other, straining hard to keep him from straightening all the way up, and ran four long steps, ramming him headfirst into the brick wall of the speakeasy. Oops again.

Frank was down on his hands and knees now, blood streaming from his broken lips and busted nose and pooling on the sidewalk. His hair had fallen into his face and it was greasy with sweat. So I tangled my fingers in his locks and dragged him halfway around the building into the alley where the speak kept its dumpster. He was trying to make a comeback now, flailing his arms at me, and I put a stop to that with a quick knee to his chest.

The wind whooshed out of Frank Talley, and he groaned and folded up like a camp chair. I went back around to the front of the speak, found the bottle of port—now empty—and returned to Frank. He was bloody all over the front of his face, and his nice suit was torn in several places.

"How you doing?" I said, squatting in front of him. Frank didn't say anything. I'm not sure he could. The one eye that wasn't closed rolled around and looked at me with no comprehension.

I broke the bottle against the ground and picked up the big-gest piece by the neck. As I lifted it, Frank shied away. He still didn't speak.

"I could take your eyes," I said. "I could cut your throat."

He closed his eyes and his lips moved without sound. He may have been praying.

"The next time anybody close to you shows up with a scar, with a bruise, with even a goddamned pimple, I'm going to be there," I said, my voice low and menacing. "I will be the last thing you see. Do we understand one another?"

Frank whimpered and tried to move himself into a more comfortable position. I thumped him on the nose with my free hand. "Do we understand each other, Frank?"

He closed his eyes and leaned his head against the dumpster. After a long moment, he nodded.

Three weeks later, Frank hit her again. This time when I saw her, the scar on her cheek was fresh and garnet red with dried blood, and her eyes were puffy from crying.

"I told you it wouldn't work," she said. I nodded and brushed past her into the house. We had to talk, and I had work to do.

Melissa filed a police report, and applied for a restraining order. Two days later, she went missing. She still hasn't been found, and Frank is a 'person of interest' in her disappearance. The cops that I know aren't saying anything, but they're obviously proceeding as though she's been murdered. They've got a witness, a guy who sometimes does them favors, who said he'd seen Frank moving a 50-gallon drum from his garage into the back of his wife's Mercedes SUV. They also have canceled checks from Frank, made out to cash, totaling a little more than eighty thousand dollars.

Nobody knows where the woman or the car—or the money—went. Except me.

The cops' best guess is that Frank killed Melissa, and then hired someone to hide or dispose of her body. I'm sure Frank had a hell of a time trying to explain where all that money went.

It took some time, but the news crews finally left the Talley's home in Mountain Brook. The cops stopped coming around every couple of hours. So here I am. It's a nice place, three stories done in Danish Modern except for Frank's office, which looks like it came straight out of the Sharper Image catalog. I have his confession right here in front of me, and I've read it nearly a dozen times to make sure there's nothing missing. It's even got his signature—a scrawl that is lethally easy to copy, let me tell you—and today's date.

Melissa didn't want to go, didn't want to leave her friends, her family. She didn't want a new identity. But I told her that's the way it has to be. I spent a lot of Frank's money setting her up with a new birth certificate, a new history, driver's license, the whole deck.

And if she can keep her head down, it'll all be okay. She'll be happy in Flagstaff or Sedona, wherever she ends up, far away from Birmingham. Maybe she can start again. Maybe she'll be able to look at herself in the mirror and not see the damage that a wrong man did to her. And in the back of her mind, she knows that if she comes back ... well, let's just say that the warranty runs out on this little job I did for her.

Frank's due back home in an hour or so. I can wait. After half a decade behind bars, waiting is one of my best things. When he gets here, Frank and I are gonna have a discussion. I expect it to be short and to the point. And when I'm done, the cops aren't gonna be able to find Frank, either.

I called in some help to get rid of Frank's body. I spent time in one of the ugliest, worst prisons in the country. I met all kinds of people with all kinds of skills. Right now there's a Ford Econoline van parked down the street, and the guys in it are very, very good at making things go away.

When I fix things, they stay fixed.

EVERY NIGHT
I TELL HIM

TONY CHARLES MADE HIS RUN on a Friday night, when the jukebox
was belting out Jason Isbell, the lights were low, and the cigarette
smoke was thick as a band of low-lying clouds. He was slugging
down Jack Daniels like the distillery was on fire, and I was at one
corner of the bar with Kat. She had her hand on my leg under the
bar where no one else could see, and occasionally she'd give me a
little squeeze.

I couldn't tell if I was frozen or on fire. I had loved Kat since
the day I'd met her in ninth grade. Twenty years, and all of a
sudden it was like she'd noticed me for the first time. She pulled
away when her husband, Scott, shambled out of the men's room.
His shirt hung untucked over his gut and sweat stood clearly on
his high, sloping forehead. He bellied up to the bar and ordered
us all another round, despite the fact that Kat and I had barely
touched ours.

"What are you two smiling about?" He asked. "Y'all are thick
as thieves lately."

Kat's smile widened.

"Lanny's trying to get me to run away with him again," Kat said. "You know, same as usual."

I nearly choked on my beer, setting the heavy mug down a little harder than I meant to. I watched their reflections in the mirror behind the bar and didn't say anything.

Scott stared hard at Kat, his eyes red and misty from the beers, and she returned his look with a level gaze, her lip quirked in that killer little go-to-hell smile that I loved so well.

"Yeah," he said, and laughed. "Right."

Kat turned her head back toward me.

"Every night I tell him, and every night he doesn't believe me." Thank God.

About that time Tony swaggered down the bar and asked Scott if he'd like to shoot a little pool. Scott said yes, and they settled on a dollar a game. It wasn't high stakes—it never is around here—and we expected Tony to lose anyway. That's what Tony Charles was: a loser. He'd been a loser ever since we'd known him in high school, and we all kind of dismissed him. Tony was all right, I guess. He was always there on the periphery of things. But you wouldn't notice if he was gone. You'd just assume he was around somewhere.

But this night was different.

They flipped for the break, and Tony won. He sank the two and three balls off a shot that cracked like a whip. We could hear it over the sound of Alannah Myles singing "Black Velvet." He ran the table with a sure hand that belied his very nature. Scott's face was waxy white. He couldn't believe it.

Through it all, Kat and I leaned our heads together, taking turns to whisper in one another's ear. Ideas and plans and sweet nothings. Things I'd only ever dreamed of us saying to one another.

Tony and Scott stayed at the pool table and each time, Tony won going away. Scott barely got a chance to put his cue on the worn green felt of the table, and pretty soon it got to him. I bought us all a round, even one for Tony, because it was such a change to see him win.

Scott didn't understand what had happened. He came back to the bar and ignored the beer I bought for him. Instead he ordered a double bourbon on the rocks, lots of bitters. It didn't take long for him to start getting mad.

"Fucker ran the table on me," he said. He was having a little trouble separating his words, so that *on me* came out as one word.

"Everybody gets lucky sometime," Kat said. She slurped the watery tequila mix from the bottom of her glass and cast a meaningful glance at me through the veil of her thick eyelashes.

Tony downed his whiskey and pushed off of the bar, heading back to the pool pool table. I don't think he ever put his cue down. He schooled a couple of college-age kids, beating them as steady as a metronome. Tony swung by us, his grin splitting his face from ear to ear.

"Didja see that? They wanted twenty bucks a game. I cleaned 'em out!" Tony bought us a round, even Scott. He was as gracious in victory as he usually was in defeat, but by this time Scott had mostly quit drinking. His face was sullen, and he was breathing hard through his mouth.

"I bet you can't do that again," Scott said. His eyes were down to pinpoints somewhere beneath that sloping Cro-Magnon brow.

Tony smiled at him. "Sure I can," he said. He had the supreme confidence of a guy who knows he's on a run, that his luck will hold.

"Prove it," Scott said. "I got a hundred."

Tony balked, just for a second, but I saw it. So did Scott, who grinned a wolfish smile. He reached his wallet and pulled out a Benjamin. Kat put her head face-down on the bar.

"Jesus," she said. "Not again." She sighed and pushed up from the bar, all dramatic-like, puffing out her cheeks and blowing her hair out of her face. She grabbed her purse and looked at me.

"You coming?"

I put a hand on her forearm, said wait a minute. I don't know why I didn't leave with her right then. I guess I just wanted to see what would happen. Maybe somewhere deep inside me, I thought Tony's streak was about to end.

"Lanny'll hold the money," Scott said, and handed me the C-note. "That alright with you?"

Tony nodded. He handed me a mix of twenties and fives and ones from the money he'd won that night. I tucked it into the breast pocket of my work shirt, and they moved to the green felt.

Tony sank the fourteen off the break, and then ran through the rest of the stripes before dropping the eight into the side pocket with a kiss as soft and chaste as a nun's prayer. Scott never even touched the table. I handed Tony the money and glanced at Kat. She shrugged into her leather jacket. I pulled on my navy pea coat, and we headed for the door.

"Goddamn it," Scott said behind us. "Make it double or nothing."

"What an asshole," Kat said, her words nearly drowned out by Tom Petty's "Won't Back Down." I didn't say anything, but we turned around to watch.

I wish we had kept going. Maybe things would have turned out differently. Maybe we'd still be together. But we didn't leave. Instead, we went back to the bar, put our backs to it, and watched the game.

Scott demanded the break this time, even though it was Tony's by right. Tony let him go for it, though, and Scott whiffed on it. When Tony tried to move in and take the shot—which was his right—Scott shoved him back a couple of paces and positioned the cue ball again.

Tony let it slide.

Of course he did. That was Tony Charles in a nutshell. You could insult him, you could push him around. Tony wouldn't do anything. When we were in high school, Scott rescued Tony one time when a couple of football players were intent on giving him a swirlie in the boy's bathroom on third hall. I came along and helped at the end of things, making sure Scott didn't get jumped after the fact. So maybe Tony felt like he owed Scott something. Whatever debt there may have been had been forgotten a long time ago, at least by Scott.

He couldn't stand the sight of Tony mooning around us, and a couple of times things had gotten physical. Nothing serious. None of us were tough guys. None of us were mean, except for Scott when he'd been drinking. But when things did get out of hand, Tony was the one who ended up with the bruises and the cuts and the scrapes at the end of the night.

Scott took his second shot, and whiffed on that one, too. The racked balls sat there, a triangular island in the middle of a sea of green felt, undisturbed as the cue ball fluttered past and found the rail, rebounding and spinning away like a lost child.

I turned around and put my drink to my lips to keep from laughing, but nothing could have disguised my shaking shoulders. Kat leaned against me, and I could feel her silent trembling laughter, too. In the mirror, Scott glared at Tony. He lined up the break for the third time, and this time the cue ball struck home.

Nothing dropped, so Tony approached the table. Scott stood his ground, his shoulders hunched and his head lowered like a pitbull about to bite. Tony took no notice, and Scott faded back toward the bar. Kat and I straightened up and turned around to watch Tony work the table again.

It was more of the same, as clean a game of eight-ball pool as you'd ever see, like watching the pros on TV, I tell you. That night, Tony didn't know how to lose. For one glorious moment, the cosmic laws that had cast him into his eternal downtrodden state were suspended by whatever perverse gods may rule us.

And then he missed.

Scott surged forward to the table. It was the opening he'd been hoping for. Tony had left a clear path to the two and the six, and Scott was able to knock both of those down. On the next shot, though, his stick wandered and bumped the eight. It rolled across the sea of green felt like an ocean liner on a collision course with an iceberg, and dropped into the side pocket.

Tony whooped in triumph, dropping to his knees in relief. Sweat stood out on the back of his blue cotton button-down shirt. He stood up, a little shaky now, and stuck his hand out to shake, but Scott slapped his hand away. The jukebox wound down. No more quarters, no more music. A dark cloud crossed Tony's face for a moment, but only for a moment. He came over, his cue dangling from one hand, and held out the other palm to me. I fished into my pocket for the thick wad of bills. His winnings.

There was a crash over my shoulder. Tony's eyes widened, and I nearly jumped out of my skin. I looked behind me, and the back-bar mirror was shattered. Beside the billiard table, Scott grunted with effort. He was firing the remaining balls from the table at Tony like he was Nolan Ryan and the World Series was on the line. The five-ball missed us all, but it took out a bottle of Bulleit bourbon and a fifth of Jameson. The next ball—I think it was the one—struck Tony square in the forehead.

He went down like he'd been shot, and a huge goose egg began to sprout immediately, stretching Tony's white ,waxy skin. His hands and feet flailed against the floor like an epileptic having a seizure, and his eyes rolled back in his head. Scott rushed forward and dropped to his knees beside Tony. He still held a billiard ball in each hand.

"Fuck," he said. "Fuck, help him."

Kat moved at the same time I did. She took the balls away from Scott, and I elevated Tony's head off the floor. I have no idea if that was the right thing to do or not. I don't know CPR. But he was coming around a little, saying something I couldn't quite catch. His brain and his mouth seemed disconnected somewhere, like when you watch a TV show and the soundtrack isn't quite in sync with the picture.

Scott fell back on his haunches, but he was so drunk that he couldn't stay there. He slid back onto his ass on the floor. Tears clouded his eyes, and he kept saying oh *I'm sorry I'm so sorry oh I'm sorry I'm so sorry* over and over again until the words faded into the background and were meaningless noise.

Tony's eyes finally fluttered open, and a few seconds later they began to focus. He grabbed Kat's arm with one white-knuckled hand and asked, "What happened?"

"It's nothing," I said. "Stay still. You're gonna be OK."

Tony tried to sit up. He rolled onto one elbow and threw up onto the sawdust. His boot-clad feet scrabbled at the floor as he tried to get them underneath him to stand.

"Maybe that's not a good idea," I said, and tried to guide him back to the floor.

"That son of a bitch," Tony said. I think I was the only one who heard him. He grabbed his cue and hoisted himself up. He listed to one side like a ship about to sink. "I won, dammit. I won."

None of us saw it coming. Scott was still down on his ass, trying to scramble back, to give Tony some room. But Tony lashed out with the fat end of his cue stick, cracking Scott in the face. His nose exploded, showering us all in blood. The cue shattered from the force of the blow, leaving long, jagged, wickedly sharp stakes of wood. Tony picked one up and went after Scott. I tried to hold him back, but he slashed at my eyes, and I fell away.

They went down in a heap, and was the only fight I ever saw Tony win. He used the shards of his cue to slash and spear skin wherever he could find it. By the time Tony got both hands around Scott's throat, Scott was beyond help.

The bartender finally came around the bar with a sawed-off Louisville Slugger. He didn't waste any time or motion. He cracked Tony across the back of the head, and our resident loser collapsed on top of Scott, shuddered twice, and lay still.

By the time the ambulance got there, they were both dead. No losers and no winners now. Kat stared, unable to tear her gaze away as the EMTs zipped the bodies into the black plastic bags, closing their faces off from the light of the world.

"Do you want to ride with them?" I asked. She nodded, and got into the ambulance. She never looked at me, and I never spoke to her again.

When the ambulance left, they didn't use the siren or the blinking lights. There was no reason to hurry.

HIS LUCKY DAY

EDDIE WHITTAKER SAT at the army surplus desk in his cramped office and tapped one pudgy index finger against the smooth, white lottery ticket. He was grinning so broadly that the cavities in his rear molars were visible. It was his lucky day, no doubt about it.

Nineteen million dollars. That's how much he was worth now. Eddie couldn't believe it. The jackpot was thirty-eight million, and there were only two winning tickets. Eddie had one. It really didn't matter who had the other. All he had to know was that half of it was his. He still couldn't believe it. It was enough for a new office. Maybe something with some nice plants, and a secretary to water them.

He pushed the lottery ticket around on his desk a little. It was the key to freedom, and, in truth, he was a little frightened by the thought. He giggled. Three stories below, he could hear the rumble of midday traffic, like rolling thunder from the ground.

Maybe he wouldn't work at all. Get a little place on the beach and watch as the world went by. No more divorce cases. No standing outside a motel room window, pointing a camera with a low-light lens, clicking away and hating himself for it. He could get

177

his teeth fixed, stop using matchsticks to pick between them after meals. Maybe buy a hairpiece, or get plugs. He could stop worrying about rent. He could buy a new car. A world of possibility opened before him. Maybe money couldn't buy happiness. But it could buy an awful lot.

Allen wasn't the only big winner in the family anymore. Allen was the one with the big downtown CPA firm. He was the one who had it all – the big house, the Mercedes, the pretty wife. He had everything, and that was just another assurance to Eddie that nice guys really did finish last. Little brother Eddie had always taken a backseat. Until now. Now, there was nothing holding Eddie back. He didn't have the money yet. But he would. He looked at the grimy office, with its warped filing cabinet and dusty baseboards. He deserved better.

Good news travels slowly. Eddie sat in his office and called everyone he knew. There was a seemingly endless procession of busy signals and phones that just went on ringing. He tried his parents. He tried Allen. He tried ex-girlfriends. There was no one to listen. He tapped a matchstick against his front teeth and thought about it for a little while. There was always Rita.

Eddie took his overcoat down from the hanger on the back of his office door and slipped into it. He picked up the lottery ticket and put it into his wallet. When he put the wallet back into his pants pocket, it didn't feel right. He pulled it out and put it into a side pocket of the overcoat, where it was easy to his hand. He locked the door to his office and went outside.

He couldn't wait for the elevator. His feet tapped and his legs shook. Finally, he took the stairs two at a time down to street level. By the time he was on the sidewalk, his pulse was pounding in his temples, and the blood rush had caused a dull roar in his ears. A fine sheen of sweat appeared on Eddie's brow, and he wiped it away with an ancient, yellowed handkerchief. He tried to get himself under control, but it was no use. His heart galloped on, like a horse without a rider. He walked two blocks to Hannigan's, a little bar he frequented, and went inside.

It was quiet in the lush darkness of the bar. Above the bar, glasses hung suspended from a ceiling rack, their globes catching the ambient light like an alcoholic's chandelier. The bar itself was an oversized horseshoe scarred with old cigarette burns. The rush didn't start until after five-thirty, when the yuppies came in to down a few before going on to their quiet lives in the suburbs. A few hardcore drinkers sat at the bar, nursing their drinks. Eddie avoided them. There was really only one person he cared to see at Hannigan's. Eddie seated himself at a small table near the door and waited for Rita.

He didn't wait long. She swept over as soon as she saw him, her strong teeth chomping down on a wad of Juicy Fruit gum. Her hair was red and teased, and there were laugh lines at the corners of both her eyes. Her tight white tee-shirt glowed in the murky darkness of the bar.

"You don't give up, do you?" She said. Her voice dropped. "It's not going to happen again, I told you. It shouldn't have happened in the first place."

"I'm not here for that," Eddie said. "I just wanted to drop in. See you."

"So you see me. I'm working. Now, you want a drink or not?"

"Sure," Eddie said, and ordered a beer. Rita brought it and left. Eddie watched the other patrons and drank most of the bottle. When he was almost finished, Rita came by and picked up the bottle.

"You've had enough," she said. "Just go, all right?"

"Can I call you? We ought to talk about the other night."

"There's nothing to talk about. You're fat, you're lousy in bed, and you've got nothing going for you."

"Rita, I need to talk to you. You gotta listen to me."

"Give me one good reason."

"I can give you nineteen million of 'em," he said, and sat back to let her figure it out. She played the lottery every week, same as him. Checked the numbers every day, same as him. She'd come to it sooner or later. He watched as understanding dawned in her small blue eyes.

"You're kidding," she said. "Not you."

"Me and somebody else. Only two winning tickets this week, Rita. You still want me to go?"

"I – I don't know what to say," she said. "This is going to take some getting used to. Maybe we should have that talk."

"No, we shouldn't," he said. A grin broke across his face, like a runny egg on a chipped plate. "I came by to tell you that you're right. It won't happen again. I'm done with you."

He threw a five-dollar bill on the table before he left.

Back at the office, Eddie tried a few more calls. He found an old address book stuffed back into a corner of the long, shallow middle drawer of his desk. It was no use. There was no one he could tell. Eddie almost gave up until he found a number he hadn't called in years. He dialed Allen's cellular number, and the phone rang twice in his ear. A worried voice picked up.

"Yes?"

"Allen, that you?"

"No, this is Jimmy Rivenbark," he said. The voice on the other end of the line was quivering like a high-tension wire. "I work with Allen. Who's this?"

"His brother, Eddie. What's going on?"

"We're at Sisters of Mercy emergency room. Allen's had some kind of attack. I thought we contacted all the family members, I'm sorry."

"It's okay. Sisters of Mercy is on West Fifteenth, right?"

"Right."

"I'll be there as soon as I can."

The drive across town took less than fifteen minutes. Eddie hurried into the lobby, his steps quick and stuttering against the hard tile floor. Ahead of him, a young woman in a nurse's cap sat at a chest-high podium that read, "Information" in large green letters across the front. The woman was reading a Stephen King novel. When Eddie approached, she put the book facedown on the desk so that should wouldn't lose her place. A blue nametag on her starched white blouse read "Erin."

"Can I help you?" She said.

"My brother was admitted to the ER," Eddie said. He gave Allen's name. "Is he still there?"

Erin entered Allen's name into the computer terminal on the desk. She looked up and smiled.

"He's not in the ER anymore," she said. "He's been taken up to the eighth floor for observation. It's room 814."

"Observation?"

"Standard procedure," she said. Erin consulted her computer again. "He was admitted to emergency two hours ago, and they're just getting him settled into a room now."

"Thanks," Eddie said, and turned to go.

"Wrong way," Erin said. "The elevators are over there."

"Thanks. I always get nervous in hospitals. I never been in one where something good happened, you know?"

"I know what you mean," she said. "I always thought that a hospital is somewhere that you come to get better, but you can never really get well in one."

"You really think so?" Eddie said.

"Sure," Erin said. "It's the smell. Alcohol and disinfectant everywhere, it's enough to make me sick, and I'm a nurse. If your brother really wants to get better, tell him to get home as soon as he can."

"I thought I was the only one who noticed the smell."

"God, no," Erin said. She wrinkled her nose. "I can't stand it."

Eddie smiled with his mouth closed.

"Thanks," he said. "I feel a little better."

"You must love your brother a lot," she said. "You're lucky. I didn't have any brothers or sisters."

"Sometimes I love him," Eddie laughed. "It's family, you know? We're not close, but we gotta be there for each other. Who else is there?

"I remember when we were kids, Allen was playing around and pushed me out of this big pecan tree out back of our house. It was high up, and we were horsing around."

"My god," Erin said.

Eddie nodded.

"Broke my arm. He got this weird look on his face before he pushed me, though. I always thought he wanted to be an only child. He almost was, if I'd landed a little different."

"I don't think I could have gotten over that," she said.

"Who says I did?" Eddie said. "But he's family. We stick together."

Eddie crossed to the bank of elevators. His left hand never left his pocket. He was squeezing the lottery ticket so hard that he was scared he might tear it in half. The elevator dinged, and the doors slid open. Eddie stepped in and pressed the button for the eighth floor. When the doors opened again, Eddie stepped out into a gray, alien world. The industrial carpeting and wallpaper were both a pale greenish gray that discouraged other colors. A young man in a red sweatshirt and blue jeans lay sprawled asleep on a gray love seat in the eighth-floor waiting room. Somehow, the dim gray furniture seemed to have leached into the sweatshirt, muting the only splash of color Eddie saw.

A tall, thin man with receding hair and glasses stood outside room 814. There was a cigarette plugged into the corner of his mouth.

"Jimmy Rivenbark," he said, sticking out his hand. "You have to be Eddie. Allen looks just like you, only thinner. Your parents already came. Surprised they forgot to call you."

Eddie wasn't surprised. He was an afterthought. Allen was two years older, and he'd always been the golden child.

"I'm gonna go downstairs, burn a cancer stick," Rivenbark said. "You okay to go in?"

"Sure," Eddie said. "Why wouldn't I be?" He pushed the door open.

Allen was pulling his slacks over his thighs when Eddie came in the room. He buttoned the pants and zipped the zipper.

"What do you think you're doing?" Eddie said.

Allen spun around, his mouth agape. Eddie remembered a similar look on his older brother's face when he was caught cheating on a freshman exam. Allen was twenty years out of college, now, though. He picked up a green pinstriped shirt from the back of a visitor's chair and slipped his arms through the sleeves.

"I'm getting out of here," Allen said.

"No you're not," Eddie said. "You're supposed to stay here for observation."

"It was nothing, Eds, just a little panic attack. You'd have 'em too, if you ever got any business. There's stress that goes along with being successful."

Allen was gaining more confidence as he stepped back into his CPA clothes. When he finished buttoning his shirt, he looked over at Eddie.

"We both know you're not going to stop me."

It rankled. Allen had been a good big brother in his own way, but he always pushed Eddie around. It was something he'd never grown out of. Allen was always in charge. Eddie tried to think of a way to stop him from leaving.

"You still think you're the big man? Still think I can't stand up to you? The whole reason I called you was to tell you I won the lottery."

"What?"

"That's right. You're not the 'it' boy anymore. I could buy and sell you anytime I want."

"Bullshit," Allen said.

Eddie pulled the ticket out of his pocket and showed it to Allen. When Allen stepped closer, Eddie put the winning ticket away.

"You don't trust me?" Allen said.

"As far as I can throw you. You're staying here. I'll stay with you."

"Listen to me, Eds. I'm not staying. If you try to keep me here, I'm going to hurt you."

"We're not kids anymore, Allen. You're staying. You had a big enough panic attack that you scared the hell out of your family and co-workers. I can stop you if I have to."

"Do it, then," Allen said.

Eddie reached for the beige phone beside the hospital bed. He picked up the receiver with one hand and tucked it underneath his chin. His left hand was still inside a pocket of his overcoat, squeezing the lottery ticket. He was about to dial the hospital switchboard when Allen hit him. The blow glanced off Eddie cheekbone, and he could feel the skin split. Blood showered over Allen's good shirt. Eddie reeled, and Allen grabbed him by the lapels. Eddie brought his knee up into Allen's groin, and the older brother sagged away, hands clutching at his own crotch. Eddie brought his hands up, aware that he'd pulled the lottery ticket out of his pocket, along with his clenched fist.

"You think that money makes you something?" Allen said. "You're still a loser, Eddie. Only difference is now you're a loser with money."

Allen hit him again, and now Eddie could see what made the cut along his cheekbone. Allen's thick gold class ring was bloody. The brothers traded blows, grunting for breath in the sterile hospital air. Allen bullied Eddie around until the younger brother was facing the only door to the room, and then hit him with a combination to the gut, and followed that with a kick to the groin. Eddie fell back against the window ledge. His hands opened, and he dropped the lottery ticket as he fought for purchase to regain his footing.

Allen charged, his body carrying forward, forward, forward.

Eddie had no choice. He ducked, and Allen's knees drove into his shoulder. In the instant Allen became airborne, Eddie realized they were both in trouble.

Eddie heard a snap high up in his chest as his collarbone broke. Allen hit the wide glass window, and the pane split in a jagged line down the center, like lightning in a night sky. The glass gave way, and Allen tumbled down, his screams growing faint as the asphalt rushed to meet him. Somewhere above, a small white slip of paper fluttered on an updraft, swung outward, away from the building, and was lost forever.

Eddie leaned out over the precipice and watched as his fortune blew away. He sagged to the floor, eyes blank and dry. His mouth was open and slack. Nineteen million dollars, gone in the blink of an eye.

It took twenty stitches to close the gash in his cheek. While the doctor sewed him up, and worked on setting his collarbone, the cops questioned him.

"It was an accident," Eddie said. "Just an accident."

That's when he overheard the nurse from the information desk. She was talking to another one of the officers.

"He told me," Erin said. "He as much as admitted to me that he hated his brother. Said he hadn't forgiven him for pushing him out of a tree when they were kids. Can you imagine someone holding a grudge that long?"

The cop heard it, too. Eddie looked around, but there was nowhere to run.

They handcuffed him in front, in deference to his broken collarbone. It was only later, when they officially charged him with murder, that Eddie broke down and began to cry.

A CLEAN GETAWAY

WHEN I HIT THE GUARD in the face with the pepper spray, he screamed like a woman giving birth. He dropped the two heavy canvas bags he was carrying and reached for his eyes. I dropped the pepper spray and scooped the sacks up and ran past him as fast as I could. No one really even looked my way. They were watching the guard, curled now in the fetal position, as he wallowed on the sidewalk and tried in vain to clear his eyes. The other guard had climbed down from the driver's seat of the armored car and was tending to his partner. I was in the clear.

Around the block, Curtis had the car idling, parked parallel to the curb and with plenty of change for the meter. I tossed the bags into the back seat and slammed the door closed. Curtis was supposed to drive away then, like nothing had happened. Instead he hit a button to scroll down the electric window.

"How'd it go?" He said.

"Perfect," I said, "if you'll get the hell out of here."

Behind us we heard the woop-woop of a police cruiser arriving at the scene, and beyond that the somewhat higher pitch of an ambulance siren. I stripped off the heavy canvas gloves I was wearing and put them in my front pocket, hanging out a little.

"Jesus, you didn't kill the guy, did you?" Curtis said.

"No. Just get moving. I'll see you in a couple of hours."

When Curtis drove away, I walked around the block and came back to the scene of the crime. The paramedics had washed the guard's face and were escorting him into the back of the ambulance. His partner was giving the cops a description of the guy who had assaulted his partner and stolen the money bags.

Good luck with that.

More cops were arriving, most of them scratching their heads in confusion at the thirty-odd men who stood on the sidewalk. We were all dressed to work, in lace-up boots, blue jeans, gray T-shirts and hard hats. Most of them were like me, in their mid-30s to late 20s. We all had canvas or cloth work gloves, and many of us wore safety goggles on our helmets. And none of the others had a clue what was going on. The cops weren't letting anyone leave until they knew what was going on, so I settled in to wait.

It took them an hour to get to me. When they did, they wanted to see my identification. I showed them a driver's license with the name Phillip Orr, and an address in Queens. They took down the phone number I gave them too. But Phillip Orr was a blank wall. It's just something I came up with for registering online. When I finally figured out how to go through with the money grab, I had a graphics guy I know make up a phony driver's license. And viola, Phillip Orr was born.

"What's your story, Mac?" The patrol officers had given way to detectives, and the one questioning me was small, with a hatchet face and a ferret's beady, calculating eyes.

"I saw an ad on Craigslist for construction workers," I said. "Said to be here at 8 a.m., dressed in jeans, a gray T-shirt and a hard hat for day labor."

"Great." He said. "Same story we got from everyone else. You see anything at all that happened here?"

"No," I said. "I was the last one to get here, I think."

There was something he didn't like about that answer. He took me by the arm and pulled me over to the line of squad cars that still sat, lights revolving, at the curb. He sat me in the passenger seat of one of the cars. No frisk, no handcuffs. Whatever had his wind up wasn't enough to make me a full-on suspect. The detective left my door open. He came around to the driver's side, sat down and read my license information into the car's two-way radio.

"Sorry about this, Mr. Orr," he said. "I just want to validate your information."

"No problem," I said. When the radio crackled again and the cop reached for it, I hit him in the face with my left elbow. His head snapped back, and he clawed for his gun. I pulled mine out of one of the pockets of the tool belt first. It was a little .25 automatic. At this range it was just as lethal as his 9-millimeter. I had the hammer back and the barrel in his ear before he could do anything.

"Take your gun out with your forefinger and thumb," I said. "Toss it in the floorboard."

He did it.

"I'm going to close my door," I said. "Then you're going to drive us away from here."

He shook his head. He had to know that the farther away we got from the crime scene, the less likely his chances of survival. I pushed the gun harder against him.

"If I go out, I'll make sure you go with me," I said. When he didn't respond, I switched the gun briefly to my left hand, then reached over with my right and closed the door. I could feel his muscles tense, but he was smart. We hadn't been in the cruiser more than a minute. The detective adjusted his mirrors, waited until it was clear, and then pulled out into traffic.

"Turn off the lights," I said. The tootsie roll up top went dark, and we slid through the city relatively unimpeded. The detective was quiet for few minutes as he drove. I gave him minimal

directions. The gun in his side had to hurt. He didn't wasn't wearing any body armor. As we rode, I cursed myself. I never should
have come back to the crime scene. I should have just hopped in
the car with Curtis and rode away. But I thought it would be fun,
you know, watch the cops mill around and wonder what the hell
was going on. I'd know better next time.

"What tipped you?" I said.

"It's 55 degrees out there, and you were the only guy sweating,"
the cop said. "You probably pulled the heist, dropped the loot off
with a buddy and circled the block. When you told me you got
there late, it made me suspicious."

"Not suspicious enough," I said.

He nodded, and grimaced in pain. There was a purpling lump
high on his cheek where I had struck him. It didn't do anything
for his disposition, either.

His cell phone rang, and I made him turn it off. A phone sends
out a signal when it's turned on, and a savvy tech can triangu-
late your position using cell towers – but only if the phone is on.
The cop wasn't liking any of this. He especially didn't like that he
couldn't get a handle on me. There was no way to turn me, no way
to fix this situation. He just had to ride it out.

"You're going to have to kill me, you know," he said. "It's the
only way I'll stop looking for you. And if you kill me, it will only
get worse for you. Kill a cop and they'll never stop looking for you."

"Shut up," I said. But he was right. The moment he'd put me in
the squad car, my options had become limited. When he decided
to check my ID through their computer, I was limited even further. And now I'd kidnapped a cop. This wasn't going according to
plan. By now Curtis was wondering where I was. He wasn't calm
enough just to wait for me.

We made a couple of turns into the warehouse district. As the
neighborhoods fell away, I could see the cop getting more nervous. A couple of times the radio in the car crackled to life, and

the detective reached for the microphone. Each time I shooed his hand away.

"What's your name?" I said.

He hesitated a fraction of a second before answering.

"Alex Kincaid," he said.

"My ass," I said. "Pull over at the curb, Alex, and show me your ID."

He pulled over like I told him to and put the car in park. He produced a leather wallet with his shield and police ID. His name was Frank Morrison, detective second grade.

"Nice try, Frank," I said. "Is that any way to start off a relationship? The next time you lie to me, I'm going to put a bullet in you."

I had Frank pull back onto the street and we drove awhile until we found a deserted alley. I had him pull in there, and I'll tell you this: I wasn't the only one sweating in that cop car. Morrison thought I was going to kill him, and if I'm perfectly honest, I had no idea what I was going to do. We sat in silence for a few moments.

"Look," Morrison said, "I know what you're trying to decide. Do you kill me? Or do you fix this some other way. Right now you're on the hook for armed robbery, kidnapping and grand theft auto. But murder puts you in another league, kid. You don't want to do that."

He was right. I didn't want to do it. I had never killed anyone before. And maybe I wouldn't have to.

"Turn the car off and get out," I said. Morrison looked so relieved I thought he was going to faint.

"You're letting me go?" He said. I took the keys out of the car and got out of the passenger side, keeping the gun on Morrison at all times. He held his hands about shoulder high, palms toward me. He was backing away, slowly moving down the alley away from me.

"Stop!" I said. "If you run, I will kill you, cop or no cop."

Morrison smiled a little and kept inching away from me.

"With that little thing, you'd be lucky to hit a billboard from that distance," he said.

So I got lucky. I aimed at the middle of the mass and squeezed the trigger. Either the gun was way off or I flinched at the last instant. Instead of a hole in Morrison's torso, I had blown a hole in his shoe. He screamed and collapsed, grabbing one of his ugly, black brogans as blood poured onto the faded asphalt.

"You shot me," he said. He was hunched over, the back of his jacket exposing a small pouch for his handcuffs. I grabbed them and used his vulnerable position to turn him onto his belly. I reached up and grabbed the left thumb, bent his arm behind him and cuffed it. Then I did the same thing with the right arm. When I had him all trussed up, I got him onto his feet – or maybe onto his foot at that point – and we limped over to the police cruiser.

Morrison didn't want to go into the trunk, but his hands were bound and he was off balance because of his injured foot. Frank was a big guy, and heavy. Finally I had him tucked into the trunk.

"I'll call 911 and tell them where you are," I said. "If you're smart, you won't come after me. Maybe you think you owe me one, after I shot you. But remember that you're alive because I let you live."

"You don't think we'll get you? We'll get you. I got your license. I got your name. I know where you live."

"You mean Phillip Orr?" I said. "That's just my little joke. My name's Phillip. Or it's not."

I slammed the trunk and returned the gun to its deep pocket in my tool belt. From another pocket I took a prepaid cell phone and called Curtis. He had a prepaid cell, too. Almost untraceable. After we were done with them today, we'd chuck them somewhere no one could find them.

"Come pick me up," I said, and told him where I was.

"That's all the way across town," he said. "What the hell happened?"

I sighed. Curtis was going to hold me down. I had known him

since we were in first grade, and there was no one else I could trust to help me with something this outrageous. We were roommates now, a couple of guys who couldn't afford to live alone in the city. He was stupid and lazy, but I could count on him. He picked me up twenty minutes later, and we headed back to his place to count the take. On the way back, I got him to call 911 and tell the cops Morrison's location.

Eighty thousand dollars. That's what we got. It took us a long time to count it all, and then afterward, we just sort of sat at the kitchen table and looked at one another. The stacks of money were separated into hundreds, fifties and twenties. Nothing smaller. It was more money than either Curtis or I had ever seen. We waited until after dark, then filled the money bags with sand and threw them into the East River. My phone followed. I wiped the hard drive on my computer and tossed it too. I'd used three different proxies to hide my IP address from Craigslist, but you can't be too careful.

We spent two days watching coverage of the "daring robbery" on the local newscasts. The security guard was going to be all right – the pepper spray had hurt, but it wasn't lethal. Detective second grade Frank Morrison fared a little worse. He'd had his big toe shot off by a robber. I snickered a little about that. The newscasters put up a not-very-good likeness of me on the screen. The day they did that, I went into the bathroom and shaved my head and mustache. And the amount of money we'd stolen kept growing with every news report.

"They say it's a hundred and twenty grand now," Curtis told me the second day. "Are you sure we counted the money right?"

"They just say that so they can make some profit back from the insurance company," I told him. That's when Curtis told me I had all the angles covered. I wish he had been right.

By the third day, the talking heads on the TV had moved on to different stories. That worried me. The media might have moved on, but I was pretty sure the robbery was still a priority with the cops. With no news coverage, I couldn't track what was going on.

We wanted no links to the job at all. And there would have been none, if Curtis had done the smart thing. But like I said before, he was stupid. He kept his cell phone – why, I don't know. He could have gotten a new one easy. But I saw him talking on it one afternoon, a few days after the robbery. I snatched it out of his hand.

"He'll call you back," I said and snapped it closed. Curtis just gaped at me.

"They can trace these, dummy," I said. "This is the phone you used to call 911, right?"

Mutely, he nodded.

"If you've had it on at all, they can use it to find us," I said. I didn't ask him why he hadn't thrown it away. Years of knowing Curtis had made me understand that screaming about it wouldn't stop his dumb behavior – it just made him feel bad. And any energy I put into anger was energy that wasn't going into figuring out how to deal with this situation.

"Go upstairs. Look out the windows on both sides of the house and tell me what you see."

Curtis rumbled up the stairs, and a few seconds later thundered right back down. He was out of breath.

"Couple of cop cars at either end of the block," Curtis said. "Nothing out back yet."

"Go get the money," I said. I went to the junk drawer in the kitchen and pulled my little .25 automatic. We still had most of the money, tucked away in a black duffel bag under Curtis's bed. I was peeping out one of the heavy blackout curtains in our living room. Detective Frank Morrison hobbled down the sidewalk with the aid of a pair of metal crutches. He and a crew of uniformed officers were just getting out of their cruisers at the far end of the block. Curtis came back down with the money. He set it on the living room floor.

"Take a look at this," I said, and pulled the curtain slightly away from the window. Curtis stepped forward to peer out, and when he did, I put the muzzle of the .25 behind his ear and pulled the trigger. The bullet never came out – instead, Curtis simply slumped to the floor. A little blood poured out of the hole in his head and stained the carpet. There was a moment when I swear he understood what I'd done. But I am still human enough to hope not. The shot froze the cops, and they all began to back toward their cruisers. Morrison hobbled as fast as he could, and I bet none of the patrol officers moved to help him.

I grabbed the duffel bag full of money and went through the kitchenette, out the back door and through the back yard. I left all the dead weight – everything that tied me to my old life – behind me.

When the cops went into the house, all they would find was the husk – the man I used to be. And that didn't matter anymore. I walked down the sidewalk, feeling the clean heat of the early spring sun on my face. Behind me, there were no footsteps.

It was a clean getaway.

SIX ROUNDS

YOU WANNA BLAME SOMEBODY, blame my corner. They coulda thrown in the towel anytime. But they didn't, so there I was, swinging away with Johnny the Jet. Johnny was supposed to fight for the title next, right? And now he's not fighting anyone ever again. That poor sonofabitch. I fucked up his career and mine, all at the same time.

What I said before, about blaming my corner? Don't do that. There's enough blame to go around. Start with me. I ain't much anymore. I fought my way up from a no-name prospect all the way to a fight for the cruiserweight title. When the champ laid me out clean with a left hook in round three, I shoulda learned my lesson right there. But I didn't. Instead I went down to light heavy, and won a couple of fights. Even though I'd been KO'ed once, I still had some name value. They put me in with Harley MacGregor for the light heavyweight title, and I did a little better. I lasted seven rounds before MacGregor turned my lights out.

That's how I came to fight Johnny the Jet—Johnny McDaniel, if you don't follow the fights. I'm still a name, right? "Black" Jack Harrison, but everybody calls me Blackjack. Two-time world title contender. But now that I'm past thirty and on my way down the ladder, I'm just a name. That's what they call me behind the scenes—a name opponent. In other words, I'm a guy the up-and-comers get to face before they go on to fight for the title. A guy who won't ever fight for the title again; a guy they expect to lose. I still got a little pride, though, and that's why you can blame me for what happened. The Jet pissed me off—and that's why he ought to take some of the blame, too.

We came out in the first round throwing stiff jabs. The lights were hot overhead, and I'd already worked up a sweat on the way to the ring. The Jet had the edge on me in speed, but I had him in power, and I let him know that early on. He threw a lazy right cross that I picked off with my left forearm, and I sunk a hook right into his gut. Muscle memory, pure and simple—it was a move I've done a million times in sparring, and a million more on the heavy bag. I never saw a black guy turn green before, but Johnny backed off quick before I could follow up.

I wasn't gonna follow up, but he didn't know that. When we engaged again, we went through the same sequence. His muscles gleamed with sweat, and his movement was like a fine Swiss timepiece—compact, with nothing wasted. He was something to see, that kid. This time I pulled my body blow a little, but the Jet flinched back and away again. He shook his head like he was confused. That's when he got on his horse and started picking me apart with those quick, annoying jabs. I let my hands drift down a little, and pretty soon he got a trickle of blood from underneath my right eye. Sweat began immediately to sting the miniscule cut, and I knew my corner was going to have some work to do at the break.

Right before the end of the round, the Jet pressured me against the ropes, and I tied him up. Johnny McDaniel was a dangerous fighter, and I was supposed to give him six good rounds of work. Getting knocked out in the first was a definite no-no. But the sonofabitch wasn't having it. He tripped me and threw me over his side in some kind of rolling hiplock. I hit the canvas hard and popped up like a jack-in-the-box.

"The fuck?" I yelled at him. "This ain't WrestleMania." The bell rang before I could get to him, and the ref stepped between us.

"Motherfucker, you better come out to fuckin' fight next round," the Jet screamed at me. "I'mma fuckin' kill you if you don't."

I said something back to him, but by that time, my corner was in the ring and trying to lead me back to my stool. Eventually I let them.

They looked at my face enough to know the cut wasn't bad, and then went to work with a Q-tip and some Vaseline to try to stop the bleeding. Sally Ray, my trainer, put an icepack on my neck. The lights were hot and I was sweating. I could smell the crowd, that kind of good Vegas crowd that still gets dressed up to see the fights, and they were buzzing with the smell of ozone and expensive cologne. The ring in front of me was blue and stained with blood—someone else's, from an earlier fight. Everything was coming in focus. I felt good. I remember thinking *If he wants a goddamn fight, I'm gonna give him one.* At some point the ref came over and told my corner that he was deducting a point from the Jet for the illegal throw. When the bell rang, I was off my stool and charging for the center of the ring.

I hurt the Jet bad within the first thirty seconds. It was that right to the body again, followed up with a pair of left hooks—one upstairs and one to the liver. Johnny sagged, but I didn't let him fall. I clinched and bulled him backwards into the turnbuckles. As soon as I was sure he wasn't gonna fall down, I threw a flurry to the body. None of the shots would have even broken an egg, but they came so fast that they looked good to the crowd. The Jet recovered quickly, taking the last few on his elbows and upper arms, so I circled away.

He came after me then, and for the first time I understood why the kid was so good. He was mad, but he was in control. He put a mouse under my left eye, to match the one on the right. Then he got a trickle of blood from my nose, and my vision started to blur. Ever been hit in the nose? The tears are hot and immediate, and there's nothing you can do to hold them back. The Jet backed me into a corner and kept the shots coming. I had my guard up, but he was relentless. One of his hooks missed my face, but the elbow that followed it was right on the money. It laid my cheek open in a shower of blood. The whole time he was hitting me, the Jet was talking to me.

"You think you gonna throw this fight, motherfucker? I'mma fucking kill you in this goddamn ring. I don't need you to throw no fucking fight. I kill you all night long, you honky piece of shit."

I didn't say anything back to him. I didn't have anything to say, and I didn't want to waste my breath. The longer I stayed in the corner, the better his odds of knocking me out. I did the only thing I could think of to get him off me. I hit him in the groin as hard as I could. Johnny screamed and clutched at his crotch, jumping up and down in frustration and pain. The ref stepped between us—just like he should have—and started to admonish me. He directed me to a neutral corner, and I stood there to catch my breath for a minute while the Jet made sure the family jewels were still in the safe.

They were, and eventually the ref restarted us, this time deducting a point from me. He warned us both about dirty tactics and told us to fight. We did, each of us working to our strengths. He stung me with jabs, but I bulled in and worked the body with half-speed hooks and straight rights. They weren't doing any damage, but they were exposing the flaws in the Jet's defense.

In other words, I was pissing him off even more than I was earlier. When the bell rang, neither of us wanted to go back to our corners. Johnny the Jet was set on murdering me right there in front of eight thousand spectators. All I wanted to do was make sure I earned the thirty grand his manager had offered me to throw the fight and look good in the process.

I sat down on my stool and watched the slow drip of blood

from my nose to the canvas. All I was supposed to do was give Johnny McDaniel six good rounds. Then I could drop my hands a little more and let him find my jaw with a nice overhand right or maybe a left hook. I'd fall, take the ten count, and move on to the next payday. The Jet would get a shot at the title. Maybe even win it. He was good.

The ten-second buzzer sounded to tell the cornermen to get out of the ring. I pushed to my feet and met the Jet head on. Tried to think about what my corner had said, but couldn't remember a word. Flashbulbs were popping behind my eyes, and I knew Johnny was landing some good combos. I was so deep into the fight that I couldn't even feel it when he hit me. I kept seeing openings, but I hesitated to let my hands go. The world weaved around me, and the only thing that I understood were Johnny McDaniel's fists. I was having trouble breathing, but in a little while it wouldn't matter.

Eventually I had to punch back. If I didn't, Johnny was gonna make good on his promise to end me right there. He swung a wild hook that he was sure would land. Why wouldn't it? Everything else he threw was landing. But this time I ducked and drove to the body again. A four-punch combination scored, and I knew I had him hurt. I went to the head with a right cross and a left uppercut that didn't have a lot on it. His head snapped back anyway. He was dazed. I clinched again, and this time it was my turn for some trash talk.

"Think you're gonna be the champ? MacGregor's gonna eat you alive, kid. Your defense is awful. You're soft in the gut—"

I backed off and went to the body two more times, and then clinched again.

"—and the head."

I cuffed him hard on the ear and watched his knees buckle. The bell sounded and I went back to my stool. He staggered to the wrong corner. His seconds had to lead him back to his seat.

"Blackjack, you sure you know what you're doing?" Sally Ray

asked while the cut man worked on the laceration on my cheek. Sally Ray knew about the thirty K. Hell, he's the one who set it up. "You don't wanna piss this kid off. He's hitting you a lot."

He gave me some water to rinse. I spit it out into a big plastic bucket.

"Fuck him," I said around my mouthpiece. My face was swollen, and I knew it would hurt the next day. It always did. "You hear him in there? He wants a goddamn war."

Sally Ray wouldn't look me in the eye. "Don't do it. You want to fight smart with this one."

Translation: We've got a lot of money riding on this. Don't blow it.

"He don't want it," I said. I wished I could spit my mouthpiece out. But that's usually a bad idea in the middle of a fight. Sally Ray shook his head, showing me he understood that the Jet didn't want me to throw the fight.

"I don't care what this motherfucker wants," he said. "You fight smart. You do not go to war. You understand me? Fight smart."

Translation: Stick with the game plan. Drop in the sixth round, just like we talked about. Goddamn it.

"I can take him," I said. "He can't defend for shit."

"Watch the overhand right." Translation: Let him hit you with his big punch. The buzzer sounded and my cornermen scrambled outta the ring. I went back out into the middle of the canvas and let Johnny the Jet McDaniel beat the hell out of me some more.

Fixing a fight is easy. There's a million ways to do it. But the easiest is this: A fight promoter approaches your manager and says "My fighter is looking for someone who can give him a good workout." Your manager, if he's smart, might answer "I got a guy could give your boy five or six rounds."

The promoter will say "Six sounds good." And from there on out, all they have to negotiate is price. The other fighter might not ever know the fight was fixed. In fact, I can tell you that the Jet didn't know until I took it easy on his gut after that first hard shot. After that, he was pissed off.

Sally Ray got the money up front, which could be a problem. The way the Jet was going at me, I had to defend myself. He was landing some hard shots, but I'm a hard-headed Irishman who doesn't have the sense to know when he's been hurt. So he kept pouring it on, and I kept doing just enough to keep the scorecards close. I wanted it to be respectable before I took the dive. There were other fights out there to lose. He threw another hook and followed it with his elbow again, the dirty bastard, and this time he caught my nose with it. The bone crunched easily, just as it had done the other four times it was broken. But now I was the one that was pissed off.

He was already beating me. He didn't have to play dirty. Ah well, as Sally Ray used to tell me when I was on the way up, what's good for the goose is good for the gander. I took the Jet's lead left on the shoulder and bulled in close. I managed to step down hard on his instep. Instead of moving my foot away, though, I kept it planted on top of his boot. There was nowhere to go. A tall, rangy kid like the Johnny the Jet liked to keep his opponents on the outside. Trouble was, the higher you get up the card, the harder it is to dictate where the fight stays. And the kid wasn't good enough to keep me off of him.

Somebody once called the art of infighting "like fighting in a phone booth." They don't have many phone booths anymore, but the principle is this sound. Every movement takes place within an eighteen-inch radius. My punches were short, sharp, and vicious. He hated being hit in the body, so I unloaded there. When his hands came down, I went left hook and right cross to his head. The cross split his eyebrow, and the sight of the Jet's blood cascading down his face made me kick things into overdrive. Back to the body, back to the head. I could see the kid's hands drop, so I teed off. I didn't hear the bell. Didn't know the round was over until the ref and my cornermen dragged me away from the Jet.

Sally Ray was in my ear the whole time I sat on the stool.
"Whaddaya doing?" He said. "Ten-round fight. You're gonna
punch yourself out. It's only the fourth round. You're on the wrong
side a thirty to be doing that shit."

Translation: You dumbass. You better come out tired in the
next round. Dance around. Let the kid jab you a few times.

"I can take him out," I said. Or that's what I think I said. My
jaw was sore and my nose was laid flat against my cheekbone. It's
a miracle Sally Ray could understand me. I could see the fight
doctor—the guy hired by the athletic commission to make sure
the fighters could safely ply their trade—talking to the Jet and
examining the gash I'd put in his eyebrow. His corner was working feverishly to stop the bleeding while the Jet was talking to the
doc, trying to keep him from stopping the fight. Eventually I was
the doctor nod to the jet and climb out of the ring.

I blew out a deep breath. I didn't realize I'd been holding it in.
We were going to be allowed to continue.

"I don't care what you think," Sally Ray was saying to me.
"Remember your camp. Remember, goddamn it. We trained for
ten rounds, and you're gonna punch yourself out by six. What the
fuck is wrong with you? You don't chase a guy younger than you.
Let him come to you."

Translation: Remember the deal. You're going down in six, no
matter whether you can beat the chump or not. Let the Jet dictate
the action in the upcoming round.

The only problem was now the Johnny the Jet McDaniel was
scared. He knew what I knew. He knew what I'd showed him.
He might be the better boxer, but I was the better fighter, and he
didn't want anything else to do with me. He wouldn't come at me,
and when I came to him, he circled away. With a minute gone
in the fifth round, neither one of us had landed a blow, and the
crowd was getting restless. I had no choice. If I was gonna let the
kid win this round, I had to walk him down.

Walking a guy down in the ring is sometimes difficult. It's

cutting off the ring gradually, backing an evasive fighter into a corner where you can unload on him. I didn't plan to unload on the Jet. Just the opposite, really. I was gonna give him his confidence back, only he didn't know it yet. Sally Ray didn't know it either. He was shouting from my corner, but I didn't pay him any attention. I flicked lazy jabs designed to do no more than back the Jet into a corner. Like any good fighter, he had ring instincts. He could sense when he was getting near the ropes. He thought I was coming to finish him, and it was fight or get knocked out.

To Johnny's credit, he fought. He caught me solid in the ribs, and I bent just a little so that the uppercut that followed caught me in the chest rather than the chin. I wobbled backward, and he came with an overhand right that landed on my forehead. Good enough.

There are places you'd rather take a hard shot, and the forehead is one of them. The arch of your skull is probably the strongest bone in your body, designed that way by God or whomever to keep precious brain matter from leaking out. But I could've won an Oscar. I went down to one knee, then slowly rolled onto my side. I had to beat the ten-count, but that was easy. Or it would've been if the Jet had kept his composure. The ref pointed him to a neutral corner and then turned back to me. I was on my hands and knees, ready to lunge to my feet at six or seven, ready to take the standing eight count.

The Jet wasn't having any of that. Quick as his namesake, he flashed around the referee and launched a boot right into my side. I felt the ribs give way and tumbled over onto my back, trying to get my breath. The Jet was on top of me before I could do that, though, hammering hard shots to my face. He straddled me and rained punches down on my unprotected head until someone— his corner, I think—pulled him off of me.

Thank God someone did. They saved my life. My corner got me to my feet and somehow maneuvered me to my stool. I don't know how they did it. I wasn't any help. The ref followed us to the corner, which is never a good sign.

"I'm stopping it," he said. "Disqualifying McDaniel. You got a problem with that?"

Sally Ray is a lot of things, mostly a sonofabitch, but he's also a quick thinker.

"Hell yes I got a problem with that," he said. "My guy's kicking his ass. The Jet wants the fight thrown out. He don't want to get knocked the fuck out. We're here to fight, goddamn it."

The ref wasn't having it.

"Your guy's hurt. He can't even fucking breathe. How's he supposed to fight? I'm stopping it. He goes down in the record books as the winner."

Sally Ray shook his head.

"You get the doc over here," he said. "If he clears Blackjack, let 'em continue. I want to see that asshole flat on his back."

The ref looked more than a little dubious. Sally Ray was giving up a sure win, and he probably had some idea why. You stay around the fight game for a while, you get pretty good at seeing the fix. But the ref finally relented and motioned for the doctor. Sally turned to me and whispered in my ear.

"I know you're hurt, kid, but you gotta come out for the next round. You do what you gotta do, but you make sure you get off that stool for the sixth."

I nodded. I couldn't really say anything, not with my ribs hurting the way they were. The doc—an older man in a sharkskin suit and rubber gloves on his hands—came over to me.

"You sure you want to continue?"

"Yes, sir." I squeezed the words out through tight lips.

"That kick looked like it hurt."

"It did." I got some breath back. "But it's mostly embarrassing. I don't want to stop like that. If I win, I want to earn it."

The doc watched me breath—or mostly pretend to breathe— for a moment, then stepped back and conferred with the referee.

After that, he climbed down out of the ring again. Must have been a lot of exercise for a guy his age. The ref came back over to my corner.

"Doc says you can fight. I'm deducting a point from McDaniel, but I'm gonna have you on a short leash out there. Rules say you get a five-minute recovery period after a foul like that. Already used about three minutes of it. When I call for you to come out of your corner, we pick up where we left off—about a minute left in the fifth."

I nodded and spent the rest of the recovery period trying to breathe while my corner worked on me. Sally Ray told me to keep my distance, which I thought was pretty obvious advice. But I was getting madder and madder while I was sitting on my stool trying to catch my breath and never really being able to. When the ref called for the fight, I shrugged off my stool and crouched low, my left arm down low over my broken ribs. I even switched stances to southpaw, to keep my left side father away from the Jet.

You ever see a cat playing with a bird whose wing has been broken? That's what the Jet was like out there in that last minute of the fifth round. He had me hurt, and he knew it. It was a good time to him. He jabbed me a couple of times, danced around a little, threw a light combo here and there. There wasn't much I could do about it. What the hell. I was going down in the sixth round anyway. About six seconds before the round ended, he clinched me up and tried to go back to my ribs. I clubbed him as hard as I could in the balls and watched him turn away and puke in a neutral corner. Take that, showoff. The bell rang as the ref signaled that he was deducting another point from me.

"Do it again, and I'll DQ you," he said, but he was grinning. Under his breath, so nobody but me could hear it, he said, "It serves him right."

My corner didn't say much, just made sure I knew the sixth round was coming up. My breath was tearing through my lungs in staggering gasps, and sweat was pouring down my body in sheets. "Gonna need the doc after this," I heard somebody say. It took me a minute to realize it was me.

That sixth round. I still don't know what to say about it. I don't know where I got the balls, but I met the Jet head-on in the middle of the ring, still standing southpaw. I tagged him with the right, but he was younger and for all of the damage I'd done to him, he wasn't the one with the broken ribs. His shots came quicker and quicker, and I began to wilt backward.

"Oh no you don't," he mumbled through his mouthpiece. He clinched me and shoved me into the corner, throwing bombs. I tried to slump down, but he pressed his weight against me, keeping me upright. He wouldn't let me fall. I was ready to take the 10 count and get out of there, but the Jet was fueled up on anger and adrenaline, and he was ready to go. I took most of his punches on my arms and shoulders, but the occasional blast got through. I could hear the roar of the crowd as they sensed the end was near. The ref was watching us closely, and I thought he might step in at any minute. He didn't, though, and the crowd's buzz began to peak.

The Jet went downstairs, then, ripping away at my left arm, trying to get me to move it. He knew I was hurt, but he wanted to inflict a little more pain before I got away to the safety of the canvas. When one of his shots got through, I felt myself turning green and empty. The world tilted, and I didn't have to fake the fall I was about to take.

But something in my body wouldn't let me fall. To tell the truth, I don't know what it was. Anger, sure. Heart? Maybe. I doubt it, though. I'd sold out on my heart a long time ago. The Jet fight wasn't the first one I'd agreed to throw. Maybe it was something else. In the ring with Johnny the Jet, I realized that he and I were two sides of the same coin. And that coin gets tossed up, up into the air, but it always comes down again, doesn't it? The Jet was on his way up, and I was on my way down. He wasn't good enough to win the title. And pretty soon he'd find himself in the same situation as me. On the downside of a career, taking less and less money to throw fights and build new contenders.

So I hit him. I hit him hard, an uppercut to the throat. The Jet stalled. I hit him in the same place, and again. He was frozen in place. And one more time. I felt his Adam's apple collapse and heard his windpipe close. It was the only thing I had left in my tank, and it staggered the Jet backward toward the center of the ring. I slumped down onto my ass in the corner, watched Johnny the Jet struggle to the ropes and try to keep his feet underneath him. He couldn't breathe, and his body was clamping up, trying to vomit, trying to do anything to just fucking clear the dead air in his lungs.

The ref didn't see what kind of trouble he was in. Neither did his corner. By the time the referee counted me out and called for the bell, the Jet was on the mat and turning gray. That's when the ring became more of a circus than it had been all night. The Jet's corner was working on him, the ringside doctor was trying to clear people away, and the TV cameramen were getting in the way as much as they possibly could.

The doc finally got the scrum pulled away, but by then it was too late. Johnny the Jet was declared the winner of the fight, even as he lay on the canvas dying.

We got out of there. Sally Ray led me up the aisle and my cut man followed. In the dressing room I collapsed on the floor. My ribs weren't just broken. They were shattered. Sally Ray called for the EMTs, but they took their time coming. Everyone was working on the Jet, trying to get him airborne again. That was a flight everyone was going to miss.

Eventually I got to the hospital. The ribs required surgery, and it was a good long time before I could take a deep breath without wanting to scream. For months, I was the most serious person on the face of the planet. I couldn't afford to laugh.

I got a visit one time from the Jet's manager, a slick thin black man who wore Armani and constantly combed his mustache with his fingers. He came to my hotel room, a little beige box where I laid my head and thought long thoughts about where I could go now that nobody wanted to book a fight with me anymore. The guy wanted his thirty thousand back.

"It's only right," he said. "You kill my meal ticket."

"Fuck you," I said. "I did what I said I'd do. I went down in the sixth."

"I was afraid you'd see it that way," he said. He took his hand— the one that wasn't busy with his mustache—out of his coat pocket. There was a knife in his hand, and he clicked it open with one smooth move.

I don't remember when I started carrying the gun. I guess shortly after I left the hospital. It wasn't much. Just a cheap .38 special, serial numbers filed off and electrical tape wrapped around the grip. I'd bought it for maybe sixty bucks, but in the dim light it looked like a serious piece of work. I took it out and held it where he could see. I didn't point it anywhere.

"You think that gun make a difference?"

Now I pointed it at him.

"Yes, I do."

He put the knife away, and I lowered the gun.

"Where'm I gonna get another meal ticket?"

"You manage fighters," I said. "You got somebody else waiting in the wings."

He grinned a little at that.

"I do, in fact."

"You better make sure he's better than the Jet. McDaniel was never gonna win the title."

It took him a few minutes to answer.

"I know that," he said. "But you gotta know that's not the point. The title fight was the money fight. He make it past you, he get a million or three for MacGregor. That where you make the money."

"MacGregor would have killed him."

"I know," he said. "And I'd still have the money."

I thought about that a long time after he left. The hotel room felt smaller and smaller to me. I sat on one corner of the bed and pulled the gun back out. Like before, I didn't point it anywhere. I just sat there, feeling its heft in my hands. After awhile, I clicked the safety off and put the barrel in my mouth. I could taste the gun oil.

I took the gun out of my mouth, wiped the saliva off on the bedspread, and holstered it. Not yet. That's not the way I wanted to go out. I still see Johnny the Jet's face in my dreams. I see him stumble back away from me, fear rising in his face as he claws at his throat. There's that one moment where he knows he's dying, and he knows nobody can help him.

Terror. I wake up to that face sometimes in the middle of the night. I killed him, and I did it on purpose, to keep him from killing me. Nobody blames me, of course. They all saw him, saw how out of control he was. But on the nights when the Jet's ghost won't let me sleep, the gun with its slippery taped grip and its loaded cylinder is a comfort. It doesn't matter anymore that I can't get a fight. I fight for my life every night, and every night so far I've won.

But I know there's a night coming where I won't win. Where the lure of the trigger will be too strong. I gave the Jet six good rounds. On the night I finally lose, one round from that gun will be all it takes.

NEVER SEE THE
STARS AGAIN

MCKINNEY GRINNED HARD as he tamped the last bit of fertilizer down inside the blue plastic drum and sealed the top. He had to be careful with the barrel, couldn't just tip it over and roll it. A wrong move with that much concentrated ammonium nitrate could blow everything sky-high before he was ready.

Instead, McKinney used a hand truck to roll the barrel next to the others. He slid the truck out from under it and looked at his work. He couldn't wipe the smile from his face even though he knew that he must look like a madman.

The barrels were identical to the ones that stored ink for the press. He nodded to himself and looked at the luminous watch dial on his right wrist. It was almost three a.m., and everyone but him had already gone. The web press hulked beside him in the dark, cavernous room.

"Here we are," McKinney said, and his words echoed in the cavernous space that had once been the heartbeat of the Herald's print operation. The press didn't answer him. It never had. Even when the goddamned thing took his left hand, yanked it between the rollers with a wet and sickening crunch as the bones snapped and gave way, the press had done nothing more than hum like a child happily slurping up the last remains of a milkshake.

That had been a bad time for McKinney, but he had fought through. Learned to do everything one-handed. It had taken him months of rehab, and when he came back to the printing room with the empty left sleeve of his shirt pinned up, there was the bulk of the press in the middle of the floor, black and solid and seeming almost to smile.

Hello, meat, it seemed to be saying. *I'll be ready for another snack, soon.*

He didn't go near the press for a long time after that, contenting himself with driving the forklift, moving two-ton rolls of newsprint into position for the other printers to attach. Every night McKinney watched for a break in the long, wet streams of pulpy paper. He'd been a good pressman, and even now when his fear wouldn't let him approach the beastly thing, he could see when the web was too heavy with ink, where a bad fold was about to gum up the works and cause a shutdown.

He knew the machine in a way that no one else on the floor could. *And it knows me. It's tasted me, and it wants more.* A hell of a thought, and McKinney tried to shake it no matter how often the idea came back. He couldn't help it. After the accident, the machine always looked hungry.

He thought no one else could see his discomfort until one night in the bar when Higgins was drunk enough to be honest.

"You're goddamn lucky," Higgins said. He was an Australian expat, always loud. But on this night he had to be. The juke box was pounding Drive-By Truckers, and the place was rocking.

McKinney put his beer down. His hand was tight on the bottle, and he had to remind himself to relax. A one-armed man didn't need cuts on his one remaining hand.

"How's that?"

"Coulda been your jack-off hand, couldn't it?" Higgins laughed so hard his face went red. McKinney just stared at him until the man stopped.

"Look, I don't mean no harm. We all understand, you know."

The bartender came by then, took one look at the dark scowl on McKinney's face, and turned on his heel. McKinney leaned into Higgins's face and growled.

"What do you think you understand?"

"Why you're scared of the old girl. If it happened to one of us, we'd never go near her again."

There was nothing left to say to that, so McKinney dropped some money on the bar and left. It was the last time he'd gone out drinking with the crew. In the weeks that followed, he made a point to get off the forklift and lay his remaining hand on the press.

Was it his imagination, or did the damned thing tremble when he touched its flank, like a racehorse ready to run?

It didn't matter. The word came down from corporate that they were moving the printing operation to a larger facility. Consolidating. They were decommissioning the press that had taken McKinney's arm. Within six months, the beast was to be sold and McKinney's job eliminated.

After hearing that news, McKinney went home and logged online, pecking away at his keyboard. A dim idea had been forming in his mind, but when he found out that the press would be dismantled and sold for parts, it was as though a fuse had lit in his brain.

You can find out anything online. Even how to make a homemade bomb. McKinney didn't cover his tracks. He didn't care if everyone knew what he did. All he wanted was revenge. It had taken him weeks of careful preparation, of putting everything together just so. And now everything was in place except one.

McKinney eyed the blue plastic barrels. He used his good—only—hand to hoist himself on top of them, sliding his hip over the top and lying down on his back so that he could look up through the blank spaces where the newsprint had once trundled. He could just make out the steel girders in the top of the printing room.

I'll never see the stars again. Once, that thought would have depressed him. Now, it only steeled his resolve. He dug carefully in his pocket for what he wanted. Then he rested for a little while, his hand on his belly, cupping the hard rectangle as though it were a fragile thing.

Six minutes after four a.m., McKinney touched the detonator, and then there was nothing but heat and light and a final thought.

He could see the stars again. He could. He could —

QUITMAN COUNTY AMBUSH

"YOU KNOW WHAT HE'S DOING, DON'T YOU?" Mikey took a hard pull from the bottle of Wild Turkey and passed it on. "Every week you see him out on the water."

"Sure," Carl said. "Man likes to fish."

The man in question was Judge Harlan Baker. If any one person owned Quitman County, it was Judge Baker. Everyone called him the hanging judge, even though nobody's swung from the gallows in Georgia since Arthur Meyers took the long drop in 1931 over in Augusta.

But Judge Baker was mean as hell, and everybody knew it. He never cut a man any slack at all. If you came before the bench on his docket, you were getting the maximum sentence. If handing out the max ever bothered Judge Baker, he didn't show it. Not on the weekend, anyway.

Walter George Lake — that's Lake Eufaula if you put in from the Alabama side — is supposed to be the largemouth bass capital of the world. And every weekend the lake's lousy with assholes trying to prove it's true. The judge is one of them. We'd been watching him for three weeks now, and if you think fishing is boring you ought to try watching someone else do it.

"Bribe money," Shaun said. "Gotta be."

"That's what y'all say," I said. "But we don't know for sure."

"Bullshit," Mikey said. "You're just scared."

Mikey could talk that way. He was the one with the gun.

I shrugged and looked away from him. No one said anything else. Carl went back to rolling a joint, and pretty soon he had it going and acrid, sweet smoke filled the air. They passed it around between the four of them. I wanted my head clear, not baked.

We took turns watching the Judge paddle a flat-bottomed aluminum boat a quarter-mile along the Georgia side of the shore, in no hurry, trolling a line in the water. Occasionally he'd drop anchor and flick a lure near the bank where the tall grass could hide bass of considerable size. He rarely caught anything, and when he did, he threw it back. The first time I saw that, I laughed and handed the binoculars to Carl, who took them with an unspoken question on his face.

Carl wouldn't have understood the irony of a man with Judge Baker's reputation practicing catch-and-release.

The Judge fished all the way over to the Alabama side, making a day of it. He packed the boat with everything an angler would need: Rods and reels, bait, tackle box, ice chest. And every time he came back from his visit across the water, he carried something extra.

Sometimes the black nylon backpack bulged, swinging pendulously. Other times, it was nearly flat. But it was always there when he came back, and it hadn't been there when he left.

There were five of us on the job, and our plan was simple: Watch him. And when he brought back a bag that looked particularly full, we'd make our move.

It was almost November and cold, with fog rising along the lake at dawn and settling back down at dusk, making the familiar shape of the shoreline something irregular and eerie. All of us dressed in camo coveralls and ball caps against the chill. Out on the water we could hear the sound of the waves change as they began to slap against the aluminum hull of the boat.

The boat slid out of the fog toward the bank, its wide flat prow coming faster than any of us expected, the hump of the judge's body slumped and inert on the bench seat near the rear.

"Now," Mikey whispered, his voice harsh with effort and fear, and Carl and Shaun ran down the half-dozen steps to the bank and laid hands on either side of the boat. Chris was right behind them, and he got the first bullet, right in the middle of the forehead. I hit the ground hard enough to knock the wind out of my lungs.

My eyes were wide, locked onto that inert mass in the middle of the boat. Now that the boat was closer, I could see that the Judge had piled up his jacket and ice chest on the bench to make a vaguely humanoid shape.

Carl and Shaun let go of the boat like it was red-hot, but it didn't matter. Big thunder rolled into two more shots, and they fell in the water, little splashes in a big lake, and the concentric circles that their bodies made would fade out of existence long before the waves reached the far shore.

Mikey, the big man with the gun, the man with the plan, turned tail and sprinted through the sparse woods surrounding this part of the lake. I could see him dimly from the ground where I'd dropped at the first sound of gunfire.

A few seconds later I saw the Judge, bare-headed and wet, slither out of the water and follow Mikey. He was grinning ear-to-ear like a goddamn skull.

When the Judge was out of sight, I scrambled to my feet and sprinted for the water. I ignored the bodies that floated nearby, prayed they wouldn't bump into me, and hoped that they were dead and not in bad need of help. What the hell would I be able to do for them?

I grabbed the boat and hoisted myself up and over the side, being as quiet as I could. Blood pounded in my ears, and I couldn't hold down the sobs that wracked my chest. Tears streamed down my face as I scrambled to push the pile off of the bench and sit. I scanned the shoreline as I dug a paddle into the water and moved away from the bank. If I kept paddling, eventually I'd come to the Alabama side.

I didn't even look down at the black nylon backpack at my feet.

TWO IN THE STREET

TWO a.m., AND LAST CALL was fifteen minutes ago. The slender guy at the bar paid with cash, peeling twenties off a thick wad that he stuffed back into the inner pocket of his cashmere coat. He looked around the bar and shook his head as if to clear it, and then he wobbled toward the door.

The wind grabbed the door out of his hand and he staggered going out into the January chill. The Rolex Oyster on his wrist caught the light as he went out and turned north up Second Ave. *Wrong way, mister.* Nothing up there except dark streets as empty as the eye sockets in a skull, all the way up to St. Vincent's Hospital. I counted slowly to ten, then shrugged into my pea coat and left my last glass half-drunk on the table, weighing down a ten for the waitress.

By the time I hit the street, he was a block ahead of me, weaving all over the sidewalk, a drunk on his way home. He paused to lean against an old Honda Civic that was parallel-parked at the curb, and then he shook himself, raised his head, and walked on. I stayed in the shadows and moved along behind him. Watching. Waiting.

The two kids that came out of the alley were lean and

hungry-looking, wolves on the prowl. Greasy T-shirts, jack boots, dirty jeans. If I'd been close enough to smell them, I knew they'd reek of weed or patchouli. The taller one had a hunting knife in his hand, and the polished steel blade caught the little ambient light there was and reflected it dully.

I skulked along under the awnings of the building, speeding up a little but not enough to make myself breathe hard in the cold night air. No reason to give myself away. Not yet.

I was close enough now that I could hear them.

"—like a donation, you know," the shorter one said and grinned at his buddy. "A little something to keep us poor orphans warm on a cold night like this."

The man in the cashmere coat wasn't having it.

"Leave me alone," he said. "I'm just looking for a good time."

"You found one," the wolf with the knife growled. I was close enough now that I could see the pitted acne scars on his face. He held the blade low, cutting edge up, like he knew how to use it. He jabbed it toward the man, his face breaking into a leer.

"Come on," the shorter one said. "Let's just get the money."

"We take the money, and maybe take a piece of him, too. He could ID us."

"He's drunk, he ain't gonna ID shit." He turned to the wobbly man in cashmere, who seemed to pull himself up to his full height. "Come on, man. Give us the fuckin' money."

"I'm not drunk," the drunk said. His voice sounded full of righteous indignation, and I grinned a little. I'd been there myself. I flipped the tail of my pea coat up and put my right hand in my back pocket.

The one with the knife made a *come on, come on* gesture with the blade, and I saw the drunk's hands go up, saw his hand dip into the coat pocket.

Good, I thought. *Give them what they want. Give me time.*

But the gun that came out of the jacket wasn't what either of those kids wanted. The first shot rolled like hard thunder along the buildings, and I could barely hear the clatter of the knife as it hit the concrete sidewalk. The next shot followed less than a second later, and then both bodies were sprawled on the concrete. The slender man in the cashmere coat stood there for a moment, the gun seemingly forgotten in his hand. Then he put it away and walked on up the street.

He wasn't weaving anymore.

I still had my hand in my hip pocket, my fingers curled around the cold metal of my Birmingham PD detective's shield. I left it in my pocket and came out of the shadows to stare down at the men lying dead on the street.

ONE IN THE CHAMBER

THE STICK WAS A .380, six in the magazine and one in the chamber. I stole it from a middle-class house in a middle-class town nobody's ever heard of, walked around with it in my pocket for a while until Montez said he had something cooking.

Montez usually had an angle, and it always involved money. We'd worked together before and always come out bucks-up and clean with the cops. I listened to his latest pitch, and it sounded good.

Of course it did. Wrap the poison pill inside something sweet so it goes down easier.

Three on the job. Jimmy drove for twenty-five percent. Montez and I were down to split the bigger slice—we carried the weight. In and out of the bank in three minutes, carrying bags that bulged with cash as we sprinted for the corner where Jimmy waited with the Charger in gear and his foot barely holding the brake.

Ten feet away, Montez pulled up short and turned so fast I nearly plowed into him.

"Come on," I said, breath like harsh smoke in my lungs. Tried to push him toward the waiting car. "Go."

Montez turned and brought up his stick, a big .40 caliber semi-auto. The bore looked big enough to carry my coffin. He squeezed the trigger and nothing happened. His eyes went wide behind the ski mask and he tried to speak. My own gun came level and I flicked the safety and fired one round into his chest.

He went down, a drunk fighter collapsing in the late rounds, and I emptied the clip into him, rage buzzing in my head like bees inside a fresh-kicked hive.

I put the .380 away and grabbed the bag of money he'd been carrying and hauled ass for the car. The brake lights were off and the car was already rolling when I caught the door and yanked it open.

"Throw 'em in the back," Jimmy yelled, but I got myself inside first in case he wanted to take off without me. By the time I slammed the passenger door, he had the accelerator to the floor and we were doing sixty toward the interstate. My hands shook and my eyes felt like they'd jitterbug right out of my head.

"What the fuck happened, man?" Jimmy wasn't looking at me. He had eyes for the road and nothing else. "You guys are booking it, next thing I know you're shooting my man in the head. What the fuck?"

I couldn't process it, either. Montez. We went to school together, hung out on the same corners. I knew his Ma, and he knew mine. He was her only boy. I closed my eyes and thought about how she'd take the news. Probably no worse than mine would have.

"I don't know," I said at last. "He tried to kill me."

Jimmy's mouth drew down in a tight line that could have garroted him if it had been any lower.

I closed my eyes again. When I opened them, we were southbound on I-65, barely under the speed limit. I cranked my seat back so he looked like the only person in the car. Three SUVs with blue lights flashing and sirens blaring came tear-assing down the highway. Jimmy pulled over and let them pass, like everyone else on the road. They never even glanced at us.

Jimmy took the next exit and found a secluded little church. Windows broken out and a door sagging like a loose tooth hanging by a thread. He parked in the gravel lot behind the building and let the engine idle. I almost got out and walked away.

"Lucky," he said, shaking his head. "Lucky as a bastard."

I didn't feel lucky. I didn't feel much of anything.

Jimmy brought out his own gun, and slow creeping sickness overcame me.

"Slow," he said. "Bring it out slow."

I did. Left the stick on the floorboard. Empty anyway. No use to anyone.

He made me get out, keeping the gun trained on me the whole time. Backed out, sprayed gravel, and sped away. The car got smaller and smaller until I couldn't see it anymore.

A GOOD NIGHT'S SLEEP

CORLEY BROWN WASN'T FIDGETING. He wasn't feigning sleep. He wasn't doing any of the million little tells a murderer's body uses to betray him. He seemed perfectly calm, sitting there and waiting for someone to come and take his statement. His hands rested on the tabletop, steel handcuffs glinting in the low light of a flickering bulb. His wide shoulders were square, and his hair was thin and dry and brown, long over the top to cover a spot of male pattern baldness. His eyes were clear and bright, and he was smiling.

It's the smile I can't forget.

It wasn't a smirk. It wasn't sarcastic or mean. It wasn't hurtful. Corley Brown had the smile of a happy man, and I couldn't understand it. Happy men don't kill their wives. They don't come home from their job at the insurance office and use a framing hammer on their wife and children. They don't leave the bodies in the living room and go upstairs to their bedrooms to nap while their neighbors call the police.

But that's exactly what Corley Brown had done.

I took the thin case file into the room with me, a few pages of notes, initial forensic details of how the Brown family had been beaten up and left where they lay. The cops who found the bodies—veterans both, guys with more than a decade on the job—had to run the other direction and thrown up. All while Corley Brown slept on, unaware.

Brown didn't stand up when I entered the room. He couldn't. The small gray table where he sat featured a large O ring bolted into the center. The chain of Brown's handcuffs ran through it.

"You ready to talk about it?" I asked as I tossed the buff-colored file embossed with the Las Vegas Metro Police emblem onto the table.

"What do you want me to say? You know what happened just as well as I do."

I dragged a chair out, turned it around and straddled it so I could fold my arms over the back. Opened the file and looked at it, not really doing anything, just letting my eyes skip across the pictures of the three victims. There was Rannie, Corley's wife, and Bradley, who would have been ten in a couple of weeks, and Abigail, who was four. None of them would be getting any older.

I took a white card out of my shirt pocket and read Miranda to him. The uniforms at the scene had already done that, gotten the arrest on video, but I had learned a long time ago that you had to be careful so that there were no questions later.

"I know what happened," I said. "What I want to know is *why.*"

Brown shrugged his shoulders and yawned. I could see molars in bad need of a dentist.

"I don't really give a damn what you want," he said. "Why don't matter, does it? *Why* just fucks everything up for you. I did it. I'll cop to it. Now let's quit fucking around. Put me back in my cell and let me get some rest."

I shook my head.

"It doesn't work that way. I ask the questions. You answer them."

Corley stared at me, gave another little shrug.

"Whatever, man," he said.

"Why did you kill your wife?"

"Are you married?"

"Sure," I said.

"Then you ought to understand."

I laughed. I couldn't help myself. I've been married for thirteen years. Some of those years were good, and some were bad. Sometimes I wanted to hug Lacey, and sometimes I wanted to strangle her. So I guess I knew exactly what he meant.

"Was there something specific that set you off today?"

When Corley said no, I believed him. Whatever happened in that gray little bungalow on Third Avenue, it had been building for a long time. I kept my eyes on his, watched how steady they were. It was unsettling. He looked at peace, the sonofabitch.

"Tell me what it was about," I said.

He laughed.

"You are like a dog after a goddamn bone," he said.

I tapped the gold shield hanging from the lapel of my JC Penney suit. "It's my business."

Corley Brown's eyes skimmed the room. He wasn't uneasy. He was just looking at his surroundings. Interview One isn't much of a room. If you've ever seen a cop show on TV, you've seen one just like it.

"I never thought I'd end up here," he said. "I thought I could wait it out, you know?"

I didn't say anything, and after a long moment, Corley Brown sighed. He looked me up and down for a moment.

"You got kids? Of course you do. You got the look. Solid citizen all around, right? I could probably tell your life story. Army, right? Used the GI Bill to go to college. Got out after twenty, caught onto the cops right away."

Almost. I'd been in the Navy. Took the exam for the fire department and the cops. Cops came through first. I didn't tell Brown any of that, though. I didn't have to. He was just warming up.

"I sell insurance. Tough game, you know? Auto, home, whole

life. Lotta stress. You gotta make sales to keep the money coming in. Pressure all the time."

Since silence was my best interrogation technique, I kept at it. I cocked my head to show I was listening.

"Rannie just—it was a lot of things. We got the country club membership, last year's Lexus. Mortgage isn't upside down, but it's close. Always fighting about money. Kids need clothes. Tennis rackets for the club. But we can't just go down to Wal-Mart and pick up a twenty-dollar stick. Got rackets? Great. Gotta have lessons. It bears down on a man.

"This time it was landscaping. We just had the yard done three years ago, but now she wanted a—what the hell did she call it?—a goddamn water feature."

Now I did interrupt. "A what?"

"A fucking fountain. She wanted to put up a fountain in the front yard, re-do the driveway into a circle with crushed oyster shells, that sort of thing. You know how much money that shit costs?"

I thought about it for a minute. The casinos and hotels all had water features, but they also had money to burn. Even if the Browns were rich, that kind of thing was just throwing money down the drain. So to speak.

"You killed your wife over a fountain?"

Corley Brown looked puzzled, puffed his lips out and blew a lock of his dry brown hair away from his forehead.

"No," he said. "I killed her because she tried to stop me from killing the kids."

My hands lost all sensation. I heard the pen clatter to the scuffed linoleum floor. I couldn't think of anything to say, so I just sat there for a moment. I tried to get to my feet, but my legs bent at unnatural angles. Finally I lunged for the door and made it into the hallway before I puked. I scrambled away from the hot vomit, my numb feet kicking at the floor. I couldn't feel anything. My bladder felt like it would let go at any moment. I put my back against the wall and covered my head with the dead sticks of my arms.

The tears came then, and I let them. Those children—those babies—I couldn't get them out of my head. A shadow blocked out the overhead light for a moment, and I peeked out from between the protective shell of my arms. Eric Church, my captain, had his hands on his hips. He was looking down at me like he'd never seen me before.

"Get back in there," he said. My captain isn't known for his soft, fuzzy side. "I'll get someone to clean this mess up."

Church put out his hand, and I reached across the thousand-mile gap between us to take it. He hauled me to my feet and slapped me on the back. In close, he whispered in my ear.

"It's the worst goddamn thing I ever heard. You've got to finish it, though. You know that, don't you?"

I did know it. It's part of what makes a cop who he is. You gotta be able to take the shit that comes with the job. It's part of being a stand-up guy, part of that thin blue line that protects society from itself. If your brother officers sense weakness in you, that they can't count on you when the shit goes down, it could spell curtains for your career. If they can't trust you—or even think they can't—then you're out. *Persona non grata.*

Church pumped my hand once, hard, and we gave each other a firm little nod. He bent and handed me the brown manila evidence folder that lay on the floor where I'd dropped it. I felt like the quarterback being asked to go back in and win the game with a minute left and no timeouts remaining. There was sweat on my neck and face, and my bladder was full to bursting.

I ignored everything else and crossed the hall back to Interview One. Opened the door. Corley Brown looked sympathetic, the asshole.

"Everything OK?" He asked. His tone was neutral, slightly concerned. No mocking sarcasm. I couldn't figure out what the hell was wrong with him.

"Fine," I said. "Right as rain." I took my seat again. I was trying to pick up where we'd left off, but I couldn't seem to find the thread of our conversation. I shuffled his file around a little and cleared my throat.

"Your wife was trying to stop you from killing your children," I said.

He nodded, his green eyes bright with earnestness.

"Of course," he said, "she was a good mother. You know how mama bears are, don't want you to mess with their cubs. I guess it's genetic." Brown paused for a moment and stared through the window to the world outside. That window was two panes thick with chicken wire sandwiched in the middle. You could see a little bit of Fire Station No. 6 across Stella Lake Street, but not much else. He wasn't going anywhere, and I still don't know what he was looking for.

"What had the kids done?" I asked.

Brown didn't answer me. He'd wound down like an old watch. He finally rattled his cuffs and said, "Can you take these off?"

I shook my head.

"Not right now. We still have some things to discuss."

Corley Brown yawned again, big enough to make me cover my own mouth.

"I'm so tired," he said. "Tired like this, it gets down in your bones like cancer, and no matter how much sleep you get, I guess it's never enough."

I grunted like someone punched me in the gut. But I didn't have anything to say, so I just listened to Brown talk.

"Bradley was a talker, like me. Talk, talk, talk all the time. He couldn't keep his mouth shut. Got in trouble for it at school and at church. And when Abigail came along, I just—some folks weren't ever meant to be parents, you know what I mean?"

I couldn't bring myself to say anything. I didn't trust my voice.

"Anyway, I put up with it as long as I could. I guess today was the day that everything snapped. I took that hammer and, well, I did what I did. I got to Bradley, and then Rannie tried to stop me. I hit her one good time. I didn't want to kill her, but, well, she got in the way."

I could see it all in my mind's eye. Corley Brown getting home from work, tired like usual. Inside the house, shrugging off his coat and tie, maybe rolling his sleeves up. All he wanted was rest, but then the twin tornadoes of his two kids blow in and make him even more exhausted. All that talk and all of that noise, the constant commotion. Maybe it didn't drive him crazy, but it drove him somewhere close and let him walk the rest of the way there.

"So that's it?" I asked. "You were just tired ... of being a parent? You kill your whole family because you're, what, too lazy to take care of them?"

Corley Brown's eyes blazed at me, spittle in the corners of his mouth.

"Do you know how long it's been since I've had a decent night's sleep? Kid cries in the middle of the night and somebody has to go to 'em, wipe their nose, get 'em water, right? Well, the other parent doesn't just lay in bed and sleep, man. Every time one of 'em woke up, I was either right there with 'em or layin' in the bed and listening while Rannie was up. All I wanted was some sleep."

And then he was done. I waited for several minutes to see what else Brown might say, but there was nothing.

"Are you sorry you did it?" I ask. I didn't need to know for the confession. I was genuinely curious.

When Corley Brown smiled at me, I believed he was the happiest man in the world. Certainly he was the happiest man I've ever seen.

"That nap," he said. "Before your beat cops got there? That was the best I've slept in ten years. I don't regret a damned thing."

There was more, but none of it mattered. I had his confession— easiest one of my career—and I was gonna do everything in my power to make sure Corley Brown spent the rest of his life locked up somewhere. The captain congratulated me when I finished my report. I didn't even have the energy to say thanks, just tipped him a mock salute and headed for the garage.

The unmarked unit is a perk of the job, a late-model Dodge Charger with buggywhip antennas and no hubcaps. It looks exactly like what it is—a cop car. But the seats are leather and comfortably low-sprung, and the AC ran cold enough to circumvent the desert heat on even the worst days.. I made the twenty-minute commute to Summerlin in silence, just like I do every day. I thumbed the button on the garage door opener attached to my visor and pulled in still thinking about Corley Brown and his hammer. Every blow freeing him from obligation, every hit a strike against the chains of responsibility that held him moored to the real world, this stark reality.

Finally, I hit the garage opener again and listened as the big door rattled closed. I shut the car off and got out, wandered over to my little workbench. I keep my tools in a big steel cart that stands about four feet high. The second drawer down holds a variety of wrenches and hammers. I took out the framing hammer, a big old one that my Dad bought for me when we worked construction together near Lake Meade the summer after I graduated high school. The steel head weighed about thirty-two ounces, all by itself. After a summer of using it, the muscles in my forearms looked like cables.

I held the hammer in my hand and swung it a couple of times, just to remember how it felt. I could still see Corley Brown and his family in the back of my mind.

The door to the house opened up behind me, and Lacey stuck her head into the garage.

"Hey," she said. "When are you coming in? I could use some help with the kids."

"Right now," I said.

Then I put the hammer back in the drawer and went inside.

DISAPPEARED

IT WAS FIVE MINUTES PAST DEADLINE, and Carly Black was still waiting on a source. Frank, her editor, wasn't giving her a hard time about it yet, but she could feel him hovering in the background, an Ivy-League vulture waiting to swoop in and feast on the body of her story.

Come on come on come ON. Her cell phone remained silent, black-screened like a shroud over her career. The desk phone sat equally mute, but that was no surprise. Hardly anyone ever called it anyway. Carly blew a stray lock of carroty red hair out of her eyes, punched in the security code on her phone, and dialed her source directly.

"I can't talk," he whispered into the phone. No hello, no apology for missing the agreed-upon time to talk.

"Me either," Carly said. "I'm past deadline here. I need those documents, or I need you on the record."

There was a pause on the other end of the call. Not a long one, exactly, but significant, or at least that's the way it felt to her. As if her source were making up his mind, whether to do the right thing or just let it all slide.

"I'll call you when I can," he said, and the phone went dead.

"Shit," Carly muttered under her breath. Then she pushed away from her workstation in the newspaper's bullpen and marched over to Frank's office, where she hoped she was projecting more confidence than she actually felt.

Frank called, "Come in," before she could even knock on his door. The office was bare bones, just a desk and a captain's chair for him, and a single metal folding chair for visitors. His desktop was bare except for a silver MacBook. No photos. No untidy stack of papers. Nothing that would, God forbid, give the place some kind of personality. There had once been Associated Press and state press association awards decorating the walls, but as soon as Frank took over, he'd had the brass plates and framed certificates put into storage.

He didn't want the paper looking back at its past, he said, but forward to its future. The Spartan furnishings in his office kept employee interactions to a bare minimum. No one but Frank was allowed to feel comfortable in his office.

"Let me guess," he said, cutting Carly off, not giving her a chance to explain. "We gotta kill the Westgate piece."

Carly nodded. The son of a bitch hadn't even asked her to sit down.

"I knew it was gonna fall through. There's a reason you were in features. You're great at the light work, give us that personal profile, some garden club bullshit. You get one real story and you can't come up with anything."

Carly's cheeks flamed red. She could feel the heat rising on her skin, knowing that her pale skin and its spattering of freckles would reveal more about how she really felt than her words ever could.

"We'll pull something from the wire," Frank said, looking down at his laptop, eyes already scanning for a replacement story. Carly stood there for a moment, but when Frank didn't look back up at her, she realized that she'd been dismissed. She waited one last awkward beat to see if Frank would show a little humanity, a little goddamned empathy for once, but that look never came, so she made the slow walk back to her desk, past the carrels that had once been full of reporters, with their inevitable stacks of papers, notebooks, recorders, half-eaten deli lunches. The place had been a madhouse once upon a time.

Not anymore.

Most of the bullpen was empty, cleaned out of anything that might have once shown any sign of life. It was almost as if the place had been hermetically sealed. Only the janitorial crew used those desks now, and even then it was only sometimes, just to take a load off during the middle of their graveyard shift.

Carly was one of the last holdouts in the newsroom, a features reporter who had always longed for the research and the chase of a hard news story. She'd been the only reporter on duty one weekend when a domestic situation had turned violent, a woman shooting her abusive husband in front of their nine-year-old daughter, and Carly had risen to the occasion, getting the cops on record but also canvassing the neighbors and building a sympathetic enough profile of the woman that the district attorney had declined to bring charges against her.

That story was her pathway into hard news, and she took to it like a politician takes to graft. She'd done five years in features, then six months on cops-and-courts, and now she was pursuing a story about a corrupt business developer who had at least one city councilman in his pocket.

Unfortunately, Carly expected that Frank would either kill the story permanently or assign it to Carson, the other hard news reporter. Carson and Frank were buddies outside of work, going hunting and fishing together a few times a year, and laughing and joking together in the newsroom. Carly wasn't sure, but she suspected that she was one of the things that particular boys club laughed about.

She settled back in at her desk and worked on a feature—her

sweet spot—about a homeless woman who had turned her life around and now helped other homeless women. The hook was that even though the woman was now employed and newly able to take care of herself, she had learned that she preferred being homeless. Carly liked the piece; It played with assumptions and the woman's viewpoint was just off-kilter enough to be interesting without being too out there. As she tried to put finishing touches on the narrative, she thought about photos to accompany the piece.

Back in the day—back when the newspaper had been at full staff or nearly so—Carly would have filled out a photo request form and sent it to the art department. But the photogs were among the first casualties in the great bloodletting of the early 2000s when the implosion of the news business began. Designers and photographers, hell, whole art departments were cut.

Editors learned to lay out pages, and reporters took their own photos. And when the typos and the inaccuracies increased, and the photos sometimes looked like humped piles of wet laundry? Well, that was the cost of doing business, right?

Carly had grown up around the newspaper, and she remembered what it had been like: sound and sometimes vulgar, with the near-constant vibration of the printing press running at full tilt in the basement beneath them.

But that was what had been, back when there was still some magic left in journalism, back before the bean-counters who hired guys like Frank had come along. All they had seen was the money, a twenty percent profit margin, and the magic soon disappeared.

Carly went home at five, along with the advertising staff (no cuts there, naturally). She parked her little Mazda in its assigned spot and walked up to her third-floor apartment. She lived alone except for a couple of cats, CJ and DJ, and her nightly routine was pretty simple: a good book—she had to look at screens all day for work, so the idea of TV at night turned her off completely—feed the cats, and then something easy for dinner. Tonight it was a can of Campbell's soup. Chicken and rice. It started bubbling in the little stainless steel pot she used most nights, and she used a teaspoon to stir the liquid and keep it from sticking to the bottom of the pot.

"Don't be scared," came a voice behind her, and Carly jumped nearly a foot into the air and spun around. The spoon she had used to stir the soup—and the one she was planning to eat with later—went flying into a corner. DJ, the most curious of her cats, went over and started sniffing it.

A middle-aged man stood at the head of her white-and-blond kitchen table. He was wide in the shoulders, a full head taller than Carly, which put him well over six feet. His skull was shorn in a military-style flattop, and his eyes were an awful shade of green, as if all life had been leached out of them.

"Get out," Carly said. She'd meant for the words to sound forceful, but instead they came out as a plea, almost a prayer. Her heart thumped in her chest, and gooseflesh rose on her arms. Her feet felt rooted to the floor. The man took no notice of her words. He wore a pearl-gray suit with a faint chalk stripe, and his shirt was blue broadcloth. His mahogany shoes gleamed in the bright lights of the kitchen.

"I'm not here to hurt you," he said.

"I don't care. Get *out.*"

The man shook his head and wiped sweat from his forehead with the sleeve of his suit. This wasn't going the way he had planned, and Carly realized he was scared, too. All she had to do was scream.

"I'm just carrying a message," he said.

"I don't want to hear it."

Carly was calming down. She didn't feel frozen to the floor anymore, and she thought that if she needed to, she could at least use her hands to protect herself. If he came toward her, she'd grab the pot of boiling soup and throw it in his face.

"I don't even know who you are."

"And you don't need to. Let's say we have a mutual acquaintance," the man in the gray suit said. "I certainly wouldn't call him a friend. I know for a fact that he doesn't feel very friendly toward you."

"Westgate," Carly said.

The man put his finger to his lips. "No names. Never can tell who's listening."

He hadn't made a move toward her, had in fact stayed stock still since the moment Carly had turned around. But there was an air of menace about him, a sense of contained violence that Carly couldn't quite put her finger on.

"I came to tell you that Paul Williams isn't gonna be a source for you anymore. He left the country unexpectedly. Won't be back for quite a while."

Carly's jaw didn't drop, but she felt the heat rise in her face the way it had earlier in Frank's office. Behind her, the soup bubbled away on the stove eye, and the rich smell of the liquid filled the kitchen.

"Who?" She said.

The man broke into a grin.

"I hope you never play poker," he said. "You'd lose your shirt."

Silence spun out between the two for a long moment before Carly asked, "How did you find out?"

"Trade secret," the gray man said. "But here's the part you should listen closely to: keep on digging into our mutual acquaintance, and you're going to find yourself on a similar trip. Get me?"

Carly nodded.

"I get you loud and clear," she said. Then, despite the strange man in her kitchen, despite his obvious threat, she laughed.

"What's so funny?"

"This. This whole thing. My editor killed the story this afternoon because P—, because my source didn't give me the files on time. You didn't have to do it this way at all."

"Well," he said, and another long moment of silence floated between them. "I guess better safe than sorry."

"You can leave now."

The man gave her a hard look, but then he backed out of the kitchen. As soon as he was out of the room, Carly opened a drawer and drew out the bigger butcher knife she had. She heard the apartment door close quietly, and she ran to it and threw the deadbolt.

Back in the kitchen, CJ had joined her sibling at the discarded soup spoon, licking away at it. Carly turned the stove eye down to low and saw that the boiling liquid had scalded the bottom of the pan. It was just as well, because Carly didn't think she could stay in the apartment one more minute. Now that the man was gone, she felt herself releasing, the shakiness and fear coming to the surface like air bubbles rising from somewhere deep beneath the ocean.

She turned the stove eye completely off, piled dry food into the cats' dish, and threw some clothes into a carry-on bag. She scooped makeup and shampoo and other necessities from the sink, tied them inside a leftover Target bag, and dropped that into the bag, too. Outside the apartment, she couldn't seem to fit her key into the lock. She kept looking over her shoulder every few seconds. The world was too big, too dark. Gooseflesh rose along her arms and the hairs at the nape of her neck stood on end as she walked to her car. The big kitchen knife was inside her purse, and Carly kept one hand on it as she fled to the safety of her car.

Carson opened the door on the third knock. He lived in a small shabby house that didn't look as if it had been cleaned since the last time Carly was there. The night they broke up. He was tall, thin, and his narrow shoulders were slightly stooped. He had a little paunch from too much beer and not enough exercise. Carly used to think it was cute to poke him above the belt-buckle and make a little fun of him. Carson was always so serious. His hair stuck up wildly every which way, and it was late enough that the stubble of his beard had grown slightly prickly when she threw herself into his arms and hugged him, hard.

"Hey," he said, pulling away from her. "What's that all about?"

Carly told him everything. Didn't hold anything back. Some of it he already knew, because Frank had discussed killing the story if Carly's source didn't come through. Of course the good old boys didn't keep secrets from one another. Carly felt her anger rise, and she tried to ride it down, push it away. It was, she recognized, a reaction to the man showing up—as if he had every right to be there—in her kitchen.

"What do you think happened to your source?"

She thought about it for a long moment.

"I think he's dead."

"Come on," Carson said. "Sure that stuff happens, but it doesn't happen here. I think you're being overly dramatic."

"There was a man in my apartment, Carson, tonight. Warning me off. That wasn't dramatic—it really happened."

"Jesus, you're shaking. Come here, come here. I believe you, okay? I believe you."

He held her then, and for the first time in the last several hours, Carly began to feel safe. They sat together on Carson's burlap-covered couch, a holdover from his college days that he couldn't bear to part with. Sentimental reasons, he once told her. It had been the first place they had made love, and Carly had been cynical enough to wonder—even in the throes of passion—just how many other women the handsome, charming young man had bedded just that same way. In the end, of course, that hadn't mattered. She and Carson had dated just long enough to decide they couldn't work together as a couple, and in fact might not actually like one another at all.

But it was to him she had come tonight, and that made a kind of sense. She could trust Carson to be Carson, to look out for himself, to be a self-absorbed prig. And that was what made him trustworthy after a fashion. He would always act in his own self-interest, and if she kept that in mind, she could deal with him.

"Wake up," Carson said, "I made coffee."

Carly opened bleary eyes to bright sunlight pouring in through the blinds in the living room. Carson handed her a thick, white mug filled with steaming brown liquid. The mug bore a logo in black-and-white: I prefer my puns intended. She took a sip, and it was perfect. Two sugars, a dash of cream.

"How the hell do you remember stuff like that?"

"What? How you take your coffee? I remember a lot of things." He shot her a meaningful look, and Carly felt the heat rising in her face again. "Let's just say you left a lasting impression and leave it at that, all right?"

Carly looked away from him, not wanting to think about it. She had been the one to end things, of course. Carson had been perfectly happy, and hadn't understood at first why Carly would want to make a clean break of things with him. There had been many talks, a lot of them late at night, with a lot of tears spilled, before they were able to shake free of one another.

"Any idea what you're gonna do?"

"I don't know," she said. "What would you do?"

Carson rubbed his freshly shaved face with one big paw. "I'd like to say that I'd follow the story. I mean, that's what every reporter thinks, right? But I'd be scared as hell."

"Well, that's fair, I guess. Because I *am* scared."

She gulped down more coffee and then stretched. The old couch really was comfortable.

"I'm thinking about calling in sick today."

Carson groaned.

"No, come on. You know that's gonna fuck up my day. Frank will double my workload."

"You haven't been pulling your weight around there for a while anyway," Carly said, but she was laughing as she said it. The truth was that Carson was a hell of a reporter, and he was just biding his time at the paper. A lot of the staff—well, the ones that were left—wondered why he hadn't left yet.

"See, this is why we broke up," Carson said. "You're mean as a snake."

"I thought it was because you didn't want to put out anymore."

Of all the things Carly could have said, that was the one thing neither of them had expected. Their eyes met, and held, and then Carson leaned down and kissed her. *He's gentler than he used to be*, she thought, and hesitated for only a second before she kissed him back. Then he was pressing against her, bearing her down onto the couch, and her fingers were underneath his T-shirt, clawing with need and desire.

When it was over, Carly couldn't help but feel a little sad. She had no regrets about what they had done, but there was a wistfulness to it, two people striving to attain something that was now beyond them.

Carson seemed to feel it too.

"I don't know where that came from," he said, and stroked her hair a little.

"Green light go," she said, and bumped her head against his shoulder. They were lying half on the couch and half-off, the weight of gravity pulling them down, down, down. He kissed the top of her head, and she snuggled in tighter against him, nearly dumping them both onto the floor.

After Carson left for work, Carly tried to figure out what to do next. If her source was burned, she had no shot at landing the Westgate story. They'd be on the lookout now, and if Paul Williams was really out of the picture—maybe even dead—it would scare off anyone else from talking to her.

First things first: call Paul. She did, but the call went straight to voicemail. She emailed him from her secure email, an encrypted account that was absolutely secure as far as she could tell, and messaged him on WhatsApp, too. If she knew how, she might have sent up smoke signals, too. But Paul wasn't answering.

Next step?

Call the cops, she thought. But what did she have? Nothing much, really, just a belief that something had gone terribly wrong for Paul Williams. A hunch, in other words. But there were ways she could check that hunch out.

"I'm sorry, we don't have an employee by that name," a chipper voice on the other end of the phone told her when she called Westgate Developers.

"He's your project manager for the Brockton deal," Carly said. "I just spoke to him yesterday."

"I'm sorry, I'm unfamiliar with him. Have a wonderful day. I'm sorry I was unable to be more helpful." There was a click, and the disembodied voice on the other end of the line was gone as if it had never been there at all.

"Shit."

Her voice was very loud in Carson's empty apartment. *Okay. What next?* Carly realized she'd have to think about this in terms of story, an investigative piece, and even if it weren't for publication, she needed to know what had happened to her source.

Paul Williams lived in an upscale condo about fifteen minutes from Carson's shabby little house. It was a cookie-cutter space, much like Carly's own, only in a much nicer neighborhood, and therefore much more expensive. Paul's car, a late-model Mercedes convertible, was parked in its assigned slot. Carly parked beside it and got out.

Something felt wrong. That sounded over dramatic, but she felt it nonetheless. The car seemed like an omen, somehow. She went to Paul Williams' front door and rang the bell, really leaning into it. Inside the bell chimed and chimed, but no one answered the door. She went around to the rear of the condo and found a small patio with white-painted wrought iron furniture and a standing ashtray filled with cigar butts. The rear door of the unit was sliding glass, and that was good.

Carly had once interviewed a burglar for a feature story on how to protect your home for the holidays, and he had shown how simple locks like the one on this kind of door were to circumvent. All it took was a plastic shim, like a disused credit card, and a little time. She had several of those kinds of cards in her purse.

She was pleasantly surprised—and more than slightly appalled—at how simple it was to pop the lock on Paul's back door. But now she was inside, and maybe she'd get some answers.

Or not.

The condo was empty. Furniture had been moved out, and recently, judging by the indentations left on the thick carpeting. She could tell where a heavy sofa had been, and a dining area table. In the galley-style kitchen, there were no pots and pans, no dishes, not even any silverware. Even the junk drawer that every good American owns was cleared out. Carly knew the upstairs would be much the same, but she was determined to check anyway.

The stairs were wide, with a support rail along the left-hand side. She took the steps two at a time, and skidded to a stop at the second-floor landing. There were two bedrooms, nothing in either one. The bathroom was bare down to the fixtures. It was as if Paul Williams had never lived there at all.

"I don't understand," Carly said, her voice echoing in the empty space.

There were two places she hadn't checked: one was a half-bath tucked under the stairwell. The only thing left behind was a couple of Magic Erasers and a bottle of toilet cleaner. The outer storage unit was unlocked, and equally bare.

Paul Williams might as well not exist, at least not here, not in this apartment. He had never been. The only proof Carly had that Paul had once lived here was his car outside.

She ran through the condo, nearly tripping over her own feet as she sprinted for the front door. She dragged the security chain free, then scrabbled for the deadbolt. When it finally snicker open, Carly yanked the door open.

Paul's car was gone.

Carly slumped back against the door jamb, feeling her knees give way until she slid down onto her butt. Was she going crazy? Surely not, right? His car had been *right there*. She put her head between her knees. Tried to think. Could she go to the cops now? Probably not, unless she wanted to look like a complete lunatic. She had even less to go on than she'd had yesterday afternoon. Cops worked off of evidence, at least in her experience. Sure they had hunches sometimes, and followed them. But she needed something for them to believe her story.

She'd made acquaintance with several cops from her brief time on the crime beat, but there wasn't anyone she could reach out to in the department, no one who would automatically believe her the same way that Carson had. She hadn't quite realized until now how much his belief in her had bolstered her self-confidence this morning. But now she was out of moves. Nowhere to go, nothing to do except fly the white flag.

If Paul ever had the evidence she needed, it was long gone along with him now. Carly gathered herself off the ground and closed Paul's door behind her. She left it and the sliding glass door in the back unlocked.

The drive back to Carson's place was uneventful, but Carly kept her hand inside her purse anyway, her fingers playing along the weighted haft of her big kitchen knife. She knew Carson had a gun that he kept in a safe under his bed, but she hadn't been brave enough to ask if she could borrow it. Maybe that was for the best. Holding the knife gave her a feeling of power, a sense that she was somehow still maintaining a bit of control over a situation that was spinning badly out of control.

But if Carly let herself think about it, that sense of any control at all was a lie, an illusion she couldn't afford to indulge. When she called Carson on his cell, he picked up on the second ring.

"Can I stay at your place again tonight?"

"Of course," he said. She could hear the warmth in his voice, the genuine sense that he would be happy to see her again. How had she missed that about him? She'd spent the last couple of years thinking of him in the same terms from the day they'd broken things off. But he'd grown; he'd changed.

Or maybe she had.

"I'm gonna go by my place and pick up some things," she said. "Like a toothbrush."

Carson laughed. "That would be good, Coffee Breath."

"Hey," she said, "just because this morning happened—"

"Doesn't mean it'll happen again," he said. "Don't worry. Message received. No pressure."

"I should go," she said. "You're trying to work. I know how you hate it when people interrupt you."

"Yeah, well, hey—I had a good time this morning. No just, you know, that."

"Yeah?"

"Yeah. I've missed you."

Carly smiled, letting a little quiet spill out between them, until Carson said "Well?" And then she laughed.

"I knew you couldn't stand it. Fine, I missed you, too."

"That's more like it. I'll see you after work."

And that was it. She made the drive over to her apartment, stewing all the while. If this were a movie, she would be more intrepid, maybe. Vow to find out what happened to Paul Williams—hell, find out what happened to her goddamned story—at all costs. But the fact was that she had no idea where to go and no idea what to do next.

In real life, sometimes there are dead ends. Something there are trails that just peter out into nothing. The Westgate story looked like it was one of those trails. Never mind the hours she had spent working Paul, slowly getting him to talk with her, the time spent laying the groundwork for the story. But nothing had come of it, and now Paul was missing, maybe even dead. She had no idea, but her natural curiosity would leave the idea alone. If someone had gotten to Paul—and obviously from the stonewall treatment and the empty apartment, they had definitely done that—could they get to her, too?

No, probably not. She was a small-town reporter, but that had some advantages. People knew her here. If she went missing, that would at least cause a stir. Carly couldn't lay claim to being a celebrity, not exactly, but folks in town knew who she was. It wasn't unusual for people, complete strangers, to try to pick up her check when she went out to eat, just because they saw her name in the paper. She never let them, though, worried that any such behavior might appear unethical.

She stopped by her mail slot on the way to her apartment. A thick manila envelope lay folded in a U-shape along the edges of the box, and she dug it out carefully. There was no return address, just her name and apartment number, which meant that someone had dropped the envelope off at the front desk. She ripped the top open carefully and peered inside.

Carly's heart leapt in her chest. It was the documentation from Paul Williams. All of the files—all of the proof that she needed for her story—right there in her hands. She stuffed the mail in her purse, atop the big kitchen knife.

She was nearly whistling by the time she got to her apartment door and unlocked it. As she entered the space, she tossed her keys onto the curio table beside the door as she always did. But this time she missed. The keys clattered to the floor. As the door swung closed behind her, Carly flipped on the lights.

There was no furniture left in her apartment. It was completely empty. Her eyes widened in fear, and she reached for the knife in her purse. She never made it. Rough hands clamped over her mouth.

Carly tried to scream anyway, for all the good it did. No one could hear her now.

HIDDEN HOUSE

I BELIEVE IN HAUNTED HOUSES. I guess I have to believe in them, after living next to one for so many years. Hidden House is a hulking wreck now, shrouded in weeds, kudzu, and trees that have grown up in the yard. But I remember when it haunted my dreams every night, and when the sounds of a man's screams could be heard in the eerie stillness of dusk.

As far as I know, there has only been one murder at Hidden House. On August 9, 1979, Jerome Baxter took a shovel and caved in the back of his stepfather's head. Jerome was arrested, tried, and convicted of second-degree murder. The court shipped him off to some prison or other, and I've never been able to find out exactly what happened to him after that.

But I know what happened to Hidden House. Two weeks after the murder, Mrs. Baxter and her other children moved out of the place. To be more accurate, they abandoned it. But I didn't find that out until later that year. I had always been afraid of Hidden House, and now that no one lived there, I was doubly so. It was a small frame house, unpainted and splintering along the wooden eaves. The windows were blank, expressionless eyes. A railed porch ran the length of the front of the house; the roof was gray shingles hung at an awkward angle. The front door was slightly askew, and it gave the place an appearance of eternal hunger. Often I rode my bicycle past Hidden House, speeding up as the watchful, restless windows came into view. None of the neighborhood kids would go inside, even though the door was unlocked.

One morning Tim Hutcherson came by. He was one of the few kids my age in the neighborhood, and we had become close friends. "I'm going to go in there today," he said. I didn't need to ask where. Hidden House crouched low in a bend of the road, almost impossible to see from more than ten yards away -- but it seemed to send out a homing beacon: whenever I went outside I would find my gaze drawn in the direction of the ugly, graying house. Tim was wearing cutoff shorts and a t-shirt, his hair done up in exotic little corn rows held in place with beads. "You want to come?" Neither of us had ever been inside the house, even though Jerome had sometimes baby-sat for our mothers. My curiosity overpowered my sense of fear.

"Yes," I said.

And that was how I found myself straddling my secondhand bicycle, staring at the gaping maw of Hidden House not twenty feet away while Tim checked around to see if anyone was watching us. I dropped the kickstand on my bike and hoisted my leg over the seat as Tim came back around the house.

"No one's around." Tim's voice was almost a whisper. "Come on." He stepped up onto the porch and rested a hand lightly on the doorknob. I stood beside my bike, one hand absently fingering the duct tape that crisscrossed the handlebars. Tim looked back at me expectantly. I joined him on the porch, the boards beneath us groaning a welcome. He pushed the door open and we got our first look at Hidden House. All was quiet and dark within. The front room had been a living room or den. A Zenith console TV sat against the far wall, its picture tube impaled by a coat rack. A love seat was overturned and the stuffing ripped out.

Pictures of the Baxter family still hung crookedly on the walls. There was a bunched-up throw rug in one corner. A three-dimensional portrait of Jesus sat on the fireplace mantle. Quickly, we went through the whole house.

In addition to the sitting room, there were three bedrooms, a bath, and a kitchen-dining room combination. The story was the same in each room. The Baxters had left everything: furniture, photos, bed linen, silverware, dishes. There were some old comic books in one of the bedrooms, and then we found Jerome's room.

"Check this out!" Tim kept his voice low, even though there was no one around. He handed me a framed photograph. It was Jerome's senior portrait; he was good looking, his skin the same shade as a coffee bean. His tightly-curled hair was cropped close to his skull, and his smile showed prominent, even teeth.

A bureau stood upright in one corner of Jerome's room. Tim began opening the drawers. "Don't do that," I said.

"Why not?"

"Jerome wouldn't like it," I said, "you looking through his stuff."

"It doesn't matter," Tim said. "He's in jail, remember?"

I nodded slowly. Somehow it did matter to me, but I didn't have the words to express that to Tim. I walked out into the hallway without saying anything else. I still had Jerome's photo in my hands. He looked so happy. Young. Free. I wished I could reach the boy that was in that photo, shake him and tell him, "This summer you're going to get into a fight with your stepdad, and you're going to do something really terrible. Whatever happens, don't pick up that shovel. You'll go to jail if you do." I hung my head and concentrated on not crying; I had liked Jerome.

I stared at the floor for a long time before I realized what I was looking at. It was a stain on the bare wooden floor, making the boards slightly darker than the ones around them. The stain was rust-colored, and I thought I knew what it was. That's it, I thought. I'm looking at where it happened. And then a hand closed on my arm.

I jerked my arm back and barely stifled a scream. It was Tim. "Scared you," he said. He grinned widely, his teeth very white in the gloom of the house.

"No you didn't," I whispered hoarsely. The hairs on my arms and the back of my neck were standing on end, a million tiny lightning rods. "Look there." I pointed at the stain on the floor.

Tim recognized what it was at once. "Blood," he said, and I nodded quickly.

"Do you think it happened here?" He said. "Or do you think it happened in one of these rooms and they fought out here?"

"No way to know, I guess."

Tim looked around. "Which one was her room?"

I pointed across the hall. "In there, I think."

He paused, as if making up his mind. "Let's go take a closer look."

We went into the bedroom, Tim a little ahead of me. The bed was rumpled and dusty. Rats had chewed at the stuffing, gathering materials to build a nest. In the bedroom it seemed the coppery, dank smell of blood overpowered every other sensation. There was broken glass on the floor, and the drapes had been torn down and left in a tangle on the floor. We looked around for a few minutes, and then Tim spoke.

"Holy sh--"

"What?" I said.

"Look over there."

Pushed against the far wall was a cheap pine dresser that sat low and humble, almost penitent. A mirror ran the length of the dresser and reflected the whole of the room. There was a woman lying on the bed.

I turned and looked at the bed, its sprawled and chewed mattress hanging half off the bed. There was no one there. I looked at Tim, and he shrugged as if to say, "I don't know how it did that either, but it's there." We looked back at the mirror.

The room was suddenly dark, and the woman on the bed was a mere shadow. Her chocolate skin melded with the shadows in a sinuous dance. Her body was Rubenesque, and she was naked. It was Jerome's mother. Dimly, I was aware of a man standing in the doorway, coming toward Mrs. Baxter. He had a thick leather belt in one hand, and he kept wrapping the belt around his fist until only about twelve inches dangled loose, the large metal buckle swaying loosely at the end.

"Gon' git it now, bitch." His voice was slurred and sluggish, like a boxer in the twelfth round of a hard fight, and I realized he was drunk.

Mrs. Baxter lay very still on the bed. "You don't gotta do that, baby. I'll be a good girl." It was a little girl's voice, pleading and frightened. The man came closer, and I recognized him as Jerome's stepfather.

"Damn right you will," he said. It seemed I could smell the rancid grapes of cheap wine on his breath. Jerome's stepfather slapped the bed with the whip of belt he held in his hands. It made a flat whap, an understated harbinger of violence. Mrs. Baxter cringed and drew her feet tight against her body, curling into a tight ball. And then I remembered the scars on her legs. I had seen them that summer when she had come up to check on Jerome while he was playing with Tim and me. They formed an ugly zebra pattern up her calves, which I had seen beneath the floral-print house-dress she always wore. The scar tissue was puckered and pink against her otherwise smooth skin. Had there been new welts on her legs when I had seen her? I believe there were.

So this was nothing new for Mrs. Baxter, or her husband, whose name I can never remember. He started by caressing her with the edge of the leather strap. He ran it up her calves, across her thighs and belly. That's when I saw the scars patterned all over her body, even her arms. I had never noticed them there before.

He kept on, lightly at first. A teasing smack against her rear, a little harder on her shoulders. Jerome's stepfather continued to hit Mrs. Baxter, moving the belt in time to his own private rhythm. I began to wince as the blows grew harder and harder, and still he beat her. Mrs. Baxter began to writhe against the bed, her body helplessly torn between two imperatives. She wanted to submit to her husband, and yet the need for self-preservation had taken over. Mrs. Baxter whirled off the bed, her hands up to shield her face. "No more, Ronnie," she said. "No more. I ain't done nothin'." She backed into one corner of the room and sat down, as if her body was suddenly to heavy for her quivering legs.

"I know you ain't done nothing," Ronnie said, his brown eyes nearly glowing in the fever-pitch of his violence. "I work all damn day at the chicken plant an' come home, you ain't go no dishes washed. You ain't got no supper cooked. You a goddamn lazy whore." The belt came down again, this time landing on Mrs. Baxter's back while she hunched in the corner. When Ronnie ripped the belt back toward him, there was a thin line of blood along Mrs. Baxter's shoulder blades and a hint of blood on the buckle of the belt.

Mrs. Baxter screamed and arched her back away from the wall. I could see the ugly rip in her flesh, and turned my head away for a moment. Tim swayed beside me, mesmerized by the mirror. His mouth hung open and his eyes were blank. I didn't want to see any more, but I had to see what happened. I turned back to the mirror and was consumed once more.

Ronnie pulled the belt back for another swing and the buckle caught in the drapes. They came down with a crash, and Mrs. Baxter scooted back toward the bed. She was sobbing loudly now, her breath hitching in long, awful gasps. Mrs. Baxter made it half-way under the bed before Ronnie caught her. His callused brown hand caught her by one ankle, while the other hand flailed away with the belt. He began to beat her bare buttocks, bringing blood with every strike. The buckle caught the back of her thigh and ripped down her leg. The wailing was horrible, and she thrashed her feet wildly to free herself from the killing frenzy of her husband. One foot caught Ronnie in the groin, and he backed away, his howls joining those of Mrs. Baxter.

"I'll kill you for that," he said. His voice had dropped an octave, and a slow grin spread across his face. In all my years before or since, never have I seen murder written so plainly across another person's face.

Ronnie crawled toward her. Mrs. Baxter was mostly under the bed by this time, but he simply caught her by the foot and began to drag her into the open. Ronnie's hands were large, with thick yellow nails that seemed luminous in the dim room. The nails were long and almost pointed, and he dug them into Mrs. Baxter's skin as he pulled her from underneath the bed. There were bloody little half-moons where his hands touched her.

Finally, he tangled his fist in Mrs. Baxter's hair and pulled her to her feet. He slung her into the far wall next to the window, and the house shuddered on its foundation. Ronnie held Mrs. Baxter against the wall and began to punch her. Jerome's mother tried to ward off Ronnie's hands, but he was too strong for her.

"No," she said, over and over. I heard her front teeth shatter after one vicious punch, and I saw the fragments of bone hit the floor and scatter.

"Please," Mrs. Baxter said. "Please, somebody help me." For a moment, I thought she saw Tim and me, standing there in her room, two innocent tourists who had stumbled on an ugly scene of death. Her hand reached out toward us, pleading.

And then Jerome was in the doorway, and there was a rusted shovel in his hands. His mouth was open wide, his scream an unintelligible howl of rage. The shovel swung in a high arc, and the blade split Ronnie's skull the way a good cleaver can split an apple. Jerome's stepfather turned and staggered to his knees. The belt was still wrapped around his right hand. He howled in pain. Ronnie tried to struggle to his feet, and Jerome hit him again. Only this time I didn't see Jerome's face in the mirror. I saw mine. I brought the shovel down again and again, until there was blood and gore splattered across the floor, until my arms were heavy leaden weights attached to my shoulders. I could feel the handle of the shovel crack and splinter. Perhaps I held the shovel, but Jerome's strength swung it. I kept chopping away at Ronnie until he stopped moving. And then I hit him some more. Exhausted, my eyes cleared, and I saw Jerome again, dragging the shovel behind him into the hall. He left a smear of blood across the floor, a red badge that would mark him forever.

He came back in a few minutes and walked over to his mother's dresser. He fumbled around in it for a few minutes until he found what he was looking for. "Here," he said to his mother. "Put this on." It was a pink housedress; he held it out to his mother at arms' length and did not look at her. Ronnie's body lay unmoving on the floor. As I watched, a fly settled on it and buzzed serenely.

Then the mirror cleared, and I shook my head. Tim swayed beside me, still drunk with the vision we had shared. "What did you see?" I asked.

"I saw Jerome's mom and stepdad," Tim said. "And I saw Jerome kill him, but it wasn't really Jerome, you know?"

"I know," I said.

"He looked like. . . me."

"Me too," I said.

Tim's legs were weak, and he started to sit down on the bed, then changed his mind. "No way," he said. "I can't stay in here. We gotta get out."

"Yeah."

We left Hidden House the way we had found it. The other kids in the neighborhood finally got the nerve to go inside, several years later. I never asked them what they saw, and they never told me. But I know no one ever went in twice. Someone came by one night and threw rocks through all of the windows, so now the house doesn't watch anyone anymore. It sits in a bend of the road, its blind eyes staring straight ahead. Through the years, it has shifted forward on its foundation so that it almost leans into the road, a blind beggar reaching for scraps of food. Sometime last year, the roof of Hidden House caved in. I can no longer bear to look at it. It looks too much like Jerome's stepfather did as he lay dead on the floor of Mrs. Baxter's room.

DADDY'S LITTLE GIRL

MOMMY ISN'T MOVING ANYMORE.

She's just lying there on the floor, face turning from blue to an awful purple color. Daddy lunged out of his chair, knocking it backward against the dining room wall. He knelt beside her, calling her name over and over. I'm screaming for her–"Mommy, mommy!"–like I haven't done since I was a toddler. I haven't called her "Mommy" in years. Now I can't think of anything else to call her.

Mommy didn't say anything when it happened. She just pitched sideways right in the middle of supper, while she was trying to take a bite of mashed potatoes. The fork clattered to the floor beside her. Now Daddy is moving around her, tilting her head back and trying to breathe down her airway the way they taught us in CPR class.

I can't move—I don't know what to do. Daddy looks up at me, his eyes wild like an animal. He tosses me his cell phone. I catch it with numb fingers.

"Call 911," he says, and I do, punching the touchscreen. The operator wants to know what the emergency is, and I tell her that my Mommy is on the floor and can't breathe. She asks me other questions—I don't remember what they are. And then she tells me to hold on, an ambulance will be here shortly.

It doesn't come shortly. The minutes tick by like decades, and by the time the paramedics get here, Daddy is just sitting beside Mommy's body, his hands covering his face as the tears splash dark salty stains against his chinos. I'm still standing by the table listening to my father sob. It hasn't hit me yet, but it will soon.

Mommy is dead.

The funeral and all that goes with it passes by like the blink of an eye. I'll turn fifteen in two weeks, and the little selfish kid part of me is screaming that I probably won't even get a party this year. I push that selfish little kid voice aside, bury it as deep as I can. Hold Daddy's hand as tight as I can. He squeezes my hand in return, his knuckles bone white where they interlace with mine. I remember crying—wailing, really—as the cemetery workers lowered Mommy's coffin into the ground. Daddy held me close and kissed my cheeks.

That night, the dreams begin. I still don't remember them, not in any conscious way. But I remember feeling like my throat is closing up with clods of red clay, and every time I try to brush the dirt away, another shovelful lands in my face. I wake up screaming.

Daddy comes running down the hallway and bursts into my room.

"Are you all right?"

I sit straight up, my eyes wide open. I'm looking for something, maybe for the man with the shovel, the man who wouldn't let me breathe. My chest hitches once, and then again, and finally the tears come. I'm not all right. Not at all. Daddy comes to the bed. The mattress sags when he sits down, and I feel his thick arms envelop me until my breathing returns to normal and the tears dry on my cheeks.

Daddy is always there for me. And I want to be there for him, too. He takes me to his bed that night, and I lie dreamless and peaceful next to him until he shakes me awake for breakfast. When we sit down at the table, something feels different. It's not just that Mommy isn't there anymore—even though that's certainly part of it. Her absence fills the kitchen and creates a gorge between us, a divide we can't quite conquer. We eat cold cereal with milk, and drink canned orange juice. We don't talk. We can't even look one another in the eye. I go to my room and get ready for school. When Daddy calls out, I follow him to the garage. He takes me to school, and then he goes to work.

We never talk about it.

Two or three nights a week, the nightmares come back. When they do, I scream in terror, and Daddy is there almost immediately. He carries me away to his (and Mommy's) bed like a knight in shining armor bearing a fairy princess away from danger. And there I sleep.

I don't understand the danger I put us both in. I can't see how Daddy is hurting. I know he is growing more and more silent, and his face is growing more and more haggard. He goes to the doctor for a prescription to help him sleep. Klonopin, the little bottle says. One at bedtime. I should see. I should know. But he is my rock. He is all I can count on now that Mommy isn't around anymore.

One night as he undresses for bed, I knock on his door. I pretended to go to sleep earlier. He is sitting on the bed, his back turned toward me. I see his shoulders shake as he cries silent tears. I understand, in my dim child's way, that he is hurting just as badly as I am. All I want to do is make that hurt go away.

I go to him, my feet padding silently on the thick carpet. Put my hand on his shoulder. He's startled, swinging his head around. His fingers find mine and interlace for a brief moment. He uses his other arm to try to wipe the tears away from his eyes. I hug him, and he hugs me back so tight I think my ribs will crack. I don't go back to my bed that night.

We sleep in the same bed, but we never touch. I don't remember much about those nights. I sleep in a dreamless haze that seems to go on forever. I feel enveloped within both of my parents. I feel safe. So safe.

Until the thunderstorm.

The clouds start to build early in the afternoon. I see them growing pregnant, dark and heavy with rain. Rumbles like heavy trucks passing make the house shiver. After dinner, the first drops of rain pelt the windows. The spatter pitter-patters against the panes. I finish my homework and change into my pajamas. Daddy is already in bed, the coverlet pulled up nearly to his nose.

"Can I sleep with you tonight?"

"You scared, kiddo?"

"Kinda, yeah."

He nods his OK, and I get in, sliding between the clean sheets and rolling away from him, burrowing deep under the covers.

I feel his hand on my shoulder. He rolls over halfway toward me and leans over, gives me a kiss on the cheek.

"I love you, kid," he says. "You're a good girl."

A smile—maybe the last real one I can remember—stretches my face. I tell him I love him, too, and say good night. I'm not sure how long it takes to fall asleep, but the rumble of the thunder and the music of the rain lull me into submission pretty quickly. A clap of thunder like the voice of God wakes me.

Lightning hit near the house, close enough for me to still smell the ozone as I come to my senses. The power is out, and the bedroom is fully dark. I can see just a little in the dark, enough to make out the shapes of the furniture. But when the lightning flashes again, I see Daddy's eyes.

He's awake. Awake and staring at me like he's never seen me before. I can see the gleam in his eye—now that I know where to look—even without the pale slash of the lightning. I don't know if he ever blinks.

I don't know how long it takes, but I finally find my voice.

"Daddy." My voice is a whisper. I clear my throat.

"Daddy—you're scaring me." The words tumble out, and Daddy shakes himself a little.

"Don't be scared," he says. His voice is a harsh whisper, as if he's straining very hard against something I can't see. "You—you look so much like your mother."

And then he tells me I need to leave, to go back to my bedroom and lock the door. I do as he says, and a little while later I hear the loud burr of his snore all the way through the walls. He can sleep, but I can't. I keep thinking about that blank look in his eyes, as if he was there but not there, and gooseflesh crawls up my legs and over the length of my body. My teeth chatter, clicking against one another, but I don't feel cold. I don't know what I feel. I pull the covers up around my ears and finally slip away into sleep.

When I wake up and go downstairs, it's bright outside, the sky that kind of impossibly beautiful blue that comes only after a hard rain. The storm is over. But the real one is about to begin.

"We're going to make some changes," Daddy says as I grab a box of cereal and dump some into a bowl. I start to say something, but he shushes me and passes me the milk. Daddy never touches me, just holds me with his eyes. I can't fight him. "When you get home from school, you're going to wear the clothes I lay out for you. Understand?"

I don't know what else to do, so I nod. I want to say no. I want to stop him, to tell him how creeped out he's making me feel. But I don't know how. I open my mouth to say something, but no words come out.

"I know you don't know how to cook yet, but we're going to work on that. I'll show you some things."

"Things have to change," he says. "I can't keep going like this anymore."

That afternoon when I get home from school, Daddy sends me upstairs. There's an outfit laid out on my bed: a striped yellow top with a pair of khaki shorts and broken-in leather sandals. I stare. I can't wear those clothes. They're too big for me.

They were Mommy's clothes.

But eventually I give in, sliding off my own grubby jeans and sweatshirt and stepping into what I think of as "adult" clothes. I look in the mirror. I'm too short and too thin, a child playing dress-up. That's all I am. I breathe in and out slowly. The shoes are a bigger problem. I never wear sandals, so the thong between my toes hurts, and I'm sure it will leave a blister. But I know wearing them will make him happy, so I put them on.

Then I go downstairs to see Daddy.

He smiles the strangest smile. And takes me in the biggest bear hug he's ever given me. He buries his face in my tumble of dirty blonde hair and inhales, like a drowning man finally breaking the surface of the deep water.

"Oh my God," he says. "Stephanie. Oh my God." I can feel his tears on my shoulder as he holds me close.

My name isn't Stephanie. That was Mommy's name.

We fix dinner together. Daddy seems more upbeat than I've seen him since the funeral, but my movements are stiff and mechanical. We pan-sear steaks and make salads so big that we can't finish them. There's ice cream for dessert. I don't eat much, but Daddy finishes his plate and mine. And afterward, Daddy holds my hand and tells me about his day. Then he strokes my hair and kisses me on the cheek.

I don't do my homework that night. Instead, I go to the upstairs bathroom and lock myself in. Tears pour down my face in a never-ending rain. I take a shower, hot as I dare. The steam boils in the room and the running water hides my sobs. When the hot water runs out, I finally get out of the tub and towel off. I put on a big old fleece robe—until I realize it was Mommy's, too. I fling the robe away from myself and wrap towels all over my body.

I leave Mommy's clothes on the floor. I never want to touch them again.

But I have to. Every night from then on, Daddy dresses me up like Mommy. I go through the motions of being his dead wife.

But every night I go into my room and lock the door. Sometimes I think I hear him pause outside it as he goes to his own bedroom, and that space in time where he stops, so does my heart.

Something is building to the breaking point. I can feel it the same way I could feel the thunderstorm building on that spring evening when everything changed. Now that summer is nearing its peak, Daddy is looking more and more ragged, like a man who's been pushed beyond his breaking point. He used to only take sleeping pills occasionally. Now he takes them every night.

When I come home from school, I wear Mommy's jeans and Mommy's dresses and Mommy's heels and Mommy's flats. Like it's a normal thing.

I cook his meals, and I hold his hand, and I let him hug me until I want to run screaming out into the street and tear my hair and tear these clothes and never stop running. There is no one to help me, and I know in time it will become almost natural. A new normal. I don't know who I could tell or who I could call. Mommy never had any family. Neither did Daddy. "A couple of orphans in the storm," he used to say to her, and I understood that he and I were now the orphans in the storm.

There's no one who could help me. No one to save me.

Except Daddy. And he finally does.

I hear him puttering downstairs on Saturday morning. That's nothing unusual. He gets up and cooks breakfast, or he works on some project or other. One time he left our toaster disassembled on the kitchen table for two weeks while he was trying to fix it, until Mommy got tired of the parts and the tools lying around and threw the whole caboodle in the garbage and went to Target and bought a new one.

I creep down the hall and peer over the banister to the first floor where I can peek like a weathervane, testing which way the wind is blowing..

I still don't feel safe there, but I have nowhere else to go. I close my eyes for a moment, but there's a sudden crash from downstairs.

I leap up, scattering covers and stuffed animals everywhere. I race down the steps into the kitchen, only to find my Daddy on his back on the floor.

For a second, time doubles back in on itself. He's lying nearly where Mommy lay in her last moments. I stop. My hands go to my face, and I feel my nails digging skin from my cheeks in long, ragged trails.

"Daddy!" I scream, and fall to my knees beside him.

He looks up at me and tries to smile.

"It's all right," he says, his voice a hazy whisper. "It's going to be all—"

And that's it. No more words. I can't bring myself to do CPR. The thought of touching his lips with mine repels me. I beat on his chest, my fists banging against his broad pectoral muscles. It does no good. I feel him shudder, feel all the life go out of him. I scream at him and cry at him and cuss at him and beg him to come back. He's all I have left.

He kicks one last time, nothing more than an involuntary spasm, and one of his house slippers comes loose. I slide my hand down his forearm to take his hand in mine, and that's when I find the bottle. Klonopin. He's overdosed, shoving as many pills as he could manage into his mouth, washing them down with swallows of Jack Daniels.

Mommy and Daddy have left me alone now, and I don't know what to do. It's a big house and a big world for a little girl all alone. I look again at the amber medicine bottle I pried from Daddy's hand.

There were still ten pills left.

I took them all. Good night.

ACKNOWLEDGMENT

A COLLECTION OF SHORT STORIES IS A WEIRD THING. While some of the stories in this volume are getting their first publication, some of them have seen daylight before. As such, I need to thank several magazines/websites for taking a chance on me to begin with.

First, thank you to Roger Nokes and the gang at *Rock & A Hard Place* press, which originally published the title story all the way back in January of 2022. Thank you to Cindy Rosmus at *YELLOW MAMA* for not only publishing me but giving valuable and insightful feedback on my stories. John Bowie at Bristol Noir took a good story of mine and made it as close to great as it could be. (If it falls short, the fault is certainly mine and not John's.) Thank you to Meagan Lucas at *Reckon Review* for giving life to "The Ghost of Buxahatchee Creek" and "Dance the Night Away." As an editor, Meagan's suggestions are never onerous and are always offered with the author's voice in mind. And as good an editor as she is, she's an even better friend. Thanks to *Murderous Ink* for first publishing "A Good Night's Sleep," and for pushing to make sure short crime fiction continues to thrive. Thanks to the crew at *The Sandy River Review* and to Suz Jay at *Flash Fiction Magazine*, as well as Amy at the gone-too-soon *Dillydoun Review*.

Thanks to Ron Phillips and *Shotgun Honey* for giving my work a home and getting eyes on my stories before I ever sent a novel over the transom. He was a little vexed by receiving an 85,000-word short story collection, but he did pretty good with it if I do say so myself.

Thanks to the people who continually support me and push me to be and do better. I love you all. That includes Misty Mathews, Morgan Hayworth, Chad Williamson, Rob D. Smith, Paul J. Garth, the fabulous Libby Cudmore, S.A. Cosby, Beau Johnson, Kent Gowran, Mark Westmoreland, Kirstyn Petras, Samm Hamilton, and the one and only Nikki Dolson. Found family is a joy.

And thank you, readers. The work of writing a story or a book is incomplete without someone to read it. While I bring my talent and experience to the page, you do the same with your own. So thank you for allowing me to come over and play. It means more than you will ever know.

One last thing: Over the past 15 months, I've lost five family members. It's been one hell of an awful time for me personally, even though I completed work on the first draft of a new novel during that time. The writing definitely helped keep me sane and keep me going during the hardest period of my life. And my last words to you (for now): Find someone close to your heart. Hug their neck, and tell 'em you love 'em. We're only here for a little while, so make the most of it.

BOBBY MATHEWS knew exactly what he wanted to be when he grew up: a writer. That led him into a career path as a journalist in Alabama, New York, Wyoming, Georgia, and finally back to Alabama before he called it quits. He's won General Excellence, column-writing, newswriting, and sportswriting awards from press associations in all four states. In addition to his journalism career, Bobby has been a PR flack, a bartender, an investigator, and roustabout.

Bobby lives in suburban Birmingham, Alabama—which truly is the Magic City in more ways than one—with his wife and two sons.

ABOUT
SHOTGUN HONEY
BOOKS

Thank you for reading *Negative Tilt: Stories* by Bobby Mathews.

Shotgun Honey began as a crime genre flash fiction webzine in 2011 created as a venue for new and established writers to experiment in the confines of a mere 700 words. More than a decade later, Shotgun Honey still challenges writers with that storytelling task, but also provides opportunities to expand beyond through our book imprint and has since published anthologies, collections, novellas and novels by new and emerging authors.

We hope you have enjoyed this book. That you will share your experience, review and rate this title positively on your favorite book review sites and with your social media family and friends.

Visit ShotgunHoneyBooks.com

FICTION WITH A KICK

shotgunhoneybooks.com

Milton Keynes UK
Ingram Content Group UK Ltd.
UKHW042304200324
439764UK00003B/61